ASHLEY HINTERMEYER

The Light Devoured

First published by Fairfarren Publishing 2026

Copyright © 2026 by Ashley Hintermeyer

All rights reserved. No part of this publication may be reproduced, stored, or transmitted in any form or by any means, electronic, mechanical, photocopying, recording, scanning, or otherwise without written permission from the publisher. It is illegal to copy this book, post it to a website, or distribute it by any other means without permission.

This novel is entirely a work of fiction. The names, characters, and incidents portrayed in it are the work of the author's imagination. Any resemblance to actual persons, living or dead, events, or localities is entirely coincidental.

First edition

ISBN: 979-8-9945497-0-4

This book was professionally typeset on Reedsy. Find out more at reedsy.com

To my husband, thank you for believing in me so thoroughly that I actually went and wrote a whole book.

To my family, please skip pages 207–209 and 226–228.

And finally, to the readers who want a book playlist, check out my website.

Chapter 1

Elayce spends the morning in her greenhouse. It's the first thing she had built when she took over the kingdom. Originally from Flora, a region in the Kingdom of Aerash, she was used to being surrounded by an abundance of flowers, plants, and crops. But Castle Vleck suffocated her in drab, cold stone. So, when she came to the castle, she had the greenhouse built and outfitted with her favorite imported plants. It was a bonus that many of the plants were used here in the castle in case anyone fell ill. Or needed to fall ill. Oddly enough, if you learn how to make medicines you end up learning how to make poisons as well.

Elayce runs her fingers through the roots of the Belladonna plant she is working with. She has gardeners to take care of the greenhouse for the most part, but she likes to get her hands dirty. It's one of her forms of meditation, spending time with the earth and her plants. Her one last connection to her home. Her village was burned to the ground by her own magic shortly after becoming queen. They deserved it after what they did. They deserved everything that they've gotten in the last three hundred years.

She plucks a few berries, placing most of them in one of the glass jars that are always waiting in the greenhouse to be filled. She tightens the clasp on the jar and leaves it on the shelf where she knows one of the gardeners will find it and bring it to her chambers. She sets the excess berries on her gardening table and wipes her hands on a fresh rag. Glancing over at the attendant, she tosses the rag on the floor at her feet, and the attendant quickly bends to pick it up and replace it with a clean rag.

Humming a lilting tune to herself, she begins crushing the berries with a black stone mortar and pestle. She loves the way mixing and creating relaxes her as she loses herself in the rhythm of the motions. Her simple actions block out the rest of her thoughts and worries. She also loves the way it builds suspense.

A deep moan comes from the man tied to the chair on the other side of the room. The gashes along his face from her nails have bled down to his neck, already beginning to clot. He's covered in dirt and sweat, but no matter what she did to him, he didn't break. Honestly, she admires that. Plus, it allows her to play a bit longer. It will not save him in the end though. He's still going to die.

She finishes crushing the berries and grabs a black goblet from a nearby shelf. She pours the berry juice into the goblet and tenderly runs her fingers over the row of vials lined up on the table. "There's not many people who can say their queen made juice fresh for them in her personal garden, you should be honored." He doesn't look like he has much left in him, but he manages to spit at her across the table. "Tsk, tsk. That is no way to treat royalty."

"You're not royalty. You're a tyrant. A demon from the underworld," he spews.

"Hmm, yes well that is just simply not true. I was born in

Flora. I'm as much a part of this kingdom as you are," she responds while mixing different liquids into the black goblet.

"If you truly were a part of this kingdom, you wouldn't be killing your people." He glances down at the goblet and then back up to her eyes, swallowing hard.

"If my people would behave properly, then I wouldn't have to kill them. Besides, I really enjoy the push and pull relationship that we have. Keeps things interesting, doesn't it?" She picks up the full goblet and walks around the table to bend in front of the bound man, eye to eye. "I sure have had fun with you this morning, but it seems your usefulness has come to an end. As a token of my gratitude for your fine entertainment, I'd like to offer you this drink. Fresh from my garden." Her voice drips with sarcasm and a smile spreads across her face, but doesn't reach her gray eyes.

He turns his head to the side and squeezes his mouth shut. She straightens, rolling her eyes. Her hand whips out and grabs him by the chin, forcing his face back to hers. She squeezes his cheeks until his lips part, her sharp nails drawing blood, and pours the potion down his throat. He chokes and sputters, but she holds his chin up so gravity works against him. She giggles under her breath as the last drop falls from the cup into his mouth. "I would love to stick around to get your full review on the refreshments, but I have other things to take care of." His eyelids are already drooping. She leans forward and brings her face level with his. "You have not saved them," she whispers to him as his breathing becomes shallower and shallower. Before the light even leaves his eyes, she straightens and glides across the greenhouse floor and back towards the castle.

Drops of blood fall from Elayce's long, black painted fingernails to the thick carpet. She doesn't notice until one of her lady's maids shuffling behind her hands her a handkerchief. The blood soaks into the white fabric, blooming across the silk threads, swallowing more and more until there's more crimson than ivory.

"Your Majesty!" A call comes from somewhere down the hall behind her. Her lip curls up in disgust, and she keeps walking in the opposite direction of the voice.

Undeterred, the raspy voice rings out again, this time accompanied by hastened footsteps and heavy breathing. Damn it, she should have stayed in the garden.

Tydas, her advisor, appears before her, out of breath with sweat dripping down his face. There's always sweat dripping down his face. She could just blow past him, but she stops and sighs, rolling her head and eyes to the side so she doesn't have to look at him.

"Report," Elayce says, noticing a mirror on the wall near them. She takes a few steps towards the mirror, but Tydas pivots to stand in front of her again.

"We're moving into harvest season, and it seems as though we will have a good yield this year. I'm sure that has to do with the Goddess blessing your rule of course, my queen."

Elayce rolls her eyes again and focuses on her own reflection in the mirror above his head. She drags a long fingernail across the edge of her black painted mouth, poking and prodding at her wrinkle free face and golden hair with the tips of her nails. Thanks to the magic that keeps her alive and young, there isn't a single flaw in her strong, defined jaw and high cheekbones. Elayce's face hasn't changed in three hundred years, as if once she came into her magic time just stopped for her. Except for her eyes. They used to be a light caramel brown, but now they are a dull dark gray, the color slowly leeching from them over time. She doesn't mind though. Her eyes used to be *his* favorite. She'd probably hate her reflection if she had to stare into them all of the time.

Tydas clears his throat and she drops her hand from her face to flick her fingers for him to continue. He hunches further into himself and trips over his tongue to keep going.

"There was another rebel attack on the wall last night, but the group of them was smaller this time and, of course, was no match for our soldiers. We captured five of them, though one of them is dead already. They refuse to speak, but we guess that they are farmers from South Garsen." He takes a breath to continue with his report, but Elayce's hand goes up into the air to indicate he should stop. The many rings and jewels on her fingers refract light from her sparks floating around them.

"I've already spent the morning with another one of our guests. What I'd like to know is how many got away?" Elayce says, raising one of her dark blonde eyebrows.

Tydas's cheeks puff up before he glances up to her glaring eyes. "Our soldiers were able to capture most of them, my queen, and they are waiting for your orders on what we should do with the rest of them. I rather think that a public hanging would do well. I can get that on the schedule for—"

"Tydas," the queen says quietly. She shifts her stance just slightly, making herself look more menacing. "Is that what I asked?"

"No, my queen," he says and nervously glances down at his report before flicking his beady eyes back up to her.

"If you are not answering what I ask, then why are you speaking at all?" A rhetorical question, one Tydas knows better than to respond to.

He clears his throat. "My apologies, my queen. Four of them

got away, and another one was killed during the attack. None of our soldiers sustained any long-lasting injuries, although a few of them were sent to the infirmary."

Her eyes flash. "Four gone and one dead already? What have you done with the body?"

"The body is already on display. We wanted to make sure it was still fresh, and that anybody who knew about the attack would understand exactly what happens when they try to defy you." His tongue darts out to wet his lips as he waits for the queen to respond.

Not that anyone worth noting has really tried to stand up to her in years. After she took over, there were many years of quiet compliance. She surprised them into submission when she put the crown on her head and declared herself the new ruler. That was when she was the most vulnerable, but they didn't know it. They never understood what it was she really wanted, never listened to her even as she told them loud and clear what she needed. So, when she had the chance to make them listen, she took it.

She hadn't even made it to a hundred years of her rule when they tried to rise up against her. It was over before it even really started. She barely broke a sweat when she ended their rebellion, turning their rebel base to ash and forcing the survivors to sweep away their own mess.

Nobody matches her level of magic, let alone the rare gift of Light Magic. She is blessed by the Goddess, after all.

You can always find some ungrateful commoners who think they are owed more than they are worth. More food, more money, more freedom. More, more, more. What they need is more discipline and more respect for the crown. If that means that they hate her for it, then so be it. It keeps her life interesting and her entertainment amusing.

"You know I hate it when the guards get to have the fun without me." Queen Elayce fake pouts and her eyes twinkle with mischief.

"But there are four—er, three, more rebels in the dungeons waiting just for you, Your Majesty. Surely that will keep you busy for a while?" His tone goes up at the end of the sentence, as if begging her to be okay with it. She stares him down, watches as another bead of sweat drips down his already greasy face. She pulls her lip back in from her pout, and turns back towards her reflection. Her eyes roam over the points in her black jeweled crown, nestled deeply within her intricately styled hair. She twirls away from Tydas, causing him to jog to keep up with her. Her velvet, jet black dress flows behind her. "We shall have a party tonight, to celebrate our guests."

Tydas attempts to bow his head, and stumbles while trying to keep up. "Of course. I will speak to the staff about getting things ready." When she doesn't say anything or break her stride, he finally takes his cue to leave and falls behind her and out of sight.

Chapter 2

She needs to get this dress cleaned. It would be a waste for it not to be seen because some rebel decided to be difficult. She'd rather go to the dungeons to welcome her other new guests, but she'll see them soon enough at the party later. She continues to her throne room instead, to get some work done before the party. Her private study lies just off the throne room, a maid will meet her there to get her cleaned up. Everyone thinks that being a queen is all parties and executions, and while she makes sure that is a part of it, that isn't all of it. Her kingdom won't run itself.

Her two guards trail her through the castle and when she arrives at her study, one stays outside the door and the other follows her in. She likes these two guards. They are nice to look at. They'd also turned out to not be complete idiots and had been in her personal guard rotation for quite a while. "Phin, could you go over the guard duty for the party tonight?" They'd had plenty of parties like this before, but she likes to make sure her guards are well informed and occasionally switch up their stations for better security.

He continues to stare at a fixed point above her head as he rattles off the details for the party. "Two guards at every entrance with a rotation every forty-two minutes, my queen.

CHAPTER 2

In the throne room, we will have one guard posted every few feet along the wall. Due to the entertainment tonight, we will have guards dressed as nobility and dispersed throughout the crowd to mingle and listen for any whispers of insurgence among the guests."

This is one of her favorite plans for guard duty. The guests have no idea who her guards are and they occasionally catch a lord or lady speaking ill of their queen. How fun to be able to provide spontaneous entertainment! They hadn't run this rotation in a while, and the nobles in attendance won't be expecting it. "Good, good. Thank you, Phin. I do hope we'll have some fresh entertainment, what a treat." Her eyes glint, but he doesn't notice as he's still fixated on the spot above her head.

She discovered a long time ago that loyalty and sharing in her enthusiasm for pain and torture don't have to go hand in hand. Although it would be nice if more of the people closest to her were as excited about these kinds of things as she is. Some of the other guards in her personal rotation will laugh along with her and even have suggestions. If she likes them, sometimes she humors them and lets them carry out the torture themselves. She could be just as amused by watching.

Phin isn't one of those guards. She leans back in her chair and flicks her hand, dismissing him back to his post. He bows his head and stands next to her door.

Darla scurries in, curtsying briefly before beginning to spot clean Elayce's dress. Her touch is light, knowing that her job is to be as invisible as possible.

Elayce turns her attention to the documents on her desk. Trade agreements between Aerash's own regions lay across the top. The council is always asking her to revise things, believing that one region is being unfairly compensated and deserves more. Always looking to see what more they could gain, and never what they could give. Her subjects think she is cruel, but they should see the inner workings of a council meeting. Silia produces the majority of Aerash's wood and paper supplies and believes that since they are the sole region to do so, that the other regions should bow down. Flora, rich in flower crops, sells their tinctures and potions at an inflated rate. South Garsen and Donnen trade in crops and animals, producing enough to feed the entire kingdom year-round. Most of the commoners didn't know that, though, since South Garsen and Donnen prefer to cater to the rich while exporting the excess. Nicen, producing most of the kingdom's alcohol, is usually too drunk to care much one way or the other.

Moving the trade agreements to the side, she focuses on the military reports that lay beneath. She recently ordered more of her people to be drafted, which brought an influx of bodies to the center of the kingdom, where Castle Vleck and the military training school reside. The council doesn't understand the order, but she is the queen and she doesn't have to have reasons for what she does. However, she isn't trying to incite a coup. She maneuvers her favor between the council members by adjusting trade agreements to appease or displease anyone she needs to take care of. It takes very little to remind these people who is really in charge. Politics is the easy part of her job really, albeit rather tedious.

She glances up at Phin, who is still staring at the same spot above her head. What is Phin like when he's not at his post? Does he sit in the barracks and silently stare at an undetermined point at the wall there too? He must have friends within the guard. His features seem to match her own and she wonders if he's from Flora, too. Phin has been around for a bit now, but she rarely takes the time to get to know her staff. Having relationships with people makes it harder when they inevitably die before you do. Being immortal can be lonely.

"Phin?"

Phin steps forward, eyes not moving from their spot. "Yes, Your Majesty."

"What region are you from?" Elayce asks. Phin's lips part slightly in surprise and his eyes flicker down to the queen before he answers, "South Garsen, Your Majesty." His eyes flicker back up before he finishes speaking.

"Hmm," Elayce hums, slowly nodding her head. "And what did you do in South Garsen before coming to train in my army?"

"My family owns a farm, Your Majesty. Cattle." He clears his throat, as if he isn't used to speaking. "But it is an honor to serve you, Your Majesty." He bows his head slightly at her.

"Do you miss home, Phin?" Elayce cocks her head to the side in genuine interest.

"Er, no, Your Majesty, this is my home." A look of confusion flutters across his features. Elayce sighs and curses herself, realizing that she's being sentimental. No doubt her trip to the greenhouse this morning is making her think about home. Rather inevitable with the three hundredth anniversary coming up. Every year, she fights with herself and her sentimentality. If only she had the power to wipe her own memories. The guard probably thinks she's trying to find a reason to claim he's disloyal and execute him.

She leans back in her chair and Phin steps back to his post by the door. She turns to look out the small window in her study that overlooks the palace courtyard. Not as beautiful as her greenhouse, but her staff keeps up the sharp edges of the hedges and makes sure the flowers are well maintained. The weather is mild in Aerash year-round, making it easy to grow and farm crops and flowers all year. Aerash is well-positioned in the world, as they are able to export many crops and necessities to neighboring northern kingdoms that can't grow crops through their snowy seasons. It's one of the reasons she chooses to not expand her rule, she doesn't want to bother with the aches and pains colder weather brings to a kingdom.

She'd visited the colder kingdoms over the years, especially when a new ruler was crowned. It's important to show face and remind them what she can do. It was always under the guise of a friendly party. They'd throw a large celebration to honor her as a guest and then ask that she show off her magic. Her magic comes easily to her, so she would oblige. She'd twirl her hands in the air and send golden sparks up. Most non-magic users don't need a lot to be impressed, and there are very few magic users left in the kingdom. None of them can use magic the way she can or she imagines her reign wouldn't have gone uncontested for so long. Especially considering she has no formal claim to the throne.

She'd make the lights go off and on, send sparks of heat rushing through the bottoms of their chairs. She would create pictures and full scenes out of the lights that flowed from her hands. Everyone would ooh and ahh, but very few had seen the full extent of her powers in years. She feels it running through her at all times of the day, and even sometimes when she sleeps. She can't remember what it felt like before this power was awakened inside of her. She'd only spent a small part of her life without it. She suspects she'll have to visit some of the other kingdoms again soon and prove good faith,

CHAPTER 2

what with building her army up. She would have to go reassure them that she doesn't plan on attacking them. Other kings and queens always think everything is about them.

A knock sounds on the door and she slides her eyes over to Phin and nods at him to open the door. She has no idea how he saw her nod since his gaze is still plastered to the wall, but he does what she wants. He opens the door and Tydas walks in.

"My queen, the mess has been cleaned up in the greenhouse. Were you able to extract anything of importance?" he asks, remaining in a slightly bowed position.

"Unfortunately, he seemed to only provide a good time, not good information. No matter, I have three more to play with. He was but a warm up for me and a warning to the others." Elayce rests her fingers along her chin.

"Of course, of course, my queen. You know exactly what to do to strike fear into their hearts." Tydas chuckles and smiles before coughing and clearing his throat when the queen's cold gaze doesn't change. "Yes, well I was just coming up to inquire about the entertainment for tonight. Would you like the three remaining prisoners brought up tonight or saved for your tricentennial celebration next month?"

Her staff is planning a big celebration in her honor, but she doesn't care enough to listen to what they suggest. When it comes down to it, she'll make a big show in front of her guests. She'll flaunt her powers to remind them what she can do, and there's usually some form of brutality to prove that she can be creative with her punishments even after all this time. It's important to her that they understand that she is the one with the crown and the power.

Elayce ponders for a moment. "Tonight. Have the guards bring them up after the feast. An execution is always better on a full stomach."

"As you wish, my queen."

Chapter 3

After dinner, Elayce lies draped across her throne on the dais above the ballroom. Both legs thrown over one armrest, torso leaning against the other as she lazily trails her fingers through the air, sending sparks of golden light through the crowded room. The guests dance to the beat of the loud music and drink Nicen wine. Many sit along the steps to her throne, entranced by the magic that she sends out into the room. The nobles never grow tired of seeing her power, and Elayce never gets tired of showing them. She loves the moments when she can show others the beauty of it. Her magic isn't just death and destruction, it can be light too. They are the ones who force her to use it as a means of controlling everything around her.

She swings her legs and rests her head against her throne, letting her hair cascade down to the floor. She senses the guards coming with the prisoners, so she flicks her wrist and the guards stationed by the entrance jump to open the doors.

"Ladies and Gentlemen," one of the members of her staff calls out as the music quiets, but doesn't stop. "Queen Elayce promised you entertainment tonight, and you shall have it!" The drunken crowd cheers, expressing the same feeling Elayce has inside, and parts down the middle for the guards to stride through.

There are three prisoners, two men and a woman. They look pretty beaten up already, many of their wounds crusted over. Nobody had dared send healers down to treat the rebels. The queen snaps her head to the man on the left. Her black painted lips turn up in a smile as she wiggles her fingers and sends slow, lazy sparks towards him. His eyes widen and he tries to get up from his knees. Elayce reaches out with her power and melds his chains to the ground, forcing him to stay down.

"No! Please, Your Majesty. No!" the girl, kneeling in the middle, shouts. Elayce doesn't break her gaze from the man as her golden sparks of power circle around him. She can feel his tremors through the sparks nearest him.

Her magic used to feel like an invasion, something that had been bestowed upon her but wasn't hers. After spending so much time with it zipping through her blood and poking at her skin from the inside, it now feels like an extension of her. Feeling what they feel and sensing what they sense. She spent so much time sitting with her power to learn it and what she could do with it. She barely needs to think anymore; her subconscious can control it well enough. The hand twirling is mostly for show. She wants people to know what's coming. The anticipation it elicits and the fear and awe that come with it is all part of the fun.

She pokes the man with her sparks, feeding on his fear and the laughter of the crowd around them. Suddenly, one of her sparks buries itself into his arm and comes out the other side. He lets out a scream that almost drowns out the music as blood begins to fall to the floor. Elayce cackles and her gray eyes shine as she watches the red spread across the marble. It's always spreading, greedy to devour more.

She can barely hear the screaming from the woman now.

CHAPTER 3

With a flourish of her hand the sparks jump to the ceiling and flutter in a circle around the room. They pop and spark and almost sing as they soar around the heads of the laughing nobles. A show, what a show. Elayce delights in it and sucks in a small breath for her big finish. Her eyes snap back to the man gushing blood on the floor, still locked in a kneeling position. Her sparks rush back to her target, aiming straight for his heart. Elayce's pulse speeds up as she anticipates the rush of feeling the last breath come from his lungs. His repayment for crossing her.

Her sparks strike in a flurry of light and a loud thump, but it isn't who Elayce had intended. The woman had jumped from her position in the center and thrust her body in front of her sparks. Elayce's mouth curves down at the corners. The room watches as the light leaves the eyes of the rebel woman and Queen Elayce's sparks seem to grow brighter in response.

"Interesting," Elayce muses out loud. The rebel man, his feet still stuck in place and with one bleeding arm, reaches his good arm towards the dead woman on the floor. Tears stream down his face, his mouth opening and closing with no sound escaping. He tries stroking her hair, but only manages to drench the tangled brown locks with blood.

Elayce's head falls back against her throne again as she laughs, reaching for a wine glass that a servant is holding on a tray next to her. "You and that face of yours had me quite mesmerized. I didn't even notice your friend here." The crowd laughs and shouts at the captives. She wiggles her fingers as she leans back and drains her cup, sending the sparks to caress the man's face. He aggressively turns his face to the side to avoid the touch. Leaning forward with her now empty cup, she giggles and hiccups before chucking the cup to the side. The sounds of the bouncing metal reverberate through the room. The servant boy runs after it and immediately replaces it with a full glass.

"Her *heroic* sacrifice doesn't even mean anything. You're going to die anyway," Elayce says.

"It means something to me. But, of course you wouldn't understand. You only know death and hatred," the man spits at her.

Elayce laughs. "You think I don't know that you're talking about love? You know nothing, peasant." He knows nothing. *Nothing*. Nobody in this kingdom knows what love is. So quick to forget what they asked her to do, what they made her do.

She feels it welling up inside of her, that power that is more than the sparks. Once it starts, it's hard to push back down and usually requires her to expel some of it. She can't keep it locked up inside, and if she lets it go here she could kill everyone around her. She doesn't mind death, relishes it, actually. But she doesn't gain anything from killing a room full of people who admire and fear her just the right amount.

She scowls, annoyed that she let this man pull these feelings out of her. She should have known that this magic would be lying just under the surface and she shouldn't have drank so much. She's been thinking about the past too much lately.

Sparks begin to dance along her skin and down her body. She quickly throws a couple up into the air, creating a light show to hide her attempt at taking some of the pressure off. "What good did love do for you or her now? She's dead and you'll soon join her. All your love has done is give everyone in this room a good show." She spreads her arms wide to gesture to the room and sparks shoot from her arms, circling the room, crackling and popping. The crowd continues cheering. They love this and they have no idea the danger they're in if she can't hold on to this magic. They dance while they watch and continue to drink alcohol, reveling in the cruelty.

Elayce smirks when she sees the crowd cheering, once again locking her gaze onto the man. "Your love won't save you." She raises her hand to command her sparks to strike the man straight through his heart when she hears a cough. She flicks her eyes to the third prisoner, who she hasn't even taken in yet. If she'd seen him from the start, this would have gone much differently. He'd been staring at the ground for most of the time, but now as he wipes the blood he coughed up from his chin, his green eyes glance upwards.

Everything stops. All the sparks that Elayce had sent through the room evaporate. She feels her breath catch in her throat. The crowd fades into the back and it's just her and those green eyes. His green eyes. The green eyes that have haunted her dreams now for centuries. She feels the rush of breath pass through her lips. A laugh rings out from far away. His eyes look up and lock with hers, but she doesn't see any form of recognition pass through them. She sits up straight in her chair, the velvet of the cushion rubbing against her body. The alcohol she drank makes her dizzy, but her enhanced senses help her stay sharp enough. She stands to move towards him, and she can feel the brush of her dress swinging against her legs. She feels the vibration through the air as he blinks, breaking eye contact for a split second and a split second too long.

Elayce takes a step forward, feeling the stone dais beneath her slippered feet. It is starkly cold and hard compared to the warm, softness that is curling up within her. She takes another step, aware of every breath, every feeling between her and this man. This man who cannot be who she thinks he is. The blond, shaggy hair and the green eyes, the slope of his nose, and the curve of his pink lips. Cracked and dry, crusted with blood. He doesn't seem too different from the last time she saw him a little over three hundred years ago. She realizes the building of power has dissipated. It's resting once again in that bottomless pit inside of her. His warmth has quelled it, as it always did.

Another step forward, and he's realized that she's going to cross over directly to him. She feels his intake of breath as she releases hers. Almost as if he's stolen her breath away. Distantly she hears someone calling her. She's dialed in to every movement he makes and every movement that takes her closer to him, but everything else beyond is a blur. Nothing matters except him.

Another step. Every strand of hair swishes as she walks. She can feel it as it sweeps across her back and caresses her face.

Her face.

Will he notice how her eyes have changed in his absence? A small part of her chides herself, this isn't really him. It can't possibly be, he's dead.

Another step forward, and she's almost directly in front of him. She's aware that her guards have all moved in closer, she can feel the shift in attention as they push her dancing puppets out of the way to get closer to her. She's mesmerized by his eyes and she can't stop moving towards him. She can draw upon her power to defend herself if she needs to. She won't have to, not against this man.

She takes the final step, and she stops directly in front of him. He's a few inches taller than she is and she tilts her head up to continue staring into his eyes.

CHAPTER 3

"Who are you?" she breathes. She feels the words leave her lips, everything else still muted in comparison to the pull that draws them together.

"Who am I? I am nobody." His words caress her. They curve through the air and land gently in her ears. She can feel his slow breathing, his calm heartbeat. How is he so calm? Does he not fear her?

"Nobody," she whispers back to him, reaching out to touch his face. Maybe if she just feels him, tastes his skin, she'll convince herself that it isn't—

"Your Majesty, this man is sick and filthy from being in the dungeons. I highly suggest that you do not make contact with him." A guard has stepped forward, his hand hovering over her shoulder. The near contact makes Elayce snap out of it, realizing that she's lost complete control of herself. She maneuvers herself out from the guards reach and away from the prisoner. The crowd has stopped dancing and moving all together; the music has ceased. Her gaze briefly goes back to the man in front of her, but before she can get trapped within his eyes again she takes another step back and clears her throat.

"Take this one back to the dungeon," she addresses the guard while pointing to the prisoner. "I will need to question him personally."

The guard nods once and grabs the shoulder of the man, leading him out of the room and back down the hallway. Elayce looks around the room and plasters a smile on her face, tossing light and sparks up into the air once again. She gestures towards the first prisoner, sending sparks through his chest without much fanfare. She doesn't have the energy to restart the show. The crowd, easily swayed, cheers again and the music starts and they dissolve into dancing. Elayce takes a deep breath and exits the ballroom, heading straight to her personal chambers.

Chapter 4

Elayce paces back and forth across her room. The fire a servant started when she first arrived does nothing to warm her now. The chill that had crept through her body once the prisoner had been taken back to the dungeons seemed to stick to her bones. At the very least, the rate at which she is pacing should warm her but it doesn't make a difference. Tydas had tried to follow her back through the halls and speak to her about her abrupt exit, but she'd dismissed him. She doubts anybody would understand what happened so why discuss it with anyone.

She needs to sleep on this and deal with it in the morning, once the alcohol has left her system. She lays down in her giant four-poster bed, across the room from the fireplace. The night's events have left her rattled. She tosses and turns, asking herself the same question over and over: who *is he, who is he?* So much energy is zipping through her, and at the same time she feels suspended in the moment when their eyes connected.

She rolls over, huffing. It's been so long since she's been unsure of what to do. She rolls over again, before finally tossing the blankets off and marching to the small apothecary attached to her chambers. Her fingers drag along the jars, not feeling the glass but the herbs and berries within them.

She pulls a few small jars off the shelf to create a sleeping tincture for herself. She tries to lose herself in the measuring and mixing like she's been doing all these years to hide from her thoughts. Instead, flashes of smiles and blood and tears keep coming to her. She has to restart the mixture three times before she finally gets it right. She chastises herself for her lack of focus, muttering about accidentally putting herself to sleep for days if she keeps making mistakes like that. Lifting the potion to her lips, she tosses her head back and drinks, almost immediately feeling its effects. Her eyes are drooping shut before she even makes it to the bed.

~

It's late morning before Elayce rolls over and opens her eyes, a feeling of discontent bubbling up within her. Sounds of water running from the bathroom tell her that one of her maids is drawing a bath for her. Mornings after celebrations are usually left open for her to freshen up and recoup, running a kingdom on a tight leash can sometimes afford her time to herself. She sits up and stretches, lazily making her way to the bathroom. A large, steaming pool is set in the floor of the tiled room, big enough for more than ten people to fit at once.

The cold tile beneath her feet helps to wake her. Elayce peels her dress and garments off from the night before and tosses them into a far corner, causing the maid to scurry across the room to remove them to be laundered.

Lavender and vanilla scents waft throughout the room, courtesy of the soapy bathwater. Elayce steps into the bath, slowly lowering herself until she is submerged up to her chin. The warmth of the water reminds her of the warmth she felt yesterday as she walked closer to the prisoner. She scowls, upset that the relative calm of her morning is already ruined.

CHAPTER 4

The prisoner would have to be brought to her this morning; she couldn't wait any longer to sort this out. Nothing would get done properly without taking care of this first.

Her eyes wander over the cavernous ceilings of her bathing room, taking in the artwork along the stone. The artwork has been there since before she took over. The scenes depict long forgotten battles with foes and blessings given to royalty by gods that nobody prays to anymore. It's unclear to her why previous kings felt like these scenes should be what someone has to look at while bathing and dressing in the morning, but seeing them gives her a sense of comfort, almost. They remind her that there has been so much that has happened in this world before her, and there will likely be so much more that happens after she is gone. Assuming she finds a way to fully defeat the Darkness that lurks at the edges of the kingdoms, of course. Maybe she will have that battle painted as a mural somewhere in the castle one day.

Her fingers dip and swirl in the bubbles, twirling in patterns that she has long since learned to use to command her magic. She should go to the training room today to blow off a little steam. Being alive for three hundred years doesn't mean that one has learned everything there is to know about combat and magic. Magic is ever changing and can have a mind of its own, even hers. The trick is to treat the magic with respect and never pretend that you know more than it does.

With her next steps in mind, Elayce finishes washing her body and stands from the bath before moving to her dressing room. The maid follows behind and begins towel drying Elayce's skin and hair as she walks. The dressing room is filled with dresses and clothes that have been collected over lifetimes. Before taking the throne, she didn't have much in the way of belongings. Most people in the kingdom don't have enough to spare on frivolities. It is quite easy to fall in love with fabrics and fancy things. Dressmakers fall all over themselves for the opportunity to dress her, regardless of the occasion. Most of the clothing she wears is black or dark blues and greens. Rarely does a dressmaker suggest the queen wear brighter clothing. While she has nothing against colors, they seem to feel that their queen belongs in dark clothing. It would be too difficult to wrap one's head around a spring daisy torturing and beheading traitors to the kingdom.

Darla comes out of the shadows to help dress Elayce. Silently, she watches the two attendants scurry about the room, gathering her stockings, undergarments, and several options of gowns to wear for the day. Rarely do any of her attendants make eye contact with her as they assist, which is probably why the only one that she actually knows the name of is Darla.

"Darla," she begins. "Tell me, are there any new rumors that I need to address?"

Darla flinches and her eyes flick up to Elayce's face and then back down to the corset she is holding up for the other attendant to tighten. "Nothing of importance, Your Majesty."

Elayce reaches up to Darla's face and drags her finger nail along her jawline, forcing Darla to look directly up at her. "Oh come, pet, do tell." There must be some gossip about what happened last night. "Or perhaps you'd like to talk about how your sister is doing?"

Darla's sister had developed an illness that should have taken her life. Darla, not yet a lady's maid then, had approached the queen and offered her loyalty and services in exchange for saving her sister. The tincture that she made, combined with the prowess of her head healer, was enough to save Darla's sister. Unfortunately, she often relapses and needs constant care. Elayce allows her sister to stay in the castle with Darla as long as she continues to prove herself loyal and useful. So far, it has turned out to be quite a good deal for Elayce.

Darla's tongue sneaks out to wet her lips and she takes a shaky breath in. "Well, Your Majesty, there were just a few whispers about the party last night. But as I said, nothing of importance. Nothing that you should spend time on."

"Out with it." Elayce lets her soothing tone drop and pushes the tip of her fingernail into Darla's skin where she still holds her jaw.

"It was just some silly whispers about leaving that rebel alive, Your Majesty. They think that maybe he used some magic to distract you, something that made you change your mind about killing him. Some think that maybe it was a protection spell or an illusion spell. It's all just whispers though, nobody really knows anything. That's all, my queen, I swear." Darla's shoulders slump as the words all rush out of her in one breath. Elayce releases Darla's face and she immediately takes a step backward and looks down at her shoes.

Elayce mulls over what Darla said. A protection spell? Probably not, she would have sensed that magic. Same with an illusion spell. Do they really think that someone else's magic would get past her defenses? After all this time as their queen, they still hope that some savior will come along and defeat her. If someone does come along and best her in battle, it won't be the hero that they're looking for. It never is. If they looked at even their most recent history, they would remember that. The fact that they don't remember is one of the reasons she's so puzzled about who this man is and where he came from.

She doesn't even try to hide what happened, they just don't care. Their hope blinds them, makes them stupid.

Elayce points to one of the dresses that's laid out for her and Darla grabs the dress and holds it up to help her into it. The corners of her mouth pull down while Darla and the other attendant put the finishing touches on her outfit and lace her hair into an intricate braid down her back.

Stepping off the dressing platform, she heads towards the door and calls for her guards. "Have the prisoner brought up to my council room." She points to the second guard. "Sweet Darla has names of some gossipers that will have to be dealt with. A few nights in the dungeons should remind them how they should be spending their time. They're lucky I don't have their tongues cut out."

When she glances back at Darla, her face is expressionless, but she can see the rush of shame that crosses over her eyes. Darla's inability to keep secrets is worth more to Elayce than the price of the herbs to heal her sister. Though she's sure that Darla wishes for any other assignment in the castle. Elayce shuts the door behind her on the way to the council room.

It isn't long before the prisoner is pushed into the council room where Elayce is already waiting. He is much the same as he was last night in his ragged, dirt-covered clothes. His hair is clumped with dirt and another dark, crusty substance that is probably blood. Her magic pulls to him and aches to reach out to comfort him. She holds back. The calming warmth of being around him settles within her, but she doesn't move from the chair she's seated in. If she remains seated, perhaps she can keep control of herself.

"Good morning," she greets the prisoner. He doesn't respond so she continues, "Shall I continue to address you as Nobody, or do you have a name?"

"I don't think my name will matter much, as I expect to be dead soon," he answers.

"Nobody it is then." She doesn't disagree with him, but she hasn't decided what will be done with him yet. "Tell me then, Nobody, why you were caught by my guards and brought here to my castle."

He looks up at her. Her heart stutters, and she is grateful that he doesn't have magic that gives him the ability to hear her unruly heart. He simply holds her gaze. Breathing with effort, he stands there, mute, in chains and covered in filth.

Elayce rolls her eyes and gestures to a chair at the opposite end of the table from her. "Have a seat. Clearly the effort of standing is too much for you." He doesn't move and the guard shoves him into the chair that Elayce gestured to. He stumbles a bit and adjusts so he is sitting properly in the chair. "I don't appreciate having to repeat myself, but I'll give you a pass this time, Nobody." As if she hasn't already given him many passes. "Why are you here in my castle?"

He spits on the table and a look of disgust settles over him. "You're a tyrant. A demon from the underworld. You need to be torn down from your throne, so that the people of Aerash can be free again."

The erratic beating of her heart slows and she feels it harden at his words. A slow sneer spreads across her face. "The same lies your friend spewed yesterday before I poured poison down his throat." She expects him to have a reaction to her words, but he doesn't. The disgusted expression stays plastered to his face, he doesn't even blink. She takes a deep breath to calm her voice. "How did you expect to remove me from my throne?"

"You won't learn any rebel secrets from me, *Queen*."

"Even if it could save your life?"

"I doubt anything could save my life anymore."

Elayce rests her chin in her hands and scrutinizes her prisoner. She switches her line of questioning, "Do you know why I didn't just kill you last night?" He shakes his head once. "Who sent you to the castle, Nobody?"

"As I told you, you will learn no rebel secrets from me."

"I don't care about the rebellion!" The screech of her chair being pushed back across the floor echoes within the room. Suddenly the room is filled with light and golden sparks that swirl around Elayce, the frustration that she feels manifesting outwardly. How is she supposed to learn who he is if he repeats phrases that have been said to her over and over by countless other rebels? The rebellion is the least of her concerns right now.

A guard clears his throat and shifts uncomfortably as the golden sparks dance around him. The queen looks up at him, glaring. Her frustration morphs into anger at being interrupted by the guard, at being driven to frustration so easily by this man who won't even tell her his name. The guard flinches under her unblinking stare. Her eyes narrow at him and the sparks move closer and circle faster. "Is there something you'd like to say?"

Using the barest movement of his head to avoid the magic circling him, he shakes his head. One single spark leaves the group and moves towards the guard's face. It seems to caress his lips, and the guard's eyes widen with fear and pain. The smell of burnt flesh fills the room and his lips, now a bright pink, stretch and contort as he attempts to pull them apart to scream. A fear-mottled moan comes from him and his hand flies up to a mouth that he is no longer able to open.

CHAPTER 4

"What did you do to him?" The prisoner gasps, a look of fear and...is that awe? Comes over him. Meanwhile, the guard has sunk to the floor, tears pouring from his eyes and across the hands that cover his mouth.

"He didn't have anything to say." Elayce's gaze snaps back to the prisoner.

"You're a monster! He didn't even speak!" The prisoner tries to gesture with his hands and his chains clank at the strain.

"A monster?" Elayce hisses. "This is what they wanted! They turned me into this, so that they could use me how they wanted. But now, you come here. To my castle. To remove me from my throne and tell me that *I'm* the monster. You want to cast me aside as if I haven't been serving the people for the past few centuries and protecting you from yourselves and a darkness that you can't even begin to imagine. You, my prisoner, have no idea what I do for you all. I can assure you that if I was gone, there wouldn't be any throne left for you to have."

Abruptly, Elayce stops and scans the room to see who's here. Other than her and the prisoner, it's just the two guards, one on the floor still. Elayce leans against the table and drops her head between her shoulders, letting a whoosh of air pass between her lips.

The words he says have been hurled at her for centuries now. Even before she took the throne, people didn't trust her. They were afraid of her power and their own powerlessness. In the end, they were right. She did betray them. They didn't deserve the kingdom, she had done as they asked and she was taking what belonged to her.

"Who did this to you?" The question shocks Elayce and her

head snaps up to look him in the eyes. The intensity in his gaze doesn't betray any feeling other than a deep curiosity.

"You...you want to know what happened to me?" The shock causes her to stumble over her words.

It's been so long since anyone asked her anything about herself and actually meant it. Does he mean it? Does he think he can figure out how to destroy her if he knows her past? If only he knew that he was already destroying her. She had to get herself together. She couldn't keep losing control of herself around him. It'd been less than twenty-four hours since this stranger walked into her life. If she wasn't going to learn anything from him, then she had to put an end to this. Soon.

"No, no I don't think it would matter much to tell you. You'll be dead soon anyway." She turns to stalk out of the room. "Take the prisoner back to the dungeon. And take him to a medic," she says, pointing to the guard. "They'll have to cut his lips apart or he'll starve to death." The door swings shut behind her.

Chapter 5

The next few days drag by. Elayce spends her time in council meetings and at small dinner parties with visiting Aerash nobles. She's irritable and distant as she tries to keep her thoughts of the prisoner to a minimum. There hasn't been another attack on the castle yet, which is odd. They had to know that she still had a prisoner alive, as his body hadn't been hung on the keep walls. Her advisor thought maybe that would drive the rebels to attempt a rescue mission, but in actuality they had been quieter than they had been in a long while.

Tydas and some of the council members at the table discuss what it could mean and argue about their concerns, but she just sits back and lets them argue. When they turn to her to see what she thinks about it, she continues to stare at them without saying anything.

"If the queen was worried, then she would say so. We should move on to more important matters," Tydas speaks on behalf of Queen Elayce, his over-sized sleeves swinging as he gestures to the council members.

She scowls in irritation, but does nothing to stop him. What is he thinking about down in the dungeons? Is he still alive? He did have injuries from the raid and the dungeons certainly aren't clean. Surely she would be notified if he died. Maybe not, there are so many people who are in and out of the dungeons. If they notified her every time someone died they might as well not leave her side.

She refocuses on the conversation in front of her, squeezing her arm to try to bring her to the present conversation. They are talking about the invitation to visit the neighboring Kingdom of Selna. Selna is a small country south of the region of South Garsen. Mostly they keep to themselves as their size doesn't afford them a large military presence. Selna and Aerash have well established trade agreements and fortunately, for them really, they never try to stir up trouble with Aerash or the queen.

"You can send a message to King Theis that I will accept his invitation." Maybe what she needs is distance from where *he* is. While the rest of the table falls into a shocked silence, Tydas doesn't show any surprise at the queen's decision.

Because her magic is well known across the lands, it is also easy to keep other kingdoms from attempting to take over her own. In the beginning, the other kingdoms had thought she was weak because she was a queen without a king, the first to declare her rule without a man at her side. It didn't take long for them to see that if she wanted their lands, she could take them without even a fight. Mostly, they stay out of her way. There is the occasional suggestion of marriage to unite their kingdoms, but she normally takes care of that by simply getting rid of the fool who suggests as much. Unfortunately, the memories of mortals were quite short and their egos quite large and it happens more often than she would like.

"Yes, Your Majesty, we will have a messenger sent out today. We will need a couple days to gather a traveling party for you, but I think you could leave the morning of the second day from now?" Tydas asks.

"Yes, fine." She waves away his approving stare. This will be her first big trip in decades, but going south will give her a chance to feel around the edges of her borders to see if there has been significant change since the last time that she was out. She can feel the pressure of her enemy, but it's weak here in the center of her kingdom. It will be good to go out and check the wards. "You're dismissed." She waves to the members of the council. Being used to her abrupt dismissals, the council members quickly get up and bow on their way out, their heeled footsteps echoing throughout the high-ceilinged room.

"My queen, you know the invitation is most likely a way to get you to the Selna court for another marriage proposal," Tydas, who hasn't moved from his seat next to her, says.

"I'm aware," Elayce sighs. King Theis is rather young and hasn't yet attempted his own marriage proposal. His father had many years ago, and no doubt told his son that the best way to protect their kingdom would be a marriage to the Queen of Aerash. As a member of the royal court, you are trained to protect your kingdom or expand your kingdom. The old king was well trained by the monarch before him and he sought out Elayce years ago when he came to the throne. He stayed without a queen for many years, hoping that he could change Elayce's mind, before Elayce forced a trade for another neighboring kingdom to send their princess out to him. The princess arrived with a note from Elayce that her patience would only go so far. A threat now a few decades past, the old king must have encouraged his son to try once again. Because surely after forty years, the queen would be looking for a companion.

Tydas fidgets his heavily decorated fingers on the table,

careful not to make any noises, most likely still suffering from the memory of the guard whose mouth had been melted shut by the queen and then cut open again by a medic. He's alive, but the gruesomeness of the punishment has sent a hush over the castle halls for the past few days.

"Speak, Tydas," she sighs, impatiently.

"I think it would be a great arrangement, Your Majesty. As the more powerful kingdom, we could use a marriage to absorb Selna as a region of Aerash. We would have the man-power to continue to protect our land, including the new area. Selna would be a great addition to your reign, Your Majesty. Our borders have been stagnant and well-held for so long." Greed wove through his words. His black velvet-clad chest puffing out with pride for his country, as if he alone was responsible for the throne's prosperity.

"If I wanted what Selna had, then I could just take it. I don't need to saddle myself with a king to get what I want," she counters.

Tydas latches on to what she said as if he was just waiting for the conversation to go this direction. "Well, then why not take it? This could go down as part of your legacy! Expand Aerash's borders! We have been idle for so long, Your Majesty. We could start with absorbing Selna, and then continue South. We could even move to Don Kemt after taking Selna. Our neighbors to the east have been complacent for years, they wouldn't see it coming. Plus, sources tell us that they're weak, trying to fight a war on their eastern border. We should take our forces and attack them—take over."

"I'm uninterested in fighting someone else's battle." Though Elayce knows that the battle happening there isn't for greed or domination. It's the Darkness closing in on the neighboring kingdom. She isn't prepared to march her army into a battle that they cannot win yet. Not without the knowledge she still seeks. Let their eastern neighbors take the brunt of the Darkness and its army in hopes that they will weaken the Darkness on its journey to her own home. Doubt floods through her at the thought that they can do anything to weaken the Darkness without magic like hers. "We have everything we need right in Aerash and anything we don't I can provide a trade agreement for."

"Yes, of course, Your Majesty," Tydas concedes for the moment, but she knows that she'll hear about it again. Probably before she even leaves for this trip.

"I'm heading to the training room," she says as more of a dismissal than to notify him of her whereabouts. He stands and bows to her as she leaves the council room and heads in the direction of the training room.

Once there, she changes into her black training gear before making her way to the middle of the black mat. As she stretches and warms up, several of her best fighters come in and start warming up as well. Nobody has magic that she can fight and practice against, but she likes to keep up on her hand-to-hand combat and dagger play. There are several racks of weapons that line the stone walls, to be used by anyone allowed in the training room. The daggers, her favorite non-magic weapons, will stay in their sheathes today, so Elayce can practice hand-to-hand. It's not a good idea to play with knives when she's distracted by thoughts of blond hair and green eyes.

Harkn, another one of her personal guards, steps onto the mat with her and raises his fists. He didn't make it to her personal guard duty without hard work, he had physically proved himself to her here in this room. Any guard who wants to reach the highest rank has to prove themselves directly to the queen in a fight. Harkn is one of the few guards who actually came out on top during his trial fight. Rarely does he best her during training, but they will often call a draw. Her captain of the guard has also earned that honor in a trial fight against the queen, but he doesn't spend much of his time in training with her anymore with the influx of new recruits.

Elayce notices the flexing of Harkn's muscles in the mirrored wall behind him as they circle each other on the mat. Mirrors help her and others training here see their mistakes better and work on their form. It also works to the advantage of the person facing them in the start of a fight. Harkn jerks forward, rushing to crash with Elayce. While her magic doesn't enhance her strength, it does enhance her balance and reflexes though she tries to tamp it down while training. It is important to be able to win in combat without relying on her magic as she never knows what could happen. Elayce shifts slightly and braces for impact, letting Harkn grab her around the waist and punching him in his side. He grunts and coughs from the hit and twists her to the ground, trying to get on top of her and pin her. She brings her knees up to his chest and heaves him away, causing him to lose grip on her and she rolls away before popping back up behind him. Both facing the mirror, she waves her fingers to him before kicking him square in the back and sending him sprawling to the ground.

"You've been missing training days, Hark?"

"I've only been missing training days with you, my queen, nobody else fights the way you do and you haven't been to training in a while."

"Excuses, excuses." She smirks and gestures for him to get up and go again. Harkn will often have suggestions for her guard rotations and how to take care of prisoners. He earned her respect in his trial fight, and she allows him to speak more freely in her presence. He is also a willing participant when she beckons him to her bed on occasion. He rolls onto his stomach and pushes himself off the floor, his black training vest allowing his muscles to ripple and swell with the effort. A smile of appreciation and challenge stretches across Elayce's face, beckoning Harkn to come closer.

Several sparring rounds later, both Elayce and Harkn are breathing heavily. Though neither of them has called it, they both walk to the side of the room to hydrate and end their session for the day.

Harkn leans against the stone wall. "Good form today, my queen."

Her gaze runs the length of his sweat glistened body. His dark hair, which started out draped over his dark blue eyes, now clings to his damp forehead. She watches his throat bob as he takes gulps of water, his eyes on her as she looks him over.

Her next distraction.

"I can think of a few more workouts we could try yet, today," Elayce says low enough, so that only he can hear.

His eyebrows raise and he sets the cup on the table beside him before taking a few slow steps closer to her. "I would be delighted if we could continue our training." His eyes gleam with mischief, but he won't reach out to touch her unless she indicates it's okay, especially where others might see.

"Then I shall see you tonight." Elayce's gaze moves deliberately to his lips and then back up to his eyes before she glides out of the training room, her body humming with anticipation.

~

The next morning, Elayce wakes up and stretches her arms above her as sparks lazily leap from her fingertips and float back down to the rumpled sheets. The clothes that were strewn about the floor before she fell asleep were cleaned up by a servant after she kicked Harkn from the bedroom. He often tries to tease and convince her into letting him stay after they are done, but she doesn't want his company once she's been satisfied. A few sparks to his backside and he's hopping out of the room to await the next time she summons him.

Tomorrow morning she would be heading out to Selna, so she just had to occupy herself for the rest of the day before she would be able to put some distance between her and the prisoner.

Nobody. Surely he has a name. She could go down to the dungeon and convince him to tell her his name so she wouldn't have to keep thinking of him as "Nobody." Or maybe she should just stop thinking of him all together and then it wouldn't matter at all.

After getting dressed, she heads to her study to get some work done. She will be gone for a few weeks for her trip, and while she can leave some of the work to Tydas while she is gone, she doesn't trust him with it all. This will be his first time filling in for her and she can guarantee he will make some decisions she will have to fix once she comes back. She grumbles at the thought.

Hours pass and Elayce remains in her study until the sun goes down and the stars come out. After pouring over documents all day, she finally leans back in her chair. Satisfied that she will leave things in a place that can't be too screwed up by Tydas. She signs the last document and nods to the page boy standing in the corner, so that he can deliver the papers to

CHAPTER 5

Tydas, who will look things over before they go to the council. Hopefully the council is appeased by what she has decided on.

Elayce feels restless and decides on a walk to stretch her muscles and clear her mind. Her feet carry her slowly through the castle halls. Dragging her fingers along the cold stone of the walls, she occasionally brushes over a painting or a mural decorating the stone. She doesn't pay much attention, winding her way through her dimly lit castle halls as her guards walk behind her. No Harkn tonight.

She's lived here for hundreds of years now and can draw the layout of the castle if asked. Every inch is familiar to her, yet none of it seems to welcome her. The walls and the floors give off cold air, despite the fair weather. Everything, the statues, relics, paintings, furniture, is well taken care of—she makes sure of it. The staff are constantly dusting, repairing, and sometimes refurbishing things so that nothing falls into decay. She traces the black lines of a vase that stands on a pedestal. It's been there longer than Elayce.

She realizes where she is, just outside the dungeons.

Her wretched feet had wandered.

The two guards standing at the entrance wait for what she has to say. She walks with purpose towards the door and one of the guards swings it open for her.

Once inside, she walks straight up to the dungeon master. "Where is he being kept?"

"Your Majesty, we did not know you were coming. We could have had him brought up to you. Why don't we bring him upstairs to you, this is no place for a queen." Dungeon Master Jarrel looks flustered and squints in the dark at Elayce. Elayce shrugs her shoulders and a group of sparks burst into the air and hover around, offering light in the dimness of the dungeon.

"If I wanted him to be brought upstairs, then I would have called for him to be brought upstairs. Bring me to him," she demands.

"Whatever you wish, my queen. Right this way."

The dungeon master turns and marches down the dark, damp hall. Moaning and hollering comes from the different cells they pass. Most could probably not see who was passing their cell doors or they would have had harsher words to yell at the queen.

"He's in a cell at the end of this hall," Dungeon Master Jarrel says, pointing behind him to a hallway so dark it appears to simply be a hole in the wall.

"Good. My guards will sit here. You can head back to your station, Master Jarrel," Elayce orders as she brushes past the three men and heads into the darkness. Wisely, none of them argue with her.

Her sparks create a bubble of light around her while she walks further and further into the shadows. They dance and dip, excited to finally be out and useful. Days spent in her study cause her magic to build beneath her skin, and now, getting closer and closer to him, she feels the pull, like a million tiny magnets straining to rip free from her flesh to get closer to him.

The hallway is so long that she gets to a point where she can't see what's ahead or what she left behind. Eventually, the cell comes into view. A wall of bars fit into a stone archway. Behind the bars sits a small room with a cot and a thin blanket, an empty tray with a silver cup on it, and a pot in the corner. She doesn't see him at first, but she hears him shuffle slowly around the corner of the door. His dirty face morphs into a puzzled expression and then one of anger replaces it. "What are you doing here?"

"It's my castle, I can go anywhere I like. If you'd like to return to our earlier conversation, the real question is, what are you doing here? In my castle?"

"As I told you before, you won't learn any secrets from me." His green eyes flash with defiance and he leans his hands against the metal bars of his cell.

"I will admit, you have intrigued me, Nobody. I have thought a lot about you since you arrived at my feet, at my celebration. For that, you have been kept alive while I decide what I want to do with you." Some of her sparks jump out from the circle and float closer to the prisoner. They shiver with excitement, causing shimmers of light to fly off and puff to the ground. "Unfortunately for you, I don't like to play these long games. I'm tired of waiting."

The sparks that had danced closer to him jump at him, but he doesn't flinch. They don't touch him and instead disappear into the metal bars that he's holding onto. Shock flits across his face when he feels the bars beneath his hands warm. At first he doesn't move, seemingly welcoming the small bit of warmth in the cold dungeon. Quickly, the bars become too hot to touch and he tries to pull away, but finds that he is unable to.

"No, no!" he shouts, pulling and tugging his hands, trying to let go of the bars. The bars begin to turn red. Elayce holds herself still so she doesn't show the war being waged within her, how much effort it takes to force her magic to harm him. The prisoner screams and writhes, using his whole body to try to separate his singed hands from the bars. "STOP. STOP, PLEASE," he screams.

The sparks pop out of the bars and the red glow dissipates immediately. The prisoner throws himself to the ground. His hands are blistered and red and he looks from them back up to Elayce who still hasn't moved. "Monster," he mutters under his breath before spitting in her direction.

Elayce inhales sharply. "I'm tired of having the same conversation with you. Tell me your name, so I can address you as I answer the question you asked last time we were here."

He regards her with a look of mistrust in his eyes from the floor. "Vaaren," he says.

Elayce freezes. "What did you say?"

"Vaaren."

For a few seconds Elayce can't do anything but gape at him. That's *his* name. "What region are you from?" He does nothing but glare back at her. "How about we make this an even exchange? I will tell you pieces of information about myself— 'who did this to me', as you asked earlier. In exchange, you will answer questions that I ask about you."

"Why would you need to know anything about me?" he asks, distrust in his tone.

"Curiosity. It's this or I find a new and creative way to rid my dungeons of another useless prisoner," she replies simply.

She can't let him see the infuriating need that she has to know everything about him. He, who looks like and has the same name as *him*. This must be some elaborate trick, but by who? Nobody remembers what happened three hundred years ago. What do they hope to gain by sending him to her?

Agree, she silently begs.

He mulls this over. Her facial expression doesn't change or give anything away. "On the condition that I can refuse to tell you anything that I think might lead you to the rebellion."

CHAPTER 5

"As I've already said, I don't care about your insignificant rebellion." After a pause, he gives her a slight nod and she exhales slowly. "Then it seems I have a story to tell." And then she begins.

Chapter 6

Before becoming queen, I was born in a village in Flora and lived in the same home all my life with just my mother and me; and when I was young, my father too. Flora was as bustling with healers and medicines back then as it is now. Gorgeous and lush, the most beautiful place in the whole kingdom. I never wanted to leave.

My mother ran an apothecary shop out of our home. There were an abundance of in-home apothecary shops, but since Flora supplied the entire kingdom with medicines, and often surrounding kingdoms, there was never an overabundance of elixirs. The king was always demanding that any excess be offered to his army who never seemed to make any progress in their battles.

Despite the war that ravaged other areas of the country, I ran wild through the gardens and the surrounding trees. I loved nature and being so close to living things that lived so differently than I did. The leaves on a plant didn't care about the war, about money or their family or status. So simple, yet so beautiful, and often with the ability to become something completely different. I learned to identify the plants and herbs that we used to make medicine. I learned to identify most plants before I even learned to read or write the same names.

CHAPTER 6

It was a game my mother played with me. She probably did it just to keep me busy, but she would send me out looking for specific plants that she needed to replenish her stock. The quicker I found the right plants, the quicker I could get to helping her do the fun part—the mixing of the ingredients.

We lived in a little three room cottage, though the main living space doubled as our shop. My father didn't help much with the medicines, he never really seemed to have a hand for it. Where my mother was soft and nurturing, my father was hard and indifferent. My father was called into active duty in the kingdom's army when I was a bit older, and I never saw him again. I know my mother received letters from him for a while, but he never wrote to me. I learned to be as dismissive of him as he was of me. I never needed anything from him.

I loved my mother though. As I said she was warm and loved teaching me how to help her. I learned everything that I could about the medicines we were making. I looked forward to being able to take over the shop one day. I knew that I could help people with the salves, balms, and mixes that we created. It felt like magic, being able to take things that the earth had given us and turn it into, sometimes, life saving potions. Nothing about our shop was out of the ordinary, really, just medicine in general made me feel like I was making a difference. I had a purpose.

Because Flora was full of others who were also making medicines, most of the time shops would pick a specialty. It ensured quality in a product, and it also had the community working together to make sure that nobody was competing—for resources or for customers. I wanted to know more than what my mother could teach me. I was hungry for knowledge. I craved the learning, the thrill of perfecting something new.

As much as I loved the steady, comforting feeling of making the perfect mixture, I also liked the heady rush of knowing that I could do more. That I could be more.

While I was still young enough to not be considered an apprentice, but old enough not to be considered a nuisance, my mother worked it out with others in our village that I would spend time learning from them. Our village was close knit and while we all knew hardships living in the kingdom at that time, generally we liked to stick together. I certainly wasn't the only child that could be found in a neighbors home learning from them. It helped especially when we'd be working on new medicines or changing recipes for old ones. Sometimes illnesses would run through the ranks of the armies and we'd have to come together to figure out how to supplement medicines with other herbs or plants so that we could stretch supplies when we couldn't grow ingredients fast enough. Or face the wrath of the king.

I was spending time with one such family, learning from the older children that lived in the household when I met Ren.

Chapter 7

The shape of Ren's name leaving her lips brings her back to the present. Vaaren is sitting against the back wall of the cell with his head leaning against it, but his eyes are focused on her. She thinks that maybe hearing Ren's name would cause a reaction in Vaaren, but he gives her nothing. He doesn't seem the least bit interested.

"That's enough for now, I think," she breathes through the tension that had coiled itself in her shoulders. Shaking the last of it off, she turns her attention to Vaaren. "Now that I've told you where I come from, tell me where you are from." It isn't a question, so she doesn't say it like one.

"I'm from Flora," he answers, stiff and unblinking.

"Your family?"

"I'm not foolish enough to tell you who my family is, Your Majesty. You can kill me before I give them up to you."

"What is your family's elixir specialty?"

"I couldn't tell you, I never got into medicine making with the rest of my family. Even if I knew, you think I don't know telling you wouldn't lead you to them eventually?" His tone begins to take on a certain undercurrent of defiance and he sniffs, brushing the back of his hand across his nose.

She assesses his words. He believes what he is telling her.

"What does a man from Flora have against his queen? I leave the merchants with more wealth than the kings of the past, do I not? You should be grateful, not marching towards my doors looking for a fight."

"Your people suffer under the strict rules you have in place. Curfews with death penalties, drafting laws that force most men in families into your army, and you can come and take what you need from us whenever you like. We are not free and we are not grateful for the terror that you bring to our towns. One could work their entire lives and not pay off their debts or be out from under your thumb. You do not care for your people and in turn, your people do not care for you. They want your rule and your threats to end with your death. I just happen to be brave enough to fight alongside those who are able." He stands up during his speech, his energy and passion rising to the surface, stopping short of spitting at her feet again.

"A noble soul for such a useless cause. A queen does what she needs to protect her people. You have no idea what is out there and what I have protected you from." She keeps her voice calm just to rile him.

"The only one we need protection from is you. Why don't you just leave Aerash? Let the people take over and rule themselves."

"I am only here on this throne because *the people* forced me to be. Your short magicless lives bind you to your shortsightedness. But I can see you're not ready to hear that today," she sneers in a low voice and turns to walk back down the hallway, her lights dancing around her. She could tell him that she was birthed by the Goddess of Light herself and he likely wouldn't change his opinion of her. Why did she even bother to tell him the truth? She got carried away is all.

CHAPTER 7

What little adrenaline he got from the exchange visibly leaves his body, and he slumps to the floor in exhaustion. He says nothing as she leaves, plunging the cell into darkness.

~

The carriage shakes beneath her as it rolls over the cobblestones on the way out of the castle walls. It would be faster if she just rode her own horse the whole way there, but that isn't the way royalty travels. It would take about four days to reach the boundaries of her kingdom, before crossing over into Selna where they would endure another two days of travel. It would be the perfect time for her to test the magic she had laid on the border.

She gazes out the carriage window at South Garsen as they pass through towns. It would be quicker to travel to Selna's capital through Flora, but she tries her best not to revisit her home region. While she loves it, and had her greenhouse made at the castle to bring remnants of home to her, Flora's townspeople have the most animosity towards her. She thought that the queen being from Flora would be something to be proud of, but the Florans make it clear they feel betrayed by her. She has even lessened their med-tax since the old kings, but they couldn't care less and instead choose to turn their backs when she rides through their towns. Ungrateful peasants.

Regardless of whether they choose to accept her or not, she's still their queen.

Images of her childhood flash through her mind, brought back in force after telling Vaaren her story. She'd been so caught up in the memories of warmth and happiness that she hadn't even paid attention to his reactions. Once she was refocused on him and the present, he quickly picked up the self-righteous attitude again.

It wouldn't be any better if she told them what she knew was coming. It would send everyone into a panic. They would probably search for another savior as they had once sought out her.

They don't encounter any trouble on their four day trek to the border. Even the rebellion knows that attacking the queen's entourage would do more damage to South Garsen than it would to the queen herself. Bursting through the door, Elayce sweeps from the carriage, causing Phin to jump back, his arm still poised to open the door for her.

"We've reached our camp for the night, Your Majesty. The guards have begun to set up your tent," he informs.

"Accompany me," Elayce orders, breezing past him and towards the ward stone that protects this part of the border. He follows without question. Everyone knows that there are wards laid by Queen Elayce to protect their kingdom, but the spots where they lay are hard to detect by anyone who doesn't have magic. While Elayce can feel the pulse and pull on her soul, they have no effect on non-magic users. They aren't meant to keep her subjects in or out, they're meant to keep the Darkness out.

The Darkness is what she had been called upon to save the kingdom from all those years ago. It had been thought that the old kings were bringing destruction to the land to punish those that wouldn't kneel at their feet. Because of the nature of her magic, the people believed she was sent by the Goddess of Light in response to the Darkness that had permeated the land, taking the lives of villagers in the night. Eventually it garnered enough strength to stay during the day, and there was no longer a way to escape it. If the cold, shadows of the

CHAPTER 7

Darkness came to you during the day that was the end.

She kneels at the black stone pressed flat into the ground. The stone is about the size of a dinner plate and shines like polished marble. A rune is carved into the middle and it glows faintly when she strokes her fingers across it. She glances back at Phin, who is standing behind her, scanning the field and pointedly not looking at her.

Elayce sits back on her heels and takes a deep, centering breath. She reaches out with her mind to the magic that feels like a part of her, coaxing it to tell her what she needs to know. She sighs with content as the magic returns, fitting back into the place it left vacant within her. It's relieving, being reunited with a part of her that has been separate for so long. She doesn't need to expend much energy to control it from so far away due to the ward stone holding it in place, but it still feels like a piece of her is coming home.

After welcoming the light back into her she begins to search for the story it can tell her. She can feel the remnants of souls that passed through the wards, flashes of faces blur together in the back of her mind as she sifts through all the information the magic has held on to for her.

There he is...the Darkness.

She can feel the Darkness as it pushes against her and tests her magic. It doesn't ever push too hard, more like a little tap here and there. She feels the strength grow behind each push as it comes back over and over again through time. It isn't at full power yet, not enough to really even test what it would take to push her wards to the ground, but it is growing. It won't be long before she will have to fight it once again.

She watches the image of a cloud of smoke rolling closer to her as if she were the stone. Stepping further into the memory, she begins to feel the wind blow from the force of the Darkness rolling in. The cloud stretches, covering the fields that lead into Selna. The stars shine down from the sky, giving off just enough light to see the fingers graze the ward, outstretched from the cloud of shadow. The Darkness brushes the ward several times, billowing up along the wall as it tests the strength before crashing gently back down to the ground and losing shape as it recedes back to the shadows. The memory fades along with the cloud while it rolls back to wherever it hides.

Elayce grunts and slumps to the ground as she pushes the magic from her body back into the ward stone. She feels the ward spring back up along the boundary, shimmering and sizzling with renewed spark after being connected so closely to her again. Phin turns to her and watches her with questioning eyes, but doesn't reach out to touch her without permission. She waves him off and rises to her feet, taking a deep breath, readjusting to how it feels to be missing that piece of her again. Using her magic doesn't usually require so much effort, but this is different. The rune on the ward stone holds a piece of her magic, so that she can be far away for long periods of time. It is also why she can accept the magic back into her and learn from it. Because it is a piece of her very being. The wards serve their purpose in holding back the Darkness, but perhaps a time would come when the pieces left behind would serve better reunited with her.

She and Phin return to camp where Elayce stalks straight to her tent. It is a lavish set up with a full bed, a room heater, a table and chairs, and even a rug covering the ground. She takes a seat at the table to look over the documents that have been laid out and calls for her dinner. While she finished up

CHAPTER 7

most things that could wait until after her trip, she had asked for the latest reports on the draft and new army recruits.

She is the only one that can fight the Darkness head on, but the Darkness will bring its own army along with it that she won't be able to focus on. Even with drafting more villagers into her army, they are not training fast enough. They will be useless to her if they are not ready to fight the Darkness's army. She pulls a fresh sheet of paper out and an ink pen, scrawling a letter to the captain of the training guard. Her pen scratches across the surface, the words coming out harsh and demanding. The training captain was a cruel man, though perhaps not the smartest. He was selected specifically by her to train the new recruits. He should have no problem with her message—train harder and train longer.

She rolls the note up and seals it by zapping it with a few of her sparks. A signature that anyone under her employ would know meant the note was directly from the queen. She walks to the door of her tent and shoves it out to where she knows Phin is keeping guard.

"Have this sent back to the training barracks immediately." There's a scraping along the ground and lumbering footsteps that get quieter with distance. With that done, she changes from her traveling clothes. Her maid is around here somewhere, but she's too exhausted to call for her. Finally ready for bed, she lays down and pulls the covers over her. There is little out here this close to the border that would be a threat to them and sleep finds her quickly.

Chapter 8

After several more days' travel, Queen Elayce and her entourage arrive at the gates of the Palace of Selna. She hasn't visited since King Theis's father was young enough to try to court her. The white marble towers of the castle rise straight into the air, looking over all who come to visit the royal family. The gates swing open wide for the queen as they approach and she is pleased by the welcome of her arrival. The carriage rolls to a stop at the foot of a grand staircase leading up to a pair of towering doors that are wide open. At the top of the stairs, Elayce sees King Theis, flanked by his own royal guards.

"King Theis," Elayce drawls as she steps out of her carriage, hand hovering over Phin's outstretched one as she gracefully descends. "How charming of you to meet me at your front door." Regularly, guests of royals are accepted in the throne room, a reminder of who holds the power in the situation. Elayce suspects that his way of greeting her at the door is all part of his scheme to woo her.

"My Dear Queen Elayce, I could no more wait to look upon your beauty than a baby bird can wait to spread its wings." He descends the stairs towards her with his broad arms stretched. When he reaches her, he grabs both of her hands in his and kisses the back of each one intently before looking up at her

CHAPTER 8

with his big brown eyes. Everything about him seems large. His features, his muscles—albeit buried under his tight clothes—even his hair is large. Styled somehow into a large curly, brown bun on the top of his head, his head being properly portioned to his large body. He towers over her when he stands to his full height, exuding warmth and welcome. "You must be famished after your travels, I have prepared a feast to be served upon your arrival. Will you accompany me to dinner, my lady?"

Smiling sweetly, Elayce replies, "Of course, Theis, but please allow me to freshen up before you sweep me away to show me off to the rabble you've gathered for dinner," dropping his title and poking fun at his effort to welcome her. He doesn't take the bait.

"Certainly! Certainly!" He motions to a servant waiting in the shadows. "Show Queen Elayce where she will be staying. I'm sure they're quite familiar to you, but just in case you've forgotten the way, this servant will show you. She will also be attending to you while you are here with us." He bows his head to Elayce, her hand still clasped in his own deep brown one. The servant scurries to get ahead of Elayce. Darla follows a few steps behind the queen, carrying one of the queen's travel cases, as well as Phin, who will remain posted outside of Elayce's room. The rest of her entourage begins to unpack her things and take care of the carriage and horses.

"I'll join you for dinner shortly, King Theis," Elayce calls out over her shoulder, not breaking stride.

Her rooms are a lavish set of three chambers connected by wide open archways. Each space has a balcony that overlooks the thriving gardens below. The gardens are so lush that she can smell the fragrance all the way in her room. She orders the balcony doors be left wide open to let the scent take over.

It's hot in Selna, but there's a beautiful breeze that comes in, causing the deep magenta drapes to sway in the wind. The kingdom itself seems to be welcoming her with its best attributes.

Elayce changes into a dark purple velvet gown with a deep V that goes clear down to her front middle. She left the modesty expected of royal attire behind a long time ago. She adorns her fingers with jewels and fastens a necklace that hangs between her breasts while Darla puts the finishing touches into her up-do. Her dress drags along the carpet as she marches to the dining hall, through the doors, and straight to the empty chair to the right of King Theis. The diners quiet as she strides past, some bowing their heads. King Theis gestures to a servant who leaps forward and pulls the chair out for Elayce, pushing it in for her to sit.

"I didn't think it was possible that you could get even more beautiful since I first laid eyes upon you, Queen Elayce, but you have proven me wrong," King Theis says, grabbing her hand and kissing it once again.

"Oh Theis, please." Elayce giggles flirtatiously and bats at his hand still trying to grasp onto hers. "Flattery will only get you so far."

"You've only just arrived after many attempts to try to coax you to visit Selna again, I have many compliments to pay you for accepting my invitation."

"I didn't say I didn't want to hear them, I said that they would only get you so far." Elayce laughs and pops a berry into her mouth.

The king laughs. "As cheeky as ever! I have waited long to be the one to hear such wit from you." Confidence exudes from the king, something she wouldn't expect from someone who

CHAPTER 8

seems to be willing to grovel at her feet.

"The palace looks the same, I've always loved the bright colors that fill your decor." The walls, floors, and most of the furniture look to be made of the same white marble as the towers from the outside. A heavy, sturdy material that could easily be mined in abundance in Selna. However, the cold marble floors are covered in brightly patterned rugs to bring in warmth. The furniture, while made of marble, is covered in bright cushions of yellows and oranges and pinks that make everything perfectly comfortable. Bright flowers bloom in vases great and small. The flowers and plants make the air feel and smell fresh, and they thrive in the warmer climate. Unlike her own castle, which is dark and unwelcome, this castle is exactly how she would have had her own styled. But after all this time it doesn't really feel like hers. The airy, flowery hall reminds her of home and makes her feel like she has space to breathe. She had forgotten just how much she loved it when she visited King Theis's father many years ago.

"I'll give your compliments to our decorator, I don't have an eye for such things," King Theis gestures to the room as he looks around.

"The pink blooms are lovely this time of year, my lord, I have never seen them so vibrant," a petite woman with white blonde hair, pinned up in curls, chimes in from a few chairs down the table.

"Perhaps they have bloomed especially for our lovely guest," Theis responds to the woman without taking his eyes off Queen Elayce. Her eyes briefly flick down the table to the woman to see her sit back in her chair and press her lips into a thin line. No doubt she was one of the eligible ladies vying for the young king's attention.

"Perhaps they have," Elayce agrees. "Their beauty is rivaled only by the flowers in my own home region." Surprising even herself with such a personal comment; maybe sharing some of her childhood with Vaaren had accidentally opened the floodgates.

"I've heard of the beautiful region of Flora, though I've never been myself, as you know. Though grateful for the healing tinctures that your kingdom offers, it would be spectacular to share more of your home with you," King Theis says.

"Well maybe if Aerash wasn't so unwelcoming," the blonde mutters underneath her breath.

King Theis's head snaps to the woman. "What would you know about such things, Lady Nenet?" Though the question invites a response, his tone doesn't. The entire table goes silent.

Her eyes bulge, perhaps surprised he had heard her. Sputtering, she says, "I only meant that—that many of us would surely enjoy the foretold beauty of Aerash. It would be a joy to travel there if that were more acceptable."

"Are you saying that you could make better decisions about the safety of Aerash than Queen Elayce can?" he challenges her.

Elayce looks back and forth between Lady Nenet and King Theis. She enjoys the King's ability to make the lady squirm almost more than she enjoys his over-the-top flattery. She revels in Lady Nenet's obvious discomfort, her sparks coming to life—doing circles in the crackling air around her.

King Theis grows more irritated with Nenet's silence. "Well?" he demands.

"I would never..." her words seem to die in her throat as the queen's magic dances closer and closer to her. She physically shrinks down in her chair, doing her best to put more space between her and the dancing lights. "I didn't mean..."

A sharp cackle of laughter bursts forth from Elayce and everyone swivels their heads from Lady Nenet and the lights to the queen. "Oh Theis, I think the girl is quite reminded of her place. The poor thing looks like she could topple from her chair if you keep this up any longer."

Lady Nenet gulps and sits up a bit straighter as the lights curl their way through the air and back to Queen Elayce. "I think I'm quite finished with dinner, let's head somewhere where we can talk without being interrupted."

King Theis stands from his chair and holds out his hand for Elayce. "Of course, my lady, let's continue our conversations elsewhere."

Elayce reaches for his hand, hovering near his, yet not quite touching, and lets him begin to lead her away. She glances at Lady Nenet, seeing the gleam of hate coming from her. Elayce smirks and flicks her other hand sending the sparks shooting straight for Lady Nenet. Lady Nenet gasps and her hands shoot up to protect her face, smacking the table and tipping her chair back in the process. She waves her arms to try and catch her balance, but the chair continues to tumble backwards and Lady Nenet flies feet over head to the floor. Her light blue skirts rustle and poof and she squeals while attempting to right herself—quite ungracefully—on the floor.

"It seems you do need another reminder of who I am, Nenet. I am a queen, and while I may not rule over the land that you live in, I am quite sure that customs here demand respect for royalty similar to that of my own kingdom. I may have let King Theis defend my kingdom moments ago, but make no mistake, I am quite capable of handling insolence on my own." Elayce's words are calm, but sharp. Lady Nenet is on her feet by the end of Elayce's speech but doesn't remove her eyes from the floor, her face bright red. Nobody speaks or even breathes as they wait for someone to make the next move.

A coughing comes from somewhere along the table. "Apologize to the queen, foolish girl," is heard between the coughs.

Lady Nenet sinks into a low curtsy. "Forgive me, Queen Elayce, I have let my emotions get the better of me today." She still doesn't look up from the floor.

Elayce watches Lady Nenet and says nothing. People around the table begin to shuffle as the silence stretches on. Lady Nenet remains bowed in the curtsy. The strain of remaining in that position begins to show as Lady Nenet's body begins trembling. King Theis quietly clears his throat and nods his head in the direction of the door. "Shall we?"

"Yes, King Theis, I'm done here," Elayce says and lets King Theis lead her away. The thump of Lady Nenet collapsing to the floor again echoes behind them.

In the sitting room, Queen Elayce and King Theis lounge on couches across from each other, the only other company are the guards. "I've scheduled a tour of the castle grounds for us both tomorrow, Queen Elayce, including the massive gardens we have that supply all the castle decor."

"I think I'll quite enjoy that," Elayce muses. The sitting room is decorated much the same as the dining room had been, white marble floors and furniture with brightly colored cushions and flowers. A beautiful marble game board sits on the table between them, left in the middle of a game from its previous players. "Perhaps a demonstration of the guard as well." King Theis nods at one of his guards, the guard leaves, presumably to give the update to the captain.

CHAPTER 8

"Is there anything else I can show you tomorrow? Your visit is so short, I have to ensure you get a good taste of what Selna has to offer. A traditional Selnan feast will be prepared for you, and I've hired a traditional Selnan troupe to entertain us for the meal. Although, it seems that you can provide entertainment enough," King Theis says.

"Most don't find joy in the same entertainment that I do, King Theis, I am surprised to hear you say so."

"While I may have never met you in person, I am no stranger to the tales they tell about you. I would be naive to believe that the whispers of the parties you host are anything less than what they say. Unfortunately, I have nothing as exciting to offer you here. I would appreciate the chance to accept an invitation to one." He smiles wryly.

"Theis, that's twice in one night you've asked for an invitation to my kingdom," Elayce points out with a laugh.

"You've only given me a few days to woo you, Queen Elayce, I'm not going to waste them being subtle." He winks at her.

Normally, Elayce wouldn't entertain such blatant attempts for her hand, but the flirting was accomplishing what she had come here to do. Distract herself from Vaaren.

"You certainly haven't been subtle, no need to worry about that. However, I think it's time for me to retire for the night. I look forward to seeing the castle grounds tomorrow." She rouses from the chaise to head back to her rooms.

"Can I escort you back to your rooms?" Theis asks.

"King Theis, charmed as I am, it won't be that easy to have me." She laughs and breezes out of the room, leaving King Theis with a smile on his face and a deep chuckle reverberating around her.

Chapter 9

Elayce watches the sweat drip down the guards' faces while they perform the demonstration for her. They didn't have much time to prepare, but the demonstration is what can be expected from a small kingdom like Selna. She can tell they don't train as ruthlessly as her army. Her eyes follow the captain, his commands bellowing through the yard and his men following him word for word.

She inspected their armor and their weapons before the demonstration, both of which were of acceptable quality. It's clear Selna doesn't spend much on their gear. It makes sense, considering Selna is rarely at war. With such a small defense, it may seem like Selna would be easy pickings, but it often gets overlooked. Selna is beautiful, and the flowers that can grow are lovely, but most of the flowers are specially grown around the castle grounds. Selna's major output is entertainment. Its citizens have talents that range from singing to dancing to great craftsmanship. The rest of the world certainly enjoys the benefits, often hiring singers and dancers from Selna to travel the world and entertain those who can afford it. Many royal dressers also send for clothing and cloth from Selna, the flowers and roots can create vivid colors in the fabrics. Even though many kingdoms revel in the luxuries Selna exports,

CHAPTER 9

it's not where monarchs will direct their efforts when looking to take over more land. They would start with areas that are more lucrative.

The fact that Selna's ruler is so charismatic can't hurt either. He's likely charmed the other kingdoms right into his pocket.

Elayce suspects this is one of the reasons Selna's rulers are always trying to propose a union with her. Elayce's army would be able to protect Aerash and Selna and the money that her kingdom brings in would be able to bolster the army that Selna has already.

The magenta flags of the Selnan kingdom flap in the hot breeze that comes through the yard, doing nothing to cool any of the men in their full armor. Thankfully, a dark magenta tarp covers where Elayce and Theis sit and watch the demonstration. A sweaty glass of water sits on a tray next to Elayce, held by a red-faced servant. She reaches over to take the glass for a sip and as her arm stretches closer to the glass, the glass starts to shake. She glances at the servant and realizes that his whole arm is shaking, causing the tray and glass to shake with it. "Relax, boy, it's too hot to waste this water by toying with you." His lips roll in between his teeth and his whole body clenches. Elayce laughs, grabbing the glass and taking a long drink.

"Maybe if you'd come visit us more, they wouldn't be so afraid of you," King Theis suggests.

Elayce laughs even harder. "Theis, if they saw the kind of entertainment I enjoyed, I think they would be more afraid."

"I'm sure some would see it for what it is, a strong queen who can protect them in their time of need."

"If only everyone appreciated my talents as much as you seem to." She settles back into her chair to finish watching the army demonstration, lazily twirling some of her sparks around the tent by flicking her fingers.

"On to the gardens now? We'll have a light lunch set for us there." King Theis stands and reaches out to Elayce. She takes it, loving that he doesn't shy from her touch even as the sparks dance around them.

With her arm looped through his, they head towards the massive castle gardens. A couple of servants trail them, holding a massive covering above their heads to shade them from the beating sun.

She truly has been looking forward to this part of the trip. There are a few buds she is hoping to take that don't grow in Aerash. She hopes to transplant them into her greenhouse. They walk lazily through the hedges and bushes, despite the heat. Elayce drags her hands over every branch she can reach, stopping often to breathe in the scents. Inwardly, she names each one that she knows—just like her mother used to have her do. Occasionally, they come across one that she doesn't know and she asks King Theis about it. Every time, a servant leans forward and whispers in his ear and then he repeats the name of the plant for her.

They come across one that she doesn't know the name of, repeating the process and waiting for the servant to give King Theis the answer for her. She can smell how sweet it is and she knows that this one is probably poisonous. "Can I take a cutting of this one? I'd like to replant it in my personal greenhouse."

The servant looks worried and steps forward as if to speak and then huffs out a breath, most likely worried to speak out of turn.

Elayce's eyes shift to the girl. "Speak, girl."

"That plant is poisonous, Your Majesty, I wouldn't want anything to happen to you," she mumbles to the ground.

"It is poisonous, how delightful. You can tell because it smells so sweet, an attempt the plant makes to lull its devourers into a false sense of security." Elayce's eyes alight with what looks to be a reflection of her sparks and a devious grin spreads across her face. "This one will fit right in in my greenhouse."

The servant curtsies slightly and steps back to her place behind the king. "I'll have one of the gardeners pack up some to take back with you, Queen Elayce," King Theis offers.

Elayce asks for three more cuttings to be prepared for her before they make it to the table set with lunch. It's in a small clearing in the gardens on a round stone patio, covered by a beautiful white awning. The table is filled with various small foods to be eaten with their fingers. A servant pulls a chair out for Elayce and she sits gracefully. Another servant sets a tray with a bowl of water, a small towel, and a small, floral scented bar of soap in front of her. She dips her hands in the water, using the soap to wash the garden from her hands before drying them on the small towel and setting it on the tray for the servant to take away.

Lunch consists of the King and Queen surrounded by flowers and a few guards and servants.

"No entertainment for lunch, King Theis?" Elayce jokes.

"I thought my company could be entertainment enough for you. Besides, I think now would be the best time for us to talk about why I've invited you here," he answers.

"I'm sure I know why you've invited me here," she replies sweetly. "How're your borders? Are you fending off attacks from other kingdoms? Or...anything else?"

King Theis pops one of the delicacies into his mouth, chewing slowly before answering. "Anything else?"

"Just making sure I'm asking the questions I need to be well informed, Dear King," she says, taking a bite off the corner of a cracker slathered with a brightly colored and delicious paste.

He adjusts in his seat, his gold medals attached to his chest glinting in the sunlight. The brown of his eyes swirling as he watches her eat, waiting to see if she'll clarify what she's asking. "I assure you that I wouldn't try to trick you into anything. I only know what a mistake that would be."

"Truly," she agrees, munching on another bite.

"There haven't been any attacks on our borders from anything like the reports from Don Kemt. As of right now, our borders are safe and secure. We are fully self-sustained in our coiffures and food stock. I am not asking for any immediate assistance. I am looking for a union between our two kingdoms, so that my people are secure...in case...in case of future threat," King Theis offers, unwilling to admit the threat that he's talking about even though they both know. The image of the Darkness poking at her ward on the border between their two kingdoms comes to mind. Either he doesn't know or he's lying.

"Why not just propose some sort of trade agreement?" Elayce asks.

"I fear that if the threat becomes too much a trade agreement wouldn't hold up as strongly as a marriage would." His gaze holds Elayce's, his voice steady.

"You don't fear you'd be giving up too much by entering a marriage with me to join our kingdoms?"

He takes another deliberate bite of the food on the table, the only sound between them is the crunching of the cracker between his teeth, the swallow. "All my life, I have been taught that my duty is to protect my people and my kingdom. Selna has never had ambitions to expand, but to let its people prosper. Same as Aerash. A union between our two kingdoms would accomplish more than Selna's goals to protect and prosper. This is exactly what both of our kingdoms need. We wouldn't be just the most powerful kingdom, but the most prosperous. I don't plan to sit idly by your side or give up my kingdom to you. I expect to be an equal partner and ruler over our newly combined kingdom."

Elayce sits back in her chair, taking in everything that King Theis said. "After all this time that I've been queen, you think that this is what I want? That expanding my rule and responsibility is enticing enough to agree to a marriage? What about my stable, well-protected borders makes you think that?"

"You don't have to fight for the expansion of your borders. You won't lose soldiers, weapons, time, or civilians in this, you only stand to gain," he offers.

"And what if I don't have the army ready to protect you too when this fight comes?"

"Reports tell me that your army is growing quite large recently."

Numbers won't matter if they aren't ready, but she doesn't tell him that. She's not sure that the new recruits will be. The Darkness wouldn't be testing her wards if it wasn't getting ready to reveal itself. But, Selna wasn't starting from ground zero. The demonstration today wasn't bad, they'd need some training on proper technique for fighting an army of darkness, but they could manage. They could also begin drafting and training Selnans into the army to supplement numbers. Selna will be brought into this conflict regardless of a marriage contract, but Elayce wouldn't let them go to battle lying down.

"I think you've said your piece, King Theis, I have much to think about," Queen Elayce answers.

A small flicker of surprise crosses Theis's face before he regains control of his features. As if he didn't think she would even consider his proposal. "Certainly take some time to think about it, Queen Elayce, but keep in mind preparations will take time." She doesn't think he means wedding preparations.

"I am well aware of the time that we have," Elayce's tone is laced with warning. He nods in deference. They finish their lunch, engaging in polite conversation and light flirting to ease the heaviness of the thought of what's to come.

~

Elayce drags her black nails through her golden blonde hair, combing through the curls that hang over her shoulder. The troupe is on the floor of the ballroom, performing one of their most famous acts for the King of Selna and Queen of Aerash and the nobles that are gathered for the show. Elayce is full from the delicious feast and is lounging in the white marble throne next to King Theis's, though hers is slightly shorter. The troupe is lively, faces painted heavily, making it hard to see any of their actual features. To their credit, they didn't balk at the queen when they saw who they would be entertaining today. A half hour into the show, the queen feels restless. She may not have seen this star Selnan troupe before, but she'd seen many traveling shows over the years and she has spent most of this trip behaving herself so far.

Maybe she should be the one to put on a show.

She flicks her hand, sending a shower of sparks exploding over the performance. The show continues, as though nothing has happened. Not even a stumble from the performers. She sends another shower, this time much closer to the performance. Again, the performers continue as if nothing strange is occurring. She looks around the room to see if anyone else is looking at her. They surely know that she is the one sending her sparks flying, even if they have never seen her magic before, they know who she is. Nobody's looking at her. King Theis has prepared his court well. Elayce is almost disappointed that nobody wants to play with her. Where is Lady Nenet? She exhales her boredom through her nose. Boredom will allow unwanted thoughts of Vaaren to creep into her mind, questions about who he is and why he looks like Ren circling obsessively.

"Entertainment not up to snuff, Lovely Queen?" King Theis murmurs, leaning over to her without taking his eyes from the troupe.

"I can think of far superior ways to spend my evening," she quips.

"The troupe is only the appetizer. I think I am far better at courting than you give me credit for." He peeks at her slyly from the corner of his eye, a small grin stretching his lips. "I want the people to know who their future queen is."

"I have given you no answer, Theis, but I can give your people a show if that's what you want." Elayce laughs. The music comes to a crescendo, the troupe's performance picking up speed, arriving at the climax of their show. Colorful flags flutter through the air, two performers waving them to add to the depth and immersion of their show. Sparks fly from Elayce and towards the flags that one of the performers is holding, the gleam reflecting the delight on her face. The instant the sparks touch the flag, it bursts into flames, showering more sparks over the whole show. Skillfully, as if it was rehearsed, the brunet performer spins the flag pole up in the air. Flames whoosh above everyone, extinguishing as it spins back down right into the performer's awaiting hand just as the music ends and the troupe hits their final pose.

The audience erupts into applause, getting to their feet to cheer on the group. King Theis politely claps, and Elayce just smirks. Pleased with the performer that was able to adapt to her spontaneous addition to the show. Maybe he would enjoy a stay at her castle. Out of the corner of her eye, Elayce sees King Theis nod to a guard at the foot of the dais. Not a moment later, the doors at the back of the room slam open as a retinue of guards march in, dragging a man between them. His clothes are soiled and ripped and bruises cover his face—one of his eyes swollen almost shut. "What is this?" Elayce turns to King Theis.

"The main course." He smiles and waves his hand as if he were offering the man up to her.

"And what did he do to deserve an audience with me?" she asks, leaning forward in her chair in excitement.

"He was a part of this troupe that was hired to perform for you." King Theis gestures towards the group of performers standing off to the side. None of them show any emotion on their faces, standing or sitting on the floor perfectly still. "But apparently felt that he could best serve you differently than the rest. Although, based on his argument I doubt he realized he would end up being your favorite part of the show."

The guards throw the man down onto the floor a few feet from the bottom of the stairs where the thrones sit. Elayce cackles with glee. "My, my, Theis, I did not expect this."

She pushes on the arms of the throne to propel herself from

the chair, gliding down the steps and to the man sitting on the floor. "Let's have some fun, shall we?" With that, her sparks burst from her in a radiant blast of light. Elayce has been pent up for too long since she arrived. Her magic has fully recovered from working with the ward stone, and she is bursting at the seams to release some energy. Sparks bounce around the room, buzzing with excitement.

Light fills the room, chasing away any shadows that had been. Some of the nobles raise their hands to their face to shield their eyes from the brightness. Cheers and claps come from the crowd, egging on the sparks that dive and dip through them. Playing and teasing, drumming up anticipation for the strike. Elayce hums with the pleasure of being surrounded by her magic, being cheered on by a new crowd in a new place. With a twist of her wrist all the sparks in the room return to her, spiraling in quick circles around the man on the floor. While his body doesn't flinch, sweat drips down his forehead and his breath quickens.

"Tell me your crime," she says to the man.

"I have committed none. I chose not to perform for a tyrant queen who murders her people," he says, shakily.

"Is it not a crime to go against the wishes of your king?" she asks.

He hesitates, his mouth falling open to answer but quickly snapping shut. There's nothing he can say to that. He switches to watching the sparks circle around him instead of the queen. A few sparks dart from the swirling tornado towards his cheek, causing him to flinch back only to be met with sparks on the other side. They draw slowly nearer to his face leading his attention back towards Elayce. "I want you to look at me while we play. I enjoy the light. I want to watch it leave your eyes."

A sob escapes from the man's mouth and tears stream down his bruised cheeks, mixing with the sweat trails. With the majority of the sparks still spiraling around him, few begin to branch off towards him. Darting in and out of the flow to prick his skin. Red dots appear where they touch, some with little puffs of smoke billowing towards the ceiling. Scraps of his clothes fall to the floor around him, burned from where the sparks came into contact. All the while, the man jumps and jerks, screaming with each spark coming in contact with his skin or his clothes. "Please! PLEASE! I'll perform, I'll do anything. Please! Make it stop!" the man begs, writhing on the floor.

Elayce's joy doesn't leave her face, but she closes her fingers into a fist, calling back the sparks to her. They gather in a swarm at her feet, cozying up to her velvet black gown draped on the floor. "I think that I have seen enough performing tonight, but there must be another arrangement we can come up with."

She turns from the begging, panting man towards his troupe. Half of the troupe remain in their places with the same expressionless face, while the other half are doing a terrible job masking their fear. "I have no use for a spineless peasant that refuses to do his job because he fears the consequences of his own failure. However, my castle could use a fresh performance. In exchange for his life, I offer employment to one of you. Any takers?"

The man who had been tossing the flags she burned during the performance steps forward and bows low to the queen. "I will serve you in exchange for his life, my queen."

Delighted, Elayce says, "Join me on the dais." She turns back to the man lying on the floor still. "It must be your lucky day, I've secured other amusement." Spinning towards the dais, the sparks shoot up to the ceiling and explode in bright fireworks that shower across the guests. Elayce takes a seat on the throne, exhaling at the delicious release of magic that has her feeling calmer.

She tosses a smile towards King Theis who had watched with a curious expression. He has never seen her use her powers this way, only minimally when she threatened Lady Nenet. He isn't showing any fear, just interest in what she could do. As much fun as Elayce had while toying with the insubordinate, she suspects it's also a way for King Theis to see a little bit more of what she is capable of. She never feels the need to prove herself to anyone anymore, but she doesn't mind showing off.

"That was certainly enjoyable, King Theis, how wonderful of you to think of me," she croons.

"Anything to please you, Queen Elayce." He nods to her and claps his hands, signaling for the music to begin playing.

The party goers immediately dip into the dance and return to their celebration. What remains of the troupe slowly carries the now unconscious man out of the room.

Sitting on the steps near Elayce's throne, the flag thrower murmurs up to her, a cruel smile on his face, "I have heard many great things about you and your kingdom. I would have gladly entered service for you, Your Majesty, without making an exchange." His muscles flex underneath his shirt as he leans towards her.

Elayce leans forward to whisper conspiratorially, "Oh, I know. But think of the guilt he will feel each miserable day for the rest of his short life, thinking that he only lives because you suffer."

Chapter 10

Arriving back at her dark, stuffy castle is a true test of her self-control. Tydas had been waiting along with a retinue of guards and servants to welcome her back. Tydas's bald head reflected the sunlight, gleaming as brightly as his eyes after Elayce confirmed that King Theis had offered a marriage proposal. He had wanted to call a council meeting right away to discuss the terms with the members and make some adjustments to the proposal. Elayce had sneered and growled at him, but he had been unperturbed—coaxing her into her study to get as many details as he could.

She told him that King Theis had expected to be an equal partner in ruling both kingdoms and that all he was truly looking for was training for his army and protection from any threats similar to the whispers from the east. No, he hadn't mentioned heirs. No, they hadn't discussed which castle would become the main home of the couple. No, they hadn't discussed any other open trade agreements or border changes. Yes, she asked about his borders and was told that they were secure.

"Interesting that King Theis is willing to give up so much for a threat he hasn't yet seen come to his own borders," Tydas muses.

CHAPTER 10

"Just because the residents of the kingdoms forgot what happened three hundred years ago, doesn't mean its leaders have. Commoners' memories die along with them, but royals keep records for their heirs. Theis was clear about his intent to save his people." Elayce sighs, rubbing her fingers along her forehead. Briefly she contemplates setting her sparks on Tydas so she wouldn't have to continue this conversation.

Ignoring her mood, Tydas continues, "You haven't outright told him no. You're contemplating it?"

"I tire of the games these kings play. Perhaps if I am married I will be left alone." Her glare bores into Tydas. She had accepted the invitation to distract herself from Vaaren, but the beautiful castle and banter with King Theis had gotten to her more than she expected.

"Ah yes, but the work of the queen is never done."

"What need do I have of you then, if I must do everything?"

"I'm merely your advisor, my queen. And currently I am advising that we call a council meeting to discuss this and send our terms of acceptance back to King Theis. This is the best case scenario, he has offered everything we wanted. Let's see what else he is willing to give."

Tydas is already scrawling notes for the meeting on a sheet of yellowed paper on the desk. The pen flicks across the paper rapidly. Elayce reaches out to her sparks, encouraging one of them to gently wrap underneath Tydas's arm and tap the paper he's writing on. A flame bursts up from the corner and quickly swallows up the paper. Tydas brushes the ash and remaining flaming paper to the floor, stomping on it to put it out. "I rescind my earlier advice. I think you need to refresh after your trip, get a massage or maybe do some training. The council members and I can discuss the contract and send you our comments before sending them off to King Theis." He doesn't look at her as he grabs another sheet of paper and begins re-writing what she had burned away.

Standing up to leave Tydas in her study, she walks directly to the dungeon.

Now, sitting here in a plush chair she demanded a guard bring down for her, she and Vaaren face each other. Is he skinnier than he was before? The shadows under his eyes have definitely darkened, she can tell by the light of her floating sparks.

"You haven't been down here in a few days, I thought you had forgotten about me." His voice is raspy from disuse and lack of drink.

"Bring water and a tray of food," she says to the guard behind her without so much as a glance. His booted footsteps disappear down the hall to call a servant for food. "I was away visiting another kingdom. I received reports upon my return that there was a rebel attack. They managed to kill a few of my guards before being captured and brought to the cells down here with you."

"Are you asking for information from me? I have been captive in your dungeon for...I thought only a few days, but it must have been longer. I know as much about their efforts as I'm sure you do," he states. Bitterness creeps into his voice, though it's clear that his time in the cell has already taken a toll on his rebellious spirit.

"I just thought you would want to be informed." She leans back into her chair. The servant appears with a tray and a table, setting it next to the queen. "Move it to where he can reach it."

The servant bows their head and shuffles the tray closer to

CHAPTER 10

the cell and then returns down the darkness of the hallway.

Vaaren looks at the tray, then turns a look of mistrust to Elayce. "What will I have to give in exchange for this?"

"We will never reach the end of our stories if you are dead from hunger or thirst. If I intend to kill you, it will be at my own hands not your own body's," she says dismissively.

He stares at her for another beat before cautiously reaching through the bars to grab some of the warm bread from the tray. Once his hand and the bread are safely back behind the bars, he gobbles down the bread like it has been days since his last meal. It probably has been. Barely swallowing and already reaching for the cup of water sitting on the tray, draining it down but being careful not to spill a single precious drop.

She waits for him to finish, studying him. His blond hair is filthy with dirt and sweat, turning it almost brown to the eye. His skin, sallow looking with sickness. His movements are quick and jerky, like he's afraid that if he gets too close to her he will be struck. Maybe he has been, she has given no specific indications for how he should be treated here in the dungeons. Many of the guards who are stationed down here have shown a nasty streak. If they didn't before they were assigned to the dungeons, kindness doesn't last long down here. The stench of piss and other bodily fluids permeates the air. Just another way that prisoners are tortured during their stay here. Some beg for the mercy of death by the queen rather than spend more of their hopeless lives down in the dark, dank halls. Once you come down to the dungeons, the only way out is death. The Queen of Aerash does not offer forgiveness.

"Are you ready to begin our exchange?" she asks him.

Taking a seat against the back wall of the cell to remain far away from her, he nods for her to begin.

Chapter 11

Ren and I became fast friends. There was little anyone could do to separate us once we found each other. I was dedicated to the study of plants and the medicines I could make with them and could sit for hours working through tinctures, experimenting with leftover supplies. Ren would sit with me while I worked, reading, studying the land of Aerash and war tactics. He loved adventure and wanted us to travel around Aerash some day, but until we were old enough to leave on our own he was content to stay by my side while I worked.

He told me about everything he was learning and reading and I explained what I was doing and trying to accomplish with my experiments. He didn't get into medicine making like I did, but he listened. Really listened to what I was saying, encouraging me to stretch the knowledge that we had of the plants we knew. If I could identify plants and know what to do with them, we could have food, mix tinctures to sell for money on the road—making my family shop mobile, and heal any injury we might encounter. He believed in what I could do, and it only bolstered the love I had for what I was already doing.

I could see his vision for our future. At first, when we were young, we would be just a couple of adventurers taking on Aerash side-by-side. As we grew older, it wouldn't be just us as two adventurers. We'd be together. Ren wasn't shy about his feelings for me. He was as sure about us as he was that the sun would rise the next day, and he told me. We moved into that part of our relationship so smoothly and so confidently. Now, while I sat and mixed potions and salves, I experienced soft stolen kisses on my cheeks. Gentle touches on my arms to get my attention when he discovered something new, back rubs when a concoction didn't go the way I thought it would. A never ending stream of encouragement and belief in me. It was like he was made to be the better part of me. The dreamer, the believer, he pushed me to be ambitious. It would be impossible for me not to love him as much as he loved me and the life he wanted for us. He filled me with light and hope. Hope that maybe Aerash had special, safe places left in it that weren't destroyed by the wars.

When we were old enough, we started making real plans to leave our small village in Flora. We wanted to start small by traveling around the region. We were going to visit other villages to learn from other medicine makers and trade some of the tinctures I had made for new recipes and knowledge on our quest to head to South Garsen.

The night before we left, I was visited in a dream by the Goddess that awakened my powers. She told me that there was a darkness Aerash's king was fighting and that he would lose. He was killing the land with his pride and that he didn't have what was needed to defeat the Darkness. That all of Aerash would be swallowed by a never ending night if I did not save it.

Chapter 12

"Do you think that telling me a story about you being in love will endear me to you?" he sneers.

"I am only telling you my history as I have said I would in exchange for yours," she replies, ignoring the sting of his tone. She sags back in her chair, almost glad to have been interrupted. Once she lets her mind wander back that far, it can be hard to remember where she is and who she is now. "Your turn."

"I have nobody at home to tell you about in exchange."

This tidbit of information interests Elayce, but she tries not to show it. "Tell me more about your childhood, you don't have to give specifics about your family."

"I was a rambunctious child. Part of the reason I never got into medicine making with my family, I just couldn't sit still. I had dreams of traveling, maybe entering the army to do it. When I was young enough to not understand what it would mean to enter your army." He described himself as a child stiffly, like he was reading from a script. Feeling drifted back into his voice when he talked about not joining her army. Interesting.

"How old are you?"

"Twenty-four."

CHAPTER 12

"What did you do if you didn't get involved with the family business and didn't enlist in the army?"

"The draft missed me somehow. I waited for it. Every time the soldiers came to town and read the list of names, I expected to be on it. But somehow, every time, I wasn't. I sought the rebels out early, I was only about seventeen. They greedily accepted my help. Any young male that hadn't been drafted yet was a blessing to the cause. When I wasn't with the rebels I was an apprentice to the town blacksmith. Something to keep me busy until I was drafted or called to a bigger mission for the rebellion. As it was, my connection was quite...valuable," he pauses, his insinuation left hanging in the space between them.

"You made weapons for the rebels, then?"

He doesn't answer, the silence damning him anyway.

"I will have to send a company out to Flora. Seems that there is an excess of weapons that could be donated to the Aerash army," she says casually, resting her chin on her hand.

His stare pierces her. "You don't even know which town in Flora I am from."

"Then they shall have to visit every blacksmith in the region." A cruel smile spreads across her face. Challenging him to give her the information that she is looking for—what town he is from. He doesn't move, but to tilt his chin down to glower at her even harder. "I suspect we're done for the night then." She rises from her chair in a swish of fabric and strides down the hall with her head held high and her pride held even higher.

~

The sweat drips down Elayce's face and bare arms. Her palms barely keep hold of the rod between them. Quick pants escape through her mouth, in time with her body's movements. Her sparks are flying all over the room, spiraling in quick, coordinated movements according to the way Elayce's mind directs them. She arches her back, lifts her arm above her head and throws the rod, hitting the target directly in the center. Her whole body lurches with the effort of the throw and she tumbles into a perfect somersault, leaping to her feet and throwing her hand out in front of her. Flying towards the target, her sparks converge into what looks like another rod, following directly behind the first. The rod bursts into flames as her sparks reach it and pummel straight through, quickly swallowing the entire target.

Harkn rushes forward and dumps a bucket of water on the fire, extinguishing the flames. "Is that the best you can do, my queen? I could throw farther than that," he teases, smirking at her.

"Be careful, Harkn, or next time I'll make you keep up with me." She tosses her head back, chugging the water from the table on the side of her personal training room. The room is empty except for her and Harkn, cleared for her to practice training with her magic. The guards are relegated to the less than impressive training rooms in their own facilities instead.

"Just getting under your skin a bit to help keep you focused." He bows his head to her and drinks some water himself before reaching for the pump to refill the water bucket.

She watches the muscles of his arms bulge with each pump of the handle, water gushing into the bucket and then waning with each pump. This room was built specifically for magic training. Magic used to be more prominent many years ago. Kings and Queens often had strong forms of some magic, used to defend their kingdoms. Or to take others. As time went

CHAPTER 12

on, magic seemed to fade. Many with magic nowadays can do little more than parlor tricks or small every day things that may or may not make their lives easier. Often, magic shows up in affinities for a certain thing. Someone may be suspected to have plant magic because their plants never seem to die or create more blooms while in season. Another may be thought to have healing magic because they can more clearly sense what ails someone. Small things that show up quietly and not always in the same way, making it hard for someone who may have never come in contact with magic before to recognize.

Since magic has become so weak, it is no longer outlawed in any kingdom that Elayce could name. Some kingdoms used to hunt magic users down and kill them or force them to enter the service of the monarchs; Elayce probably would've ended any kingdom still practicing this after she had come to power. She was much more rash in the earlier days of her reign. Elayce believes that magic sensed it was in danger and receded from the humans it used to bless, flowing back into the earth or to the Gods and Goddesses from where it first came. She can feel strong magic in the hum of the earth and she knows that it's all around. This is something that she learned slowly over time. Nature and the energy that flows through everything can bolster her powers and assist her in pulling more from the depths of her own well of powers. All you have to do is trust the magic instead of fearing it.

She never had any interest in finding other Magic Wielders in her kingdom, though she does have a few in her service. There's a healer that's been with her for almost a hundred years, Merda. She may look like she's one hundred years old, but she most certainly doesn't act like it. Merda isn't afraid to break anyone who reminds her of her age either—before healing them right back up and daring them to say anything to her about it again. Merda came to Elayce's castle on her own, offering her services to the queen in exchange for a rather comfortable lifestyle in the castle. Recently, her kingdom has been graced with a rather talented chef that she thinks must have an affinity for nature and plants because he really knows how to season a meal.

While she benefits from some of these lesser magics, most wouldn't be useful in a battle against the Darkness. If she ever got wind of someone with magic in the way that she could wield, she would ride out to see them. She could offer them so much, lessons in magic and a place to train, without requiring anything in return from them. She would never, ever force them to fight for her. That had been a choice she hadn't been given. She understands what it means to be given gifts that you do not want and to be used for them. Turning those gifts into burdens before you ever had a chance to learn what you could do.

It took many years after the battle that chased away the Darkness for her magic to come back in full. She had depleted it so fully and she hadn't trusted it enough that she thought she had spent it. Maybe it wasn't meant to remain with her in the force that she needed it to defeat the Darkness. The blessing from the Goddess may have been only for the battle and then deserted her when she took the throne for her own. It had worried her, though she didn't show it. Maybe it had been punishment for burning down her village.

She snapped at everyone around her, barked orders, and threatened death. They were so stunned that she had taken the throne that nobody even questioned her orders for hangings, beheadings, and isolation in the dungeons instead of using her

CHAPTER 12

powers. She acted strong and made what she had of her lights and sparks dance around her for show; the threat had been enough. They had seen the pile of ash left where her village had once stood, they weren't taking any more chances.

Slowly, her powers started to come back. She felt less and less drained week by week. Confidence started to fill her with the return of her defenses. Rage and grief still consumed her and her actions. She had lost so much and she was alone. Elayce lashed out with new strict laws and a short temper, setting the stage for how she would run the kingdom. Even she didn't know what direction each day would take; there was nobody she trusted to help her through it, not even herself.

The silence that radiates from this training room is what eventually brought her here. Few were left in the castle once she took over and even fewer knew what to do with her. This room was built when powers were mighty and used in battle. Fire magic, water and ice magic, and a few times even blood magic ran through royal blood lines. It was built by powerful Magic Wielders to withstand different types of magic, so their wielders could practice and hone their skills. Even Elayce doesn't understand the runes etched into the floors and walls that keep it standing. When she walks into this room, the silence fills her up, forcing her magic to jump outside of her. She can concentrate on just her magic with no outside distractions. It's easy to practice here, allowing her to test out different things. No matter what kind of magic she throws and where, she has never been able to damage the room. She learned to trust her magic and herself.

She tries to come here often, even after all this time. Especially with the Darkness threatening its return.

Practicing magic wielding isn't the only way that she is

preparing herself. Elayce has spent time trying to teach herself other kinds of enchantments. Runers have the rare ability to read, create, and use runes. A Runer could teach another Magic Wielder how to use runes, but only they can create them. This is how her ward stones worked along her kingdom's boundaries. Years ago, she had commissioned a very old Runer to draw on to the stones and teach her how to leave a bit of herself behind to use them as defense against enemies. She hasn't heard rumors of or seen a Runer in over two hundred years.

It has been a while since she pored over any of the rune books she kept in the restricted section of the library. Energy might buzz through her, but her body is waning. She grabs a towel to wipe the sweat from her face before flinging it to the ground, brushing past Harkn on her way out of the training room and to the books.

Chapter 13

"Your Majesty?" Tydas and the other council members are all staring at her.

"Hmm?" She looks up from the point on the table she had been staring at.

She's exhausted. Darla had come looking for her last night and found her in the library long after she would have regularly gone to bed. Darla had snuck in timidly, tip-toeing across the floor like a mouse. Squeaking "Your Majesty?" into the dark, barely candle-lit cove where Elayce was settled with her books. Elayce had jerked awake, her lights flaring and blinding Darla until Elayce remembered where she was and realized Darla wasn't there to attack her, but to wake her up and bring her back to her rooms.

"Council Member Arvij is wondering what you think about the proposed changes to King Theis's proposal?" Tydas clarifies.

"What I think is that we reject the whole proposal. Same as I've done for the last three hundred years."

Murmurs echo through the room.

"Well, why don't we invite him to the anniversary celebration, my queen. He did say he would love to come see Aerash." He nods his head and looks around the table, encouraging the council members to nod their heads as well. "You could give him an answer while he is here. It would be proper etiquette to at least give him an answer in person," he says.

She growls, leaning towards Tydas with a menacing glare. The lights floating around her lean forward too, creeping closer and closer to Tydas. He doesn't flinch, even as the sparks get close enough to reflect the grease on his face. The council members, however, all lean away from her. One of the chairs begins to wobble on its hind legs, the occupant throwing it off balance. A whimper comes from Gresha, Nicen's council member.

"Queen Elayce, this proposal is nothing but good for Aerash. This could be your legacy, expanding the borders of Aerash peacefully."

"I am my own legacy," she growls.

Tydas has enough self-preservation to look ashamed. He looks down at the table, shuffling the papers in front of him so he doesn't have to meet her eyes. "Of course, Your Majesty."

"Send him an invitation to the celebration then. He can join us next month, and I can tell him no while he's here." She leans back against the chair, her sparks withdrawing to float behind her.

"I will have a formal invitation drawn up and sent to Selna," Tydas says, his energy renewed. Greed could always find a bright side.

"In fact, why don't you send invitations to the royal families of all of our neighbors. Norde, Istin, and Don Kemt would surely love to join the momentous celebration," she declares, not to be outdone by Tydas.

"We haven't had any visiting royals for decades!" Arvij, South Garsen's council member sputters, resulting in a coughing fit.

"Then I expect you will all have much to prepare." She secretly hopes that this will keep them busy enough to leave her alone for a while. It will also give her the chance to meet with the neighboring rulers and settle any rumors about why she might be building up her army. Briefly, in the beginning, she thought that being queen would mean that she would be free to do as she pleased. That she wouldn't be bothered, begged, cajoled into doing the work for others. Quickly, she learned that she had the wrong idea of what it meant to be a queen.

She glances to where Tydas is sitting, furiously scribbling away on the paper in front of him. He leans so close to the table that he doesn't have much farther to lean before his head touches it. "Tydas?"

"A wonderful idea, Queen Elayce. Marvelous. I will bring this to the celebration committee at once and they will begin their adjustments." He jumps from his chair, still scribbling on the paper, pressed up to his hand. "We'll have to have the extra rooms cleaned out? Hire more staff, they'll bring their own staff? No, we should hire more staff..." His mumbling cuts off when he walks out the door and turns the corner heading, no doubt, to find the Head of Staff to alert them of the changes.

Elayce looks from the empty doorway to the council members still seated quietly at the table with her. "Yes, well, I could use a drink," Gresha mutters. Not a surprising comment coming from the Nicen council member. She scoots back her chair, her pleasantly plump form covered in an unflattering shade of pale green. She scoops the papers up and marches off, her boots clacking across the tiled floor of the council chamber.

Seeing that Elayce doesn't stop her or say anything about

her departure, the rest of the council members begin to mutter excuses for leaving and grab their things to leave as well. Elayce does her best to make them uncomfortable with her silent stare as they shuffle out.

She drops her head onto the back of the chair, exhaling slowly. Her time in the library last night hadn't produced any new information. Not that she much expected that to happen, she's been studying the same texts for years. The pressure to figure out how to take care of the Darkness is growing, and she can do nothing but train and raise an army. There is nobody to talk to, no legends to chase after, no whispers of one last hope. She is the legend. She is the answer to defeating the Darkness. Or, she thought she was.

~

The clang of metal fills Elayce's ears. Phin stands behind her staring off into the distance. Captain Barton stands on her other side, watching the newest recruits spar in the training room they are all standing in. Some are fighting with weapons and some are fighting in hand to hand combat. It's clear from the slow jabs and loud grunts that many of the men have been training hard all day already.

"Did you receive my letter while I was away?" Elayce asks Captain Barton. His brown eyes, too small for his wide face, slide over to hers.

"Yes, Queen Elayce, I did. I have implemented new training times. They get up earlier and train later. I've tasked more senior members of the guard to rotate through training and exercises with them."

"It doesn't look like it," she comments.

He clears his throat. "They were completely untrained when they were drafted just a few weeks ago. No matter how hard

CHAPTER 13

we train, they will need time."

"We don't have time," she snaps.

"If there is something specific they need to be training for, then perhaps you should inform your training captain."

"Your job is to follow my orders."

"My queen, I cannot prepare them for a threat I do not know about."

He isn't wrong, but she isn't planning on confirming the rumors about the Darkness yet. She still doesn't know how to defeat it this time, and she doesn't want to create widespread panic. Men will desert the army and her people will begin rioting if they knew what was coming again.

"Phin, call Captain Nolan and tell him to meet Captain Barton and me in Barton's study." Phin nods and leaves the sparring room to relay the message. "Your study, Barton." Elayce takes off without waiting for him.

When Captain Nolan enters, Queen Elayce is seated at the chair behind Barton's desk while the training captain sits uncomfortably on a small brown leather couch on the other side of the room, stroking his red mustache. He bows to Elayce after closing the door behind him.

"Captain Nolan," Elayce greets him.

His curly dark hair, speckled with gray, flops across his face when he stands from his bow. He walks forward to stand in front of the desk, his large form blocking the room from her view. His hands are clasped behind his back, causing his large upper body muscles to flex and protrude. His jet black eyes pierce his surroundings, roving the study rapidly. Captain Nolan has been with the guard since he enlisted when he was eighteen and quickly caught Elayce's eye with his skilled combat maneuvers. It didn't take long for him to join Elayce's personal guard, and not long after that for him to challenge her to a trial fight for the captain of the guard position. He has held the position since he was twenty-five, nobody daring to challenge him and then Elayce to a trial fight to take over his position.

"My queen," he says, finally taking a seat though not looking any less alert.

"What I'm going to tell you doesn't leave this space." She makes eye contact with Barton and then with Nolan before continuing. "Since you're the only ones who will know, I will know if either of you speaks of it outside this room. Then I'll have to find a new captain of the guard and a new training captain. Understand?"

They both nod.

"The Darkness is returning."

"The Darkness?" Barton's eyes bulge, and his mustache flutters with his exhalation. "The thing you defeated three hundred years ago during your ascension to the throne?"

Elayce says nothing. Unwilling to admit that if the Darkness was back, then it means she didn't really defeat it. Captain Barton swallows, realizing what he just insinuated.

"Well you can just...defeat it again." His voice cracks and he clears his throat, continuing in a deeper tone. "Right, Your Majesty?"

"If we do not wish for it to return again, I believe that I will have to do things differently," Elayce says.

"You've had all of this time to train and prepare. Everyone knows you're the strongest Magic Wielder in the land. Surely you can vanquish the Darkness with ease this time." Barton's voice keeps getting higher as he talks. He stands from the couch and paces back and forth across the tiny room.

CHAPTER 13

"Barton, sit. Your cowardice is stinking up the room." Captain Nolan rolls his eyes. Barton may be the training captain, but he hasn't seen a real battle before. Most of the men haven't seen anything like what will be coming. The army generally spends their time training, taking care of rebel skirmishes, and enforcing the laws of the kingdom. Nothing would prepare them for the army that the Darkness will bring.

"I thought the rumors from Don Kemt were false." Barton sinks down on the couch in a huff.

"I never said they were," Elayce answers.

"You never said they weren't!" Barton retorts.

"Watch yourself, Captain," Nolan warns Barton. Turning back to Elayce he says, "How can we prepare?"

"The wards I have around the kingdom are holding for now. I will need all six collected before the Darkness comes to our kingdom—I can't be separated from any pieces of my magic during this fight. When King Guydor comes next month, I'd like us to meet with him to talk about the attacks he's been experiencing. See if we can learn anything from him."

"He won't share that information for free."

"I'm aware. We'll offer him protection."

"We don't have the men to send to Don Kemt, Your Majesty," Barton chimes in.

"I said we would offer him protection. As in King Guydor and his family. Not his whole kingdom," Elayce explains.

"You think the king would abandon his kingdom?" Barton's panic is still evident in his voice.

"I don't doubt for a second that he would choose his own safety over his kingdom. He will believe that once I have defeated the Darkness, he will get to return to his throne."

"There will be nothing left to rule," Barton cries.

Nolan strokes his beard, ignoring Barton's protests. "And will he get to return to his throne?"

"Ask me again once this war is over." Elayce smiles conspiratorially. Barton's jaw clenches and he sits back against the back of the couch. "Now you know the threat that we face, Captain Barton. Are you capable of training the new recruits or shall I find someone who is?"

Barton grimaces, his face looks a little green. "I will do what I can, Your Majesty." He stands to head out and gives a little bow before disappearing out of his own study.

"See to it that the recruits are ready to face the army of the Darkness by the celebration next month. I have a feeling we don't have much longer than that."

"Yes, Your Majesty." Captain Nolan stands and bows deeply on his way out.

Chapter 14

The clacking of booted footsteps along the tiles breaks her concentration. She glances up from the book to see Dungeon Master Jarrel standing before her.

Intrigued as to what he could be out of the dungeons for, she gives him her full attention. "Speak."

"He is asking for you, Your Majesty," Jarrel says.

"The rebel prisoner?" Jarrel nods. "And why are you delivering his summons to me?"

"He says that he has information he's willing to share with you in exchange for a brief time outside of his cell," Jarrel explains.

"Interesting," she murmurs. She'd been really focused on this rune in her book, it looks very similar to some of the symbols from her training room. Cross referencing it with some of the other books stacked on the table with her, she thought that maybe this could be something that could help her in her fight against the Darkness. She's just guessing at everything, but maybe eventually she could guess right. Or eventually a Runer might come forward and she could hire them to help her. "Bring him up, then. See to it that he's bathed first." Her nose wrinkles, remembering the smell the last time she was down there.

Jarrel nods and retreats from the room.

A short while later, the prisoner is pushed roughly into a seat down the table from her. Close enough that they can speak, but far enough away that if he were to lunge for her the guards could comfortably back her up. His hair is still wet from the bath, and without the blood or dirt covering him any longer she can see bruises lining his skin. Some are yellowing and healing and some look fresher.

"Not enjoying the accommodations we have for rebel visitors?" Elayce asks him.

"A...break would be nice," Vaaren answers, looking a little sheepish.

"A bit early in your stay to be needing a break, isn't it?"

"I can give you some information in exchange."

"We already have a deal where I gain information from you."

"I..." Vaaren pauses, glancing behind the queen. His eyes slide over to the man tied up against the wall. She looks to where his eyes roam, seeing Captain Barton's head loll to the side. Dried blood cakes his cheeks and neck. Small burn spots cover his arms and what was left of his hair and mustache is charred and patchy. His eyes are closed, and if it weren't for the wheezing breaths slipping from his mouth it would be hard to tell if he were still alive.

"Who is that?" Vaaren asks Elayce.

"A coward who needed to be reminded who he was serving," Captain Nolan answers, moving forward from his position in the shadows. Elayce smiles cruelly.

"Have him moved to the public viewing cages for the next twenty-four hours," she says to Captain Nolan.

"The public viewing cages?" Vaaren asks.

"He may have earned his wounds in private, but his punishment will be public. This is what happens when you are an incompetent fool who questions their queen," Elayce says matter-of-factly.

"If the coward lives through that, he will be sent back to training camp and begin with the new recruits," Nolan adds, beginning to untie the ropes from around the former training captain.

"He won't live another twenty-four hours without medical attention, look at him!" Vaaren gestures towards the unconscious man, as if Queen Elayce was unaware of the state she left him in.

"If he can't stand a little torture then maybe he was never fit to train my army." Elayce shoves the book that she was reading to the side, shifting Vaaren's attention to it.

"Is that a book of runes?" he asks.

A look of shock crosses Elayce's face. "You recognize this?"

"I..." Vaaren starts, glancing back and forth between Barton and Elayce, swallowing hard. "I'm a Runer."

Vaaren is a Runer?

The word seems to echo around the room; Elayce is stunned into silence. The air around her seems to pause as well.

"I could...I could help you with what you're looking for. If you let him get medical attention instead of sending him to the public viewing cages." Vaaren gulps. A war rages in his eyes, seemingly unsure if this is a fair trade. "And you don't harm any more blacksmiths from Flora."

"What makes you think I need your help with this?" Elayce demands.

"Unless you're a Runer, I don't see anyone else in this room helping you with what's in there." Elayce watches the confidence slowly slip back into Vaaren's posture. She had given the wrong answer; should have blown off his offer immediately. Now he knows he has bargaining power.

Without taking her eyes off Vaaren, she says, "Captain Nolan, take Barton to the infirmary. Merda should be able to fix him right up. He's stripped of his title and he starts his training over."

Vaaren holds eye contact and sits back against his chair, crossing his arms over his chest.

"And," Elayce grits out, "end the Blacksmith Order in Flora."

"Yes, Your Majesty." Captain Nolan doesn't hesitate. He signals to two guards on the other side of the room to come take Barton from the room. Barton groans and wheezes as they pick him up and carry him out, Captain Nolan on their heels. The guards' exit leaves Vaaren and Elayce alone in the room.

"Thank you," Vaaren says.

"Don't thank me, Nobody, you will do your fair share to uphold your end of the agreement," Elayce snarls. She doesn't try to keep calm anymore. She might have agreed to the terms of the deal, but out of desperation, not choice. Vaaren flinches at her words. She flings the book across the table to him, but he catches it before it slams into his chest.

"What are you looking for?"

"You don't need to know in order to help me with what I need."

He opens the cover of the large, black book. "How can I help you find what you need if I don't know what you're looking for?"

"You're going to teach me what you know about runes and I will tell you when I've found what I need."

CHAPTER 14

"You don't know what you're looking for?" he asks her, his eyebrows raising and disappearing behind his shaggy hairline.

She glares at him. "You better get started before I change my mind."

He clears his throat and looks down at the book on the table in front of him, then at the stack of books sitting on the table next to her. "Are these all the books you have on runes?"

"No." He looks down again at the book in front of him, studying the first page. "When did you find out you were a Runer?"

He looks up at her. "Shortly after I joined the rebellion."

"Do they have other Runers?" she asks.

He doesn't reply.

She sighs. "How did they know you were a Runer?"

"They have tests for the people that join the rebellion. When you have a limited number of resources, people being one of them, you have to know what you have and how to use them."

Elayce hears the truth in his words. It is a much smarter strategy than she would've expected from the rebels. They haven't been much of a threat. They must have fewer resources than she thought.

"Why would they allow a Runer out on an attack mission?" A valid question. Runers are so rare that he would be much more valuable to the rebellion kept safe and alive. Out of her reach.

"I wasn't supposed to be a part of the mission that night. Something happened and I ended up with the group to replace another rebel who didn't show; I was the only one available. Turns out, they had been caught past curfew by the guards near their hometown. Things like that happen often, but the missions still need to be carried out." Elayce notes the tone of hollowness in his voice, attributing it to the failure of the mission. "It wasn't even supposed to be an attack mission. We were meeting an informant; they gave us information on a civilian that needed a safe space to hide. I wanted to go back for them another night, I didn't have a good feeling about it. The lead said that we could wrap the whole thing up and then be done with it. Not have to worry about sending out another party later. We got caught by a patrol and it turned into a fight near the wall."

"You weren't even trying to break into the castle?" Confusion floods her at Vaaren's admission. The report she received from Tydas had been wrong. She wonders if that had been intentional or if the guards who had been there had misinterpreted what the rebels were trying to do.

"No," he says.

She can't imagine sending someone as rare as the first Runer she's met in centuries on a recon mission. Nothing could have been more important to them than the skills that a Runer could offer them. She studies his face again. Ren's eyes, the same shade of green. She used to hold leaves from her plants up to his face, comparing the green of his eyes to that of the plant she was holding. He'd laugh and ask what medicines he could be mixed in to. Suddenly, she didn't want those green eyes to look away from her anymore.

"Would you like to hear more of my story?"

Chapter 15

I had felt the magic come alive within me when the Goddess reached forward with her long, spindly hand and touched my chest with just the barest tip of her finger. It felt like my blood was being electrified and ignited, traveling from the point of contact with her finger all the way to my fingers and toes. I thought my flesh would peel off, burning and melting from the inside out. The intense sizzling faded slowly, so slowly, until I could feel the magic settling into a gentle buzzing under my skin. When I touched things with my bare skin I would leave burn marks behind, but thankfully didn't set anything on fire. I didn't know anyone in my village that I could go to for help. We didn't know anyone in the kingdom that we could go to for help. Even then magic was becoming so rare, that people like us didn't know much about real Magic Wielders.

Through the dark, I ran to Ren's to tell him about the dream that I had had. I was a sobbing mess; afraid to let him touch me at first. I didn't want to hurt him or set him on fire. I wasn't yet able to project my magic. Ren had been so calm. He sat with me and let me tell him what I had dreamed about. He never questioned what I told him, that the Goddess had visited me and that she told me that I was to defeat the Darkness that was coming. I could tell he was concerned for me, but he was also excited. Immediately, he began flipping through pages of his books. He made connections to previous stories and fables about heroes and adventurers, his excitement growing and growing. He really thought that this was what we were meant to do.

"This is it, Laycie! This is going to be our big adventure!" he'd said, jumping up and pacing around the small, bare room.

His enthusiasm helped to dissipate some of my anxiety. I was able to finally stop crying and think about what had happened. What the Goddess had asked me to do.

"I can't do this," I told him.

"You have always wanted to help people. Think about how many people you could save." He reached for my hands, pausing at the last second before touching my still sizzling skin. Instead he pleaded with his eyes. Even though he wasn't able to hold me, I still felt like he was. His gaze was so warm and familiar and he enveloped me in it. His excitement convinced me that I should accept what the Goddess had told me. I didn't want to disappoint Ren. If he believed I could do it, then maybe I could.

"Okay," I whispered. "We need help though. I need to figure out how to use this. How to control it."

We had to be careful about who to tell. Magic had been disappearing from the world for a reason, and we didn't want my powers to be discovered by the wrong people. We knew that no matter what lay ahead, it was dangerous, we weren't too naive to think otherwise. We first told my mother, who had a network of people she trusted within the community. She used her network to get a message to the rebellion. My mother believed the rebellion had the best chance of helping me accomplish what the Goddess had tasked me with.

CHAPTER 15

The rebellion had been working underground against the king for some time. He was cruel and, as I had said, obsessed with his own power. He was starting wars on several fronts and stealing citizens in the night to draft them into his quickly dwindling armies. The towns on the outskirts of the kingdom were constantly under attack from neighboring kingdoms, but the king never sent his armies to protect the people. Often, he would send his forces to sneak into the enemy territory and attack their towns, trying to gain ground while his people were offered up as lambs to the enemy. Recently, it had been getting worse. It felt like the wars were coming to a crescendo. While more and more Aerashians were being stolen from their beds and forced into the army, likely to never come home, Aerash was showing signs of failing. Though the king would never admit to failure, instead blaming the people and his soldiers. The rebellion was working to overthrow the king and then would attempt to broker peace with the neighboring kingdoms.

I knew why the tides had turned, though. I knew that the king was not only fighting the war he had started for land and glory, but he was now fighting a war against the Darkness. The king couldn't do both, but he would never admit to it. With my burning skin, it was easy to convince the rebels that the vision I told them about—my visit from the Goddess—had been real. They were desperate for an edge, a sign that led them to their victory. I had been presented to them on a gold-plated platter. They turned me into their symbol, their savior. They placed all their hopes on me and started planning their next moves.

Chapter 16

She grows quiet, done with her storytelling for now. He had sat quietly through her whole story, captivated by her, just like she wanted. The room had grown dark as she spoke, the sun falling below the horizon and the stars beginning to peek out. Long shadows stretched across the room, cast by the glittering lights spaced along the dark walls.

"Had you always planned to betray them?" Vaaren asks quietly, breaking what Elayce had thought to be comfortable silence between the two of them.

"That's a lot of judgment for someone who hasn't heard the whole story."

"Everyone knows what you did. You killed the king and stole the throne for yourself, killing some of the rebel leaders to get them out of your way."

Elayce sighs. "Then I guess I won't need to tell you the rest." She stands and begins to walk out of the room. Another person who won't listen to her, letting their preconceived notions drown her out.

"Where are you going?" Vaaren calls after her.

Elayce addresses a servant who arrives in the room at the sound of her retreating footsteps. "Show Vaaren to one of the guest rooms, post a consistent guard watch as well."

CHAPTER 16

"You're not sending me back to the dungeons?"

"Would you prefer that I do?" She turns her head over her shoulder but doesn't quite face him, and he doesn't answer her question. Tired from reliving her past, and her present, she leaves him and heads towards her rooms, alone.

~

She spends the next morning in her greenhouse. She'd called Harkn to her rooms last night, but even his company hadn't made her feel better. Vaaren's words last night—*"Had you always planned to betray them?"*—felt like her own sparks had ruptured in her heart. She tried reminding herself that even though he had so many similarities to Ren, he wasn't Ren. This was some trick that someone was trying to confuse her with. She just didn't know who, or how. Regardless, the accusations that spewed from his mouth didn't hurt any less. She was having a difficult time separating Vaaren from Ren, but it was clear that Vaaren was never going to listen to her. He had sat quietly while she was telling him about herself and not heard anything she said.

She squeezes the jar she is holding until it bursts into glass fragments that fly across the room. She lets out a frustrated cry and slams her hand down on the bench in front of her. Blood from the cuts on her hand smears across the top. After a pause, she traces her fingers in the bloody mess, drawing a rune she remembers from her studying. She waits for something to happen, maybe a tug from her magic or any indication that it might work. But nothing does.

She screeches and grabs the edge of the bench, flipping it along with everything on it. She flings out her arm, launching sparks at the overturned table. They streak through the air, smacking into the table with such force that it slides back along the floor before hitting the wall and bursting into flames. The flames quickly claim the wood and move up the wall grabbing onto low hanging shelves. Elayce doesn't move, watching the flames burn the plants she's so lovingly tended to. The jars of berries and plant cuttings that she's collected fall and shatter on the ground. Some make it to the floor intact and roll away, as if searching for a safe place to hide from the flames. Don't they know there is no safe space near the queen?

A guard runs into the green house, screaming for the queen to get to safety outside. She ignores him, entranced by the dancing oranges and reds. She reaches out again, calling the sparks forth, and points to other areas of the space that aren't yet drowning in flames. Sending her magic to wreak destruction. More sparks, more flames. The temperature rises, causing the glass walls to begin to shatter and smoke to pour out.

The guard throws his arm over his face, trying to prevent himself from inhaling any smoke. He reaches forward and grabs her wrist, trying to pull her to safety. She immediately wrenches her arm from his grasp, sending him careening away from her. He trips over broken pieces of debris and tumbles to the ground. The force of his fall shakes the space around him and burning pieces of the building come crashing down on top of him, trapping his limp body in the corner of the quickly crumbling room. Elayce stares at where the guard is now buried beneath a flaming pile of debris, rubbing her wrist where he had touched her.

Another guard runs into the room, face covered with his arm. The smoke is getting thick enough that Elayce has a hard time seeing who it is at first. His head swivels back and forth searching for Elayce and the other guard. Elayce lifts her palm, sending lights into the air and lighting the way for the guard. His head snaps to her and she sees that it's Phin. His arm stretches to her through the smoke and gestures for her to follow him. Briefly, her gaze slides over to the corner where the other guard is still buried and unmoving. She sends her sparks ahead of her towards Phin to light his way and follows him out of the greenhouse.

Outside, she stands with Phin at a safe distance from the crumbling structure. The greenhouse is still burning, fully engulfed in flames. Much of the glass of the roof and walls has shattered, the metal frame twisting and falling in on itself. There isn't much else near the greenhouse, so they just let it burn itself to the ground. The fire will go out with it. Elayce stares at the mess she made. Her anger burns away as quickly as her plants, leaving her feeling empty. Phin says nothing of the missing guard, standing silently next to her with his gold uniform covered in soot and ash.

Tydas comes tromping across the lawn to stand next to them. He doesn't say anything, just gives Elayce a questioning look with a raised eyebrow.

"Have it rebuilt and restocked before our visitors arrive for the celebration next month," she says, without explanation.

"With all the preparations the staff are working on to welcome the visiting royals, we don't have anybody to spare to rebuild, Your Majesty," Tydas says.

She whirls around to face him, ash pluming off of her gown and hair. "I said. Rebuild. And restock my greenhouse. Before our visitors arrive." Though they are around the same height, she somehow towers over him. Her eyes reflect the sparks that are dancing around them both; their fast, energetic movements are a direct contrast to her deadly demand. The usual mocking that accompanies her threats is gone.

Shrinking into the collar of his shirt, Tydas chokes out, "Yes, of course, Your Majesty. I—I will make sure that it is done."

~

She dismisses the servant once she's done washing the ash and soot from her blonde tresses. It had taken three washes to return her hair to its natural shine and softness. When she had looked in the mirror, covered in the grime from the fire, she had been transported back to that day in her village. The day that she burned it to the ground. The only thing missing this time were the tear streaks that had washed away the grime on her face. Her eyes stared back at her, soulless and gray.

She had removed her clothes, ordering them to be disposed of. The smell of smoke could never be washed out of them. The bath had been drawn for her as she had undressed, and she didn't hesitate to step into the steamy pool of water. That floral, clean scent washed over her, at first just mixing with the smoky scent that clung to her. She relaxed with her head back on the tile while the servant had washed her hair. Slowly, so slowly, the scent of smoke and the memories of screams faded away.

Now, she lies still in the bath, alone but for one of her servants just outside the bathroom. The bubbles from the added soap float on the top of the water; they pop and grow again with little swishes of her limbs underneath the surface. Maybe she could just stay in here, disappear with the bubbles. Never have to answer any more questions, or have responsibility for things she shouldn't be responsible for. She sends a breath of air towards a particularly tall tower of bubbles across the tub and it wobbles. She frowns and takes a deep breath in and pushes it out, sending a wave of air over to it. This time it

CHAPTER 16

topples over, some of the bubbles popping and dissolving into the water. She makes a satisfied little grunt and leans her head back again, closing her eyes.

How long could she stay in the bath before someone would come looking for her because they needed something? Being queen has always been cumbersome. She can fight and push her way into certain things, get rid of demanding advisors and nosy servants. But there's always another advisor or servant standing behind them ready to take their place and ask for the same things. She took up the crown, so she has the responsibility to keep it up. The endless complaints, needs, or wants all come to her. Maybe magic disappeared because nobody should be made to endure hundreds of years of this.

It will all be over soon if she can't figure out how to defeat the Darkness anyway.

She should just leave, let the Darkness come. She trusted them at the beginning. They let her down. They've done nothing since then to prove they're worth saving. Her mind drifts to Theis, a man who offered to give up any real power he had to save his people. Not his kingdom, because he'd be giving that up as well, but the people who live there. Too bad he's hundreds of years too late.

Vaaren's face comes to mind. A puzzle for her to solve. When she tells him about what happened all those years ago, when he is silent, she forgets that he isn't Ren. That they aren't sitting outside in the garden and she isn't reading him a story. He listens to the adventure with such rapt attention that she almost feels the loving cocoon that used to surround her when she was close to him. But then he speaks. His voice and cadence the same as Ren's, but his words soured with hate. What is the part of him that's fake? His looks? His words? His soul? His soul that is still inherently good, she just happens to be on the wrong side this time. Her nostalgia has her continuing to go back to him again and again. If she can get through to him, maybe she can get answers to her questions about him.

She can't forget about studying the runes. It's the only hope she has left. She knows that runes can stretch and push her magic in new ways that could give her an edge against the Darkness. She doesn't know *what* that edge may be, but she has to hope that the answer lies in the books that Vaaren can read to her. Maybe once she's finally truly completed the Goddess's task, the Goddess will return and deliver her from this life.

Chapter 17

The only sound in the room is the soft turning of pages as Vaaren sifts through one of the heavy rune books. Sun streams in through the windows behind him; Elayce watches the dust fly off the pages and float in the air around him. His shaggy hair is clean and falls silkily over his face. He's wearing fresh clothes, servants garb with golden trim along the edges of the shirt and trousers. She taps her nails against the glossy, dark table and sighs.

"Have you found anything yet?" she asks.

"Don't you think I would have said something if I had?" he answers her, not taking his eyes from the pages.

"No, actually," she says, stretching her hand in front of her to admire the rings on her fingers.

He sighs and looks up. "It's slow work. I haven't had time to learn anything on my own. Everything I'm looking at is new. My ability allows me to read and learn, but it's not instant. It takes time to understand what I'm looking at."

She shifts her outstretched hand and gives him a disapproving look through her fingers. She has no idea how a Runer's magic works. She just thought that he would know things instantaneously. He could be lying to her for all she knew about it.

"Explain," she demands.

A look of contemplation comes over his features. Then he shoves the book towards the queen and scoots his chair along the edge of the table to be closer to her.

He points down at the page. "See there's a rune here. But, when I look at it, I don't know what it means. There are all these other symbols on the page," he slowly points to different markings on the page, "and all these other symbols come together to tell me what this rune can do. When I concentrate, when I use my Rune Magic, these symbols...they come off the page and move around. They tell me the story of the rune that's on this page and how it can be used. By myself and by others."

She stares down at the page, concentrating on it and willing anything to move. She calls her magic to her skin, careful not to call anything that might burn the book, just the very essence of her magic. But nothing on the page stirs.

"What?" he asks her.

"I thought that maybe if I knew how it worked then I could use my own magic to see what you could see."

"If that were to work, I'm sure someone would have figured that out long ago," Vaaren says. He brushes his fingers through his hair, pushing it off of his forehead only for it to fall straight back across his eyes.

She grunts in annoyance.

"Talk me through what you're seeing."

He hesitates before focusing back on the page in front of them. After a few seconds he begins to point at things that Elayce assumes he can see, but she cannot.

"Here, this is telling me that this rune can be used as a warming spell." He drags his finger along the page to another space that looks empty to her. "This part is telling me that the temperature of the room the Runer draws this rune in will determine how long the spell lasts on its own." Again, he slides his finger to another spot on the page. "And this piece here is saying that Magic Wielders that use fire can imbue their magic into it, making the runed item last until the Magic Wielders soul leaves this plane of existence." He continues to explain that the rune disappears from the page and redraws itself over and over on the page so that the Runer can see exactly the direction and order the strokes have to be created in for the rune to come out correct. He flips the page and she sees the same exact rune on it.

"When I concentrate on this page, I can understand that drawing the same rune in a different order allows the rune to be different. In this case, it's more powerful—this rune would allow the user to start an actual burning fire, rather than creating an object that gives off heat." He flips the pages backwards twice. "This rune is the same, but weaker because of the order a Runer draws it in. It's got a certain number of uses instead of a time frame of consistent use." He rubs his fingers along his jaw line while he studies the page.

"The way these books are written—it makes sure that a Runer could learn the magic all on their own. They would never need a teacher."

All those years she had to learn about her magic on her own through trial and error. Many errors.

"Smart way to ensure Rune Magic always has a chance to come back," Vaaren comments. He blinks slowly and yawns, covering his mouth and leaning away from the queen. "Sorry, Your Majesty. I'm not used to using this magic so much. It's taxing."

Elayce frowns. She hadn't expected Rune Magic to be taxing. It's been so long since she'd expended magic to exhaustion, and she doesn't know of anyone else who expends magic while using it the way she does.

"This is going to take quite a while if you have to rest between readings, let alone creating the rune once we find what can help."

His eyes are guarded and she wonders if he's lying. "I'm sure with more use, I will be able to stretch my limits."

"I'm sure," she says, more of a threat than an agreement.

"When will we be studying again, so I can be prepared?"

"Whenever you're rested."

"Should I have someone...call for you then?" he asks, likely remembering being chastised the last time he called for her.

"Notify the guards whenever you're rested enough to study for a bit. They will notify me and bring you here, where the books are being kept. Take notes of the things you find. That way if I am unable to join you for each session, I can look over them when I have time."

With somewhat of an agreement between the two, he nods to Elayce and a guard comes over to escort him back to his rooms. They're just down the hall, but she doesn't trust him enough to get there without a guard at his back. She ordered his chains be kept off for now, but the minute he proves that he needs them they will be back on.

Once he's gone, she pulls the book over to her again. She tries once more to use the energy of her magic to speak with the book. When she reaches out, her magic hits a wall around the book. She caresses the wall, searching for an opening but she doesn't find one. Whoever wrote this book centuries ago made sure that only a certain type of magic can commune with it.

CHAPTER 17

This book and the other rune tomes are likely older than even she is—especially if they are written so that a Runer doesn't need a teacher. She fingers the pages of the book, but the pages are sturdy and without any trace of aging. Likely runic magic is in use, holding the book together and protecting it from being lost to time.

She should find the book that holds the rune drawn on her ward stones for Vaaren. It's possible that he can tell her more about the rune and if it has better uses or if a stronger version exists. He can even draw more for her to use if she decides to take over the rule of Selna as well. Will Vaaren do that for her? She'll never force him into it. Now that she knows the magic he possesses, she won't use his powers against his will. Fortunately, they've come to a mutual agreement. Had it been too easy? No, he seems the type of person that would sacrifice himself for the greater good. His magic use for the life of the ex-training captain and the promise to leave the blacksmiths alone. His treatment is much better, too—now that he isn't staying in the dungeons. At any point if he chooses to stop helping her, then he will be returned to the dungeons. She will allow him to make that choice if it comes to that.

It has been a long time since a magic user of any kind has chosen to reveal themselves to her, although she suspects that the performer she acquired in Selna has an affinity for fire magic in his blood. He likely doesn't know that and there isn't a reason to tell him either. He'd already said that he would've chosen to serve her and will continue to do so. He will be a star performer at the celebration in a few weeks when the visiting royals come, and he will be paid handsomely for his services.

She wonders if runes can enhance the lesser magic that he or others like him seem to possess. She would have to ask Vaaren to pay attention if he came across anything like that in her books.

Boots click in the distance, getting louder as they approach her. The dragging sound of a cloak accompanies the footsteps. As the tall, broad outline of Loras, her Head of Staff, comes into focus, Elayce pauses. It's rare that he comes to speak to her directly instead of going through Tydas.

"Your Majesty." He bows low, his arms sweeping the green cape out to the sides making him look like he grew wings.

"Loras, it has been a while since you've come to address your queen."

"The coming celebration calls for us to speak in person," he explains in his deep voice.

"Are you and your staff incapable of making decisions on your own?" Elayce challenges him, knowing full well that she will have to sit in on some of these planning meetings anyway. When you take on the role of both king and queen, you are required to oversee all aspects of the running of the kingdom.

"We only wish to make sure that everything is up to your standards, my queen." He remains in his deep bow, only tilting his head up to look at her.

She motions for him to stand, rolling her eyes. "By now you would think that you would understand the standards. I don't ask for anything other than what befits my reign as your beautiful, benevolent queen."

"Yes, of course," he says in a flat, emotionless tone as he stands from his bow.

"When is this meeting you wish me to attend?" she pouts, disappointed. Clearly he is not going to engage in any games.

"The committee is meeting in an hour," he says. She glares at him and he coughs into his hand. "I mean, whenever the meeting would fit into your schedule," he amends, not making direct eye contact.

"Perfect, I will meet you in an hour. Make sure staff are ready. You're dismissed," she says and waves her fingers in a scooting motion. He gives a slight bow, turns and rushes out, his cape flowing behind him on an invisible breeze.

When she enters the throne room an hour and a half later, the committee is already in full blown discussion of the coming festivities. The discussion pauses momentarily while they all bow to her as one and wait for her to seat herself on her throne.

"Your Majesty." A small woman in a golden gown that flutters just above the floor steps forward as she addresses the queen. "As the designer for the tricentennial festival and celebration, I believe we should stick to the kingdom's formal colors of gold and gray. With so many visiting kingdoms, it is imperative that we show our pride for our country. We don't want to show any favor to the other kingdoms by using their colors in the celebration."

"Fine, next." *What a waste of time.*

The woman steps over to a table off to the side that holds different fabrics of yellows and grays, pointing to several servants that shuffle the bolts around based on her direction.

Another woman steps forward and bows to the queen. "The entertainment will be robust. Parties following the great feasts every night leading up to our formal celebration on the final day of the tricentennial. I have made arrangements to include our new flag thrower and he has asked for additional performers to be with him. Shall I oblige his request?"

"Why not?" Elayce answers sarcastically.

The woman's cheeks turn scarlet and she bows her head slightly before stepping back, allowing the next committee member to walk up. This time it's Dungeon Master Jarrel.

"Dungeon Master Jarrel, I didn't expect to see you on the committee. Don't you have better things to do than plan parties?" Elayce needles.

"I am only here to discuss the other entertainment for the week, Your Majesty. With the rebellion having gone nearly silent we don't have any rebels to send up for you as requested." He squeezes the hilt of the sword attached to his belt, his knuckles turning white. The black hairs on his mustache flutter with his rapid breathing.

"Was there not an attack while I was away in Selna?"

"There was, but the rebels have died. Either in the attack or in the dungeons," he says.

"Feeble things."

"Indeed, Your Majesty." He clears his throat.

"How do you propose we show our guests a true Aerash experience, then?" Queen Elayce asks.

"Well..." Jarrel's face takes on an ashy look. "There are other prisoners that you could make an example out of. Or, there is one rebel that is still here in the castle."

Elayce's eyes flash, she hasn't told anyone what Vaaren revealed himself to be. She isn't sure what her advisors and guards think she is doing with him behind closed doors, but it isn't any of their concern. She'll have to check in with Darla on that. "Right now, Vaaren is more important to this kingdom than you are, Jarrel. Perhaps you would like to volunteer to be the entertainment for our guests?"

He winces. "Your Majesty, I didn't mean to offend you. I was only trying to accommodate your wishes."

"And my suggestion doesn't?" she asks. The small crowd of servants and workers heads swivel back and forth between the queen and the dungeon master.

"I am no rebel, Your Majesty. I am your loyal dungeon master," he stutters over his words. Elayce doesn't respond. "I will speak with Captain Nolan. He and I can come up with a solution that will work for you."

"Delightful," Elayce answers, her gaze already moving from the dungeon master and looking for the next servant. After what feels like forever, Loras announces that the majority of the details have been approved by the queen and she is welcome to take her leave.

Chapter 18

"We need to make the trip now, Nolan," she says.

"We'll need some time to prepare a traveling group to send with you," he responds, his tone coming as close as it ever would to frustration. It's not often he argues with Queen Elayce, so she lets it slide.

"I don't want a contingent of guards to go with me. I want only a few to come. This mission has to be covert." It's time to retrieve the ward stones from around her kingdom. She can feel it, like a tingle on the back of her neck. The Darkness is coming soon and once the festivities start and the guests arrive she won't be able to leave. Now is their only chance.

"Then I will be the one to go with you," he says, pounding his fist on the table they're seated at.

"No, I need someone I trust here at the castle," she argues.

He breathes deeply, his fist on the table unclenching and clenching again. "Fine," he relents. "But I am hand-picking the three guards that are going along."

"One."

"Two," he says, no room for argument this time.

"Only because I'm also bringing Vaaren," she says smiling.

Two is fine and she knows it. A group that small can stay hidden in the shadows well-enough, but also be adequate to

CHAPTER 18

defend their position if needed. Two guards for Vaaren and she could handle herself. This trip wouldn't be announced, even after she left they would maintain that the queen was readying the castle for her visitors. The only trouble they'd encounter on the trip would be whatever they started.

She told Darla this morning to handle packing a saddle bag for a trip that would be less than two weeks. Now she just has to tell Vaaren. As if on cue, a guard escorts him into the room.

She grins. "Do you know how to ride?"

~

Elayce, Vaaren, and their two guards, Lind and Pax, are halfway to the first ward stone in Selna before they stop to camp for the first night. They'll start in Donnen and go around Aerash, ending in Silia on the border of Don Kemt where the threat is the highest. She didn't answer Vaaren's questions before they left, and there were many, so she's prepared herself to be peppered with them at the first chance he gets. They rode hard and there wasn't much opportunity to talk.

As the guards put up the tents, Elayce and Vaaren sit next to a fire. While the weather is warm enough, the darkness brings a chill with it that they want to fend off.

"Won't the fire attract unwanted visitors?" Vaaren asks, stoking it with a long stick.

"No one that I wouldn't be able to handle," she assures him.

"I wasn't worried about my safety."

"Well I hope you weren't worried about mine," she counters, chuckling.

He glares at her. "Why did you bring me along? Wouldn't it be easier to travel without me?"

"As I told you, I didn't want to be separated from you that long." She pauses, clears her throat. "We need to continue going through the tomes."

"Right," he says distrustfully. He looks over at the heavy tomes that are in the saddle bag, now on the ground near her tent. "Seems a big risk to take me and the tomes out of the castle."

"I can handle whatever we come across. I'm sure you'd be delighted to see my powers in use." Her lights flicker around her, excited at the thought of showing off for Vaaren. She has so much more control and prowess than she did three hundred years ago. Not that there's any way Vaaren would know that. "Anyway, now that I know you exist, I would find you anywhere."

He blinks back at her. She turns her head, letting her hair drape across her face to hide the blush that spreads across her cheeks under his gaze.

"Because you're a very valuable asset, of course," she finishes. Gods, what is she saying? Being outside the castle is making her forget who they both are.

He lets the awkward pause stretch between them, before finally giving a small nod and turning his attention back to the fire. If he did more of the talking, maybe she wouldn't be making such a fool of herself.

~

They make it to the ward stone just before the end of the third day, and as she predicted, they don't encounter any trouble.

"What will happen when you take the wards down?" he asks.

"Captain Nolan is working on sending out more troops to our checkpoints along the borders, but we've come to the time when the magic will do more within me than here at the border." She gets down on her knees next to the small stone. Taking a deep breath, she repeats the process she did when

CHAPTER 18

Phin was here with her.

The spark of magic responds and jumps to her. It longs to be reunited with her and quickly settles within her pit of magic. She sighs contentedly, a feeling of fullness washing over her. She looks out across the field, scanning for any rushing enemies, but nothing looks amiss. She hands the stone to Vaaren.

"You're giving this to me?"

"Relax, I just want you to study it. Maybe there's a better way we can use this magic. A way that doesn't force me to leave a piece of myself here?"

He rubs his fingers along the now dark rune. "Whoever drew this knew what they were doing. I'm not sure there's a better way."

She nods. Figures. It would have been too easy. Vaaren tucks the stone into a pack on the side of his horse, pulling out an apple he feeds to the mare. His horse is a dark brown mare, and though fast, is the slowest of the bunch. She is, however, carrying several rune tomes so that could account for some of it. He clucks, patting her shoulder and running his fingers through her mane.

"This is as safe a spot as any to camp for the night, Your Majesty," Pax says. He waits for her to nod and then begins to set up her tent.

Vaaren starts collecting whatever brush he can find to start a fire. They purchased ingredients to cook a meal that will last them until the next town they come across. With just the saddle bags on their four horses, they don't have space to carry a lot of extra supplies.

Once Vaaren's gathered enough to make a little fire, Elayce sends a few sparks over to light it.

"That is convenient," he remarks.

"Magic doesn't have to be feared and hated," she says, leaning back on her hands and looking up at the stars.

"Just the person using it."

Elayce rolls her eyes. "Don't ruin this peaceful night with your whining."

He pulls a rune tome from the saddle bag and brings it near the fire, angling it so the flames light up the pages. He's laying on the ground on the other side of the fire from her, the book propped up on his legs so that she can see the pages over his head. They read together in silence. She cringes when he folds the corner over on a page before flipping to the next one.

"Is there a problem?" he asks without turning around to look at her.

"No."

"Your shadow cringed," he says, flipping to the next page.

She crosses her arms and looks out over the field. Has he no respect for literature? It's not even his book. It's her book.

"I can feel your indignation from all the way over here," he says.

She scoffs, rolls her eyes again.

"You don't usually have a problem saying exactly what's on your mind." Another page flip.

"That doesn't sound like the compliment it should be," she retorts, running her fingers through the long grass at her feet. She cannot maim her Runer.

"Hmm," he replies.

Maybe she could maim him a little bit. "Interesting advice coming from you."

"I don't really wish to share my innermost thoughts with someone like you."

CHAPTER 18

"You don't even really know who I am." The grass begins to blacken and shrivel beneath her touch, resentment flowing out of her.

"I don't need to know who you are to know that what you do is wrong."

The fire begins to grow, forcing Vaaren to roll to the side to get away from the flames. He glares at her and she shrugs innocently.

Pax and Lind make their way over to the fire and begin cooking the meal for the four of them. Nolan told her he specifically chose these two because they had been on more covert missions that required them to be on their own for a while. They would be used to making camp and taking care of the group as well as understanding what it meant to stand watch. So far, they have been doing a good job. They remain quiet for the most part, not questioning anything Elayce demands. Nolan must have given them clear instructions.

However, she doesn't want to continue bickering with Vaaren right across their laps, so she turns instead to playing with her lights. She sends them bobbing and weaving around the camp, trying to keep herself entertained. Maybe she'd even attract some trouble and a different form of entertainment. She smiles to herself. She doesn't kill innocent people, despite what Vaaren thinks. She just has very high standards for everyone around her and very high consequences for when they aren't met. It's the best way to keep things running smoothly.

Sometimes, it's the best way to protect people from themselves. Besides, her standards are high, not impossible.

~

The morning dawn wakes her before the night watch does.

She crawls out of her tent and stretches, admiring the bright world around her. Everything feels so alive and serene. She loves the way it makes her feel, standing in the endless expanse of nature. She feels, not small, but a part of something bigger. An endless loop of life and death that trundles on through time. This is her kingdom to protect. The wild animals, the birds, the lush trees and the thick, green grass. If the Darkness were to take over, there would be nothing left here. Black shadow would eat through anything living, leaving behind desecrated landscapes where life would be incapable of thriving.

Upon seeing the queen awake, Pax wakes Lind and Vaaren to begin the chore of clearing their camp to move out. She can't remember the last time she'd been to Flora and they'll be crossing into the region tomorrow. Hopefully, they won't have to ride through highly populated areas. When they need food, she'll just send one of the guards in on their own while she stays outside the town lines. She isn't interested in being cajoled by the Florans, better to just avoid them all together.

Elayce mounts her own steed, black and tall. She doesn't ride much, or really care for animals. Her life-span is so much longer and it's quite rough to get so attached to something that will die so long before you do. She does always have a primary steed ready for her when she does go out. The horse is almost always the tallest in the herd. This particular one happens to also have a mean streak. He keeps nipping at the other horses, sometimes even the guards. Somehow, he seems to sense that nipping at Elayce wouldn't be the best decision for him. If she ever had a favorite animal, this one is certainly at the top of the list.

He trots forward, stopping near where Vaaren is stuffing one of the books back into the saddle bag.

"Are we to keep riding straight through until nightfall?" he asks her.

"I'd like to get this trip over with as quickly as possible. Do you have a problem with that?" she retorts.

"I can't do much studying while I'm riding," he answers simply, shrugging his shoulders.

"Perhaps you could sleep on your horse, so that you can study when we camp at night."

He scoffs and she glares. For the better part of the day, the only noise that accompanies the group is the beating of the hooves.

~

"So you're hiding," Vaaren says. His arms are crossed and the look he's giving the queen would never be misconstrued as respectful.

"I am not hiding. It will just be easier if I stay here while Pax goes into town to get food for us."

"There's an inn here we could stay at," he adds.

"We can't risk being recognized," she points out.

"It's close to nightfall. We can send the guards ahead to buy what we need and rent a few rooms. We can join them after the sun sets."

She scoffs. "There's nothing wrong with camping outside the town lines." She shifts her weight from foot to foot. The area is warm enough, but there isn't much cover here. They crossed into Flora not that long ago. The mixture of nerves and relief upon returning to her home land created a twist of knots in her stomach that she's been trying to ignore. She'd prefer to keep riding to get past the town, but it's too late to get too far away at this point and they need to replenish their stock of supplies.

She takes in the sweet smells of the wild gardens around them. She wouldn't mind laying in the gardens all night, protected by the flowers that grow tall around them. But it's been almost a week since she's slept in an actual bed and with the harsh riding they've all been doing...well a real bed does sound nice. She could easily clear the entire inn for the group and pay for the innkeeper's discretion. Her heart races at the thought of being in a Floran village, unease creeping its way into her stomach.

"Coward," Vaaren mumbles, barely loud enough for her to hear.

She narrows her eyes. She is not a coward. "Guards, go on ahead. Buy the supplies we need and clear the inn for us for the night. Make sure the innkeeper is discreet."

Vaaren mimics her expression.

She sighs. "Fine, just rent out a few rooms for us."

Vaaren lifts an eyebrow.

"Offer gold in exchange for their discretion."

Vaaren nods and Elayce shakes her head, turning back to her horse to finally be released from Vaaren's gaze.

Come nightfall, Vaaren and Elayce make their way slowly into town, leading their mounts behind them. Both have drawn their hoods up over their faces to offer some cover from anyone still prowling the streets late at night. They pass a few guards who nod their heads briefly instead of a full salute, Lind and Pax must have warned them ahead of time the queen would be coming through.

The inn is a stone building in the middle of town. A stable boy is waiting at the doors for them and holds out both his hands, waiting for the reins. The queen's horse reaches forward to nip the boy's hand, but he is quick to move out of the way, reaching around and taking the reins from Elayce. He bows quickly, walking around to the side of the inn with both animals in tow.

Vaaren is already up the steps of the inn, holding the door open for Elayce.

"See? This isn't so bad," he says to her quietly.

She sniffs and walks past him into the inn. The entrance to the inn leads into their dining area. It's quiet, only a few hushed whispers from conversations being held in the shadowed corners. Pax and Lind rise from the bar when they see Elayce enter. They gesture to the stairs, but now that she's here, she isn't ready to head up quite yet.

She takes a seat at a table in the corner, leaning against the back wall. The men join her, but she waves off the guards. She can handle herself in a dimly-lit inn and they should take the chance to recharge before they continue on their journey.

The room itself is cozy, decorated with hand carved trinkets and mounted animal heads. A small fire blazes in the fireplace in the center of the room, sending light and shadows across the room in an intricate dance of give and take.

For the most part, she and Vaaren are ignored. She's able to absorb it all in peace. Flowers sit in a hand carved, wooden vase on each table. She reaches out to stroke the soft petals of the flowers that sit on their own table. The periwinkle color of the petals stands out in contrast to the dark wood that surrounds them. She drags the vase closer, inhaling the scent of the flowers. She opens her eyes to find Vaaren staring intently at her.

"What?"

"Nothing," he says, shrugging, but he's not looking at her like it's nothing. He's looking at her like he has a million things he wants to ask. She looks back at the vase and away from his prying eyes.

"This is my home. Was my home."

"You could have had a new castle built here in Flora if you loved it so much."

She winces. "It would have been too painful to stay."

"Is it painful for you to be back?"

She twirls the vase, appreciating the small sprigs from every angle, avoiding his gaze. It isn't like how she thought it would be, being home. The innkeepers have kept their promise for discretion, and nobody here knows who she is. She can almost pretend like this is a normal night, before her powers invaded her body and she put the crown on her head. But that's not how things are. She isn't sitting in a tavern with Ren having a drink at the end of the night, talking about the future they want to build together.

She is here to uphold her duty to protect the kingdom with the help of a man who says he hates her. He who makes her feel like her body is on fire, making her forget everything that she's toiled over for the last three centuries. If he were anyone else, he'd be dead already. But she could never bring herself to harm him. She might not know who he really is, but her magic senses something about him and she long ago learned to trust it.

"I'm ready to retire now," she says, standing from the table. He stands after her, but when she doesn't hear his footsteps behind her she turns around to look at him. He glances down to the vase on their table. He bends over, closing his eyes and inhaling the scent of the flowers, just like she did. She looks away before he catches her staring and they head upstairs to bed.

Chapter 19

After almost two weeks, they make it to Silia. The woods here are dense and their pace of travel has slowed. Even though it's daytime, the light doesn't find its way through the thick canopy above them and it's quite dark and damp. She lights their way as best she can with her lights, but there's nothing to be done about the air that clings to them.

They've run into no trouble so far and the ward stones from Flora, Nicen, and South Garsen are safely tucked into the saddle bag on Vaaren's horse. She's a little surprised that Vaaren hasn't tried to make a run for it, but he's faithfully traveled along with them day after day. Every morning she wakes looking for him, just to make sure he hasn't slipped away into the night. He's always right where he was when she went to sleep. Sometimes with a book left open across his chest, as if he fell asleep reading. It catches her off guard, so early in the morning and out in the wilderness. One morning, she almost brushed her lips over his before she remembered who they were. Thankfully, he hadn't sensed her nearness and had remained sleeping long enough for her to scramble back to her own tent.

They will reach the final ward stone soon. She knows where it's laid, but something doesn't quite feel right. She hasn't said anything to the others, but she can't quite feel it the way that she normally feels the ward stones when she gets close. It still feels very far off. Maybe the density of the trees is messing with her somehow.

The air, though damp, has grown quite cold in the last few minutes. Must be the lack of sunlight. Vaaren's horse stops, takes a few steps back. She whinnies and shuffles, fighting against Vaaren's direction to go forward. The hair on the back of Elayce's neck stands up.

"Wait—" A shout erupts from behind her, cutting her off. Lind is on the ground, scrambling to get back up. His horse rears and takes off into the woods. Its cries echo back to them, hoof beats stopping in their tracks. Then she sees it.

It's on all fours, black as the night. It blends in with the surroundings and ripples of shadow pulse off of it, making the edges of the creature blur. Its eyes, black but still glowing. It creeps closer to them, a growl emanating from its chest. Deep and rumbling. Pax is on his horse still, trying to regain control of the terrified beast. His sword is drawn, but he's distracted.

The creature lunges, shadow trailing behind it so it's impossible to tell how big it is. Elayce reacts, almost too late. She sends a shower of sparks towards it. It's already knocked Pax off of his mount, but the creature whips around to face Elayce. A pained hiss rips from its lip-less mouth. It leaves Pax, turning to prowl towards the queen instead. She shoots out more sparks, sending them spinning around the creature, trapping him in. For the first time since it's shown itself, it looks unsure. She squeezes her hands together, drawing in the spinning vortex around the creature. It huddles closer in on itself, trying to avoid the sparks. Eventually, it has nowhere to go and hisses and screams as the sparks overtake it. The screams, ear-shattering screams, almost cause her to lose her focus but she doubles-down, squeezing the creature until it winks from existence.

She looks around, Lind is helping Pax to his feet, blood dripping down his cheek. Lind's mount is surely gone by now. Somehow, Vaaren has managed to stay on his.

"What was that thing?" Vaaren asks.

"A part of the Darkness's army," she says. She glances over to Lind and Pax, but as they've been the whole trip, they remain expressionless. Lind is trying to help Pax wipe away the blood on his face.

"How is it here?" he asks.

"I don't—Quiet." She spins around to look out beyond the trees. There's more than one, she can feel it. She sends her lights to illuminate more of the forest around them, finding shadow leaking towards them from every direction. She gestures to the guards and they close in around her and Vaaren, standing back-to-back. One may not have been a challenge for her, a few more probably won't be either. But she doesn't just have to protect herself. She has to keep Vaaren alive. If she loses the Runer, she'll have no hope of defeating the Darkness.

She hears jaws snapping in the distance, coming closer and closer. Maybe the creature hadn't been crying out in pain, but in warning to its pack. How many can she fight off? The guards have no way of killing the creatures on their own, they can only deflect and maybe distract long enough for her to come over and kill them.

Several long jaws poke through the shadows at the same time. Glancing around herself quickly, she spots at least ten.

Enough of this, she will not be hunted.

She sends her sparks out in an explosion of light. The

creatures pounce. She hears metal squelch against something, hissing and barking and shouting all around her. Regular weapons won't work against these beasts. She conjures a sword made of light, leaning down to swipe at the creature attempting to bite her steed. It screeches, black blood leaking from the gash that she opened in its flesh. Three more turn her way to defend their pack member. She slides from her saddle, rolling to the ground and slashing the creature in a flurry of sparks as she hops to her feet, killing it. The stallion rears and rushes one of the creatures, crushing it between its head and a tree. The creature scrambles, pulling its thick black claws through the horse's neck. Her sparks go flying, straight through the head of the creature, sending black blood spattering everywhere.

She spins, trying to find Vaaren. He's swinging a sword from the back of his horse. Where he got the sword from, she's not sure but she's glad he has something. She lunges for him, but another creature jumps in front of her, swinging his claws and opening a long, shallow gash across her stomach. Damn it! She needs to focus. Hopefully Vaaren can manage to keep them away until she can fight her way to him.

A scream comes from behind her and she knows it's Lind. She tries to send sparks out to help him, but she can't tear her eyes from the creature in front of her. If she focuses on everyone at once, they will all lose. She punches the creature, coating her hand with a layer of sparks before contact. Her hand goes straight through the creature's mouth, the jaw coming to rest on her arm like a bracelet.

She shakes it off, hearing Vaaren's horse whine and scream in front of her. A thud echoes around her and she looks up to see Vaaren's been thrown from the mare and is being circled by two of the shadow creatures. Their shadows grow thicker and Vaaren begins to disappear from view.

"No!" she screams, sending a wave of light out from her. The creatures nearest her disintegrate into formless shadows, leaving her free to run to Vaaren.

The sound of flesh being torn from bone rings out behind her, but she keeps moving. If she's counting there's still five creatures left, and two of them are circling Vaaren. A wave of nausea flows through her and she briefly remembers the gash across her stomach. Not now.

Suddenly, she's tumbling forward and immense pain shoots through her shoulder. She screams, reaching for the creature that's attached itself to her arm. She rolls to the side, shaking it off. A dagger of light appears in her hand and she slams it down into the creature underneath her. She feels it go limp between her legs and drags herself forward.

Get to Vaaren, get to Vaaren.

A scream comes from the shadows he's hidden within. A scream means he's alive still. With her good arm, she releases a wave of light but it's not as strong as she wants it to be. It forces the two creatures to back up from Vaaren, bringing him back into her view. He's barely conscious, bright red blood leaking from a wound on his arm. One of the creatures took a bite out of him.

Her focus lasers to the creature that has flesh hanging from between his teeth. The creature's tongue lolls out to grab the hanging flesh, pulling it into his mouth. She watches him swallow and then...smile. The creature is smiling at her, like it knows what it's doing. Maybe it does.

She keeps her gaze locked on the creature, standing there, breathing what it doesn't know will be its last breaths. She staggers to her feet, feeling the warm blood from her injuries drip down her cold body.

"Tell your master to fight his own battles," she says to the creature. It cocks its elongated head to the side, as if it's listening to what she has to say.

And then she explodes. A wall of light bursts from her body in every direction, lighting the forest up in a way that can surely be seen by the nearest town. The nearest trees catch fire, bursting into flames, quickly crumbling and falling under the force of the blast. The shadow creatures scream as they disappear and she hopes the creature had time to relay her message to the Darkness before it was wiped away.

If not for the fires burning around them, they'd be plunged back into darkness once her wall of light extinguishes. She rushes to Vaaren, who's barely breathing, but alive. Taking stock of their situation, she looks around to see that her horse is the only other one still alive. Vaaren's mare is laying on her side a few feet from them. Thankfully, she didn't run off with the rune tomes. Behind her Pax and Lind are dead. Lind is covered in deep gashes that match the claws of the creatures and Pax's middle has been torn away as if the creatures were eating him before she disintegrated them.

She tries to haul Vaaren up, but his unconscious weight is too much for her weakened state. She huffs and then clicks her tongue. Her horse snorts and trots over, blood from the scratches on his neck starting to crust over already. She pats his side, going to fetch the books from the dead mare to transfer to her saddle bags. The forest around her is still burning, she needs to get them out of there quickly before the smoke and exhaustion overtake them all.

After she's moved everything over, she shakes Vaaren's

shoulder.

"Vaaren," she whispers into his ear. "I need you to wake up and help me. I need to get us out of here, but I can't get you onto the horse myself."

Thankfully, he stirs a bit. Moaning and gasping when he moves his injured arm.

"Come on, just a little bit more," she says, hauling him up by grabbing under his arms. He screams, and she can almost feel the pain in it. She's sweating, the heat from the fire and the strain of trying to move both of them is too much. He wobbles on his feet and she does her best to keep him upright.

"No, you don't," she heaves him towards the horse. "You can pass out again once you're in the saddle."

With a final thrust, she and a barely conscious Vaaren are able to hoist him onto the tall steed. She pulls herself up behind him, trying to hold him upright as best she can while guiding the horse out of the burning woods.

Chapter 20

When she wakes next, she's in a bed that isn't her own. Her body is sore and she can feel her magic low in its pit. The sun is peeking in behind a white, lace curtain covering a small square window. She looks to where the sun stream lands and finds Vaaren laying next to her in bed. He looks so peaceful and relaxed, his breathing deep and even. She matches her breathing to his, feeling a calm settle over her being this close to him. His eyes shift slightly behind his eyelids. She reaches out and gently brushes the hair off of his forehead, her fingertips graze over the dried blood from a scratch that stretches down his face.

The night before comes rushing back to her. The woods, the shadow creatures, Lind and Pax lying dead, and then riding her horse as fast as she could to the nearest town with Vaaren plastered to her front.

She had drained herself so fully, and Vaaren couldn't hold on to consciousness, they had to stop for the night. She had tried to keep her hood low to hide her identity, but she practically dragged Vaaren into the almost full inn and she's sure someone saw her. At the very least, the inn keepers know who she is. And they know that she brought an unconscious, injured man into the last room that they had. With one bed.

CHAPTER 20

She groans, rolling out of the bed. She barely had the energy to get them to the room last night and wrap their deepest wounds, let alone get cleaned off before passing out in the bed next to him. They're both still coated in black and red blood. Her dress is stiff with it, and she grimaces at the way it clings to her in the oddest way. If she hadn't been so drained, there was no way she would have passed out still wearing it. She had to leave most of their supplies in the forest in favor of carrying the gold and the tomes as well as two people on one horse. Maybe she can have the innkeeper send for new clothes for the both of them.

She's about to head down to demand the innkeeper help her when a low moan comes from Vaaren. She spins around on the bed, folding onto herself to sit next to him, peering over his face. His eyes blink open and then he startles a bit.

"Hello," he groans.

"How are you feeling?" she asks.

"I've been better," he says, his hands roam his own body, feeling for injuries. "Where are we?"

"At an inn in Fender. I couldn't ride us all the way home after last night. Our injuries are slowing us down; we might have to camp another night before we make it back to Castle Vleck."

His hand skates along the makeshift wrap that covers the bite marks in his arm and his own bare chest. He blushes.

"I had to wrap your wound," she explains. Lucky for both of them, she didn't have enough energy last night to truly appreciate his body.

"Lind and Pax?"

She shakes her head.

"The horses?"

She shakes her head again.

"What's left?"

"We have my horse and the books," she confirms. He grimaces.

"What happened? Why were there shadow creatures in Silia? What about the ward stone?" he asks, sitting up suddenly and swinging his legs off the bed. She grabs his shoulder to keep him sitting.

"I'm not sure what they were doing there. They must've come over from Don Kemt. As for the ward stone," she pauses. "We have to get back to the castle. I'll have to make do with missing just a small sliver of my magic."

"We were so close," he says.

"I don't think we were," she admits, removing her hand from his shoulder to wring her fingers instead.

"How so?" He twists, so that he can see her face.

"Something didn't feel right, we should have been close to the ward stone. But it's like it wasn't there." Her shoulders sag. Frustration funnels through her, and maybe a bit of embarrassment. She hates feeling out of control.

"What does that mean?" he asks, brows furrowing.

Someone could have found it, hidden it, stolen it. Maybe someone found a way to neutralize it. It doesn't make any sense though, she doesn't know anyone with the power to have done that. Or, she didn't until she met Vaaren. She glances back up at him. "I don't know."

"We should get going, then." He shifts closer to the end of the bed until he's able to fully support himself standing upright.

They grab their few belongings and make their way downstairs. She spies the innkeeper.

"Do you have spare clothes we could buy from you?" She keeps her head low, allowing the hood to cover her face. She gestures to her crusty clothes.

"Yes, Your Majesty," the innkeeper says, scuttling away.

Elayce groans inwardly. Of course the innkeeper knows who she is. Thankfully, there seems to be nobody else around. She finds a chair at one of the dining tables to sit and wait for the innkeeper's return.

"I thought you might threaten the innkeeper for identifying you out loud," Vaaren says, sitting down in the chair next to her.

"Well, I need her to fetch the clothing," Elayce responds.

He shrugs, choosing to look around the sparsely decorated room while they wait.

The innkeeper returns shortly with a change of clothing for both of them. The outfits are commoners' clothing, but clean. She can't remember the last time she wore something this drab. They take turns changing in their room before heading out to find the stables. The stable hand is there, already saddling up her horse. The innkeeper must've told them Elayce and Vaaren would be on their way out.

"One horse," Vaaren muses.

"It was good enough for you last night," Elayce answers.

She mounts and then looks at Vaaren, leaning her head to indicate he should get on behind her. He hesitates and she sees him glance around them. For a moment, she thinks that he might run, but instead he grabs the back of the saddle and hoists himself up behind her. The warmth of his thighs settles around her and his arms snake around her middle, careful to avoid the wound on her stomach. She stiffens slightly at the touch.

"It's very tall," he says, his breath caressing her neck.

"Hold on tight," she says, a small smile spreading across her face. Thankfully, he can't see her expression. She pushes her heel into the animal's flank and they take off.

When they stop to camp for the night, both are exhausted and not any less sore than when they woke up. They don't even bother to make a fire, instead Elayce lets her sparks float around them, creating a cocoon of warmth. They sit quite close to each other. With nobody else to keep watch, it's the safest option. She catches him gazing at the sparks as they float lazily through the night.

"I could have left you to the shadow creatures last night, you know," she says. Perhaps not the smoothest way to start a conversation.

"You need my rune knowledge," he says, still focused on the spinning sparks.

She's not going to admit that he's right. "I could have found a different way to get what I need."

"You didn't save the guards though." He's squeezing his knees to his chest.

"I can't save everyone," she mumbles, letting some of the sparks drift over her body, finding comfort in their touch.

He looks at her, the moving lights casting strange shadows across his face.

She sighs. "I didn't plan to betray the rebels."

Vaaren shifts his whole body so he's facing her, giving her the confidence to keep going.

"When Ren and I offered to help, they promised that they would protect my mother. I didn't want my choice to be a part of this rebellion to bring harm to my mother. They sent guards to protect her in her home around the clock, I even checked several times to make sure that they were upholding their end of the deal. They always had two guards posted outside our front door, and they would follow her when she went to the market. I thought she was safe..." Elayce trails off, looking down at the small space between hers and Vaaren's leg. Brown, damp grass poking up between them.

"After the battle with the king, the Darkness—he said something similar. About how I couldn't save everyone. At first I thought he meant...well I realized that he was talking about my mother. I rode out to her cottage as quickly as I could. When I got there, the weapons and shields from the rebel guards were cast aside. The door was wide open, hanging off its hinges."

She can still feel the rush of cold that she felt when walking through the doorway, and she shivers. His hand comes to rest on her arm and the usual flood of warmth she feels from being near him almost chases away the chill of the memory.

"They said they would protect her but when it came down to it, they abandoned their posts. They abandoned her, leaving her defenseless and unaware in her own home. I never should have trusted them to begin with. I should have protected her myself." She hesitates, she's never spoken this aloud to anyone.

"When I found my mother, murdered in our home. I..." She pauses again, swallows, squeezes her eyes shut. Without opening her eyes, she continues, "I lost control...of myself...my magic. I collapsed and the emotion just bled through me. I couldn't think about anything else. I couldn't feel. My magic exploded around me. The town. The town burst into flames. I couldn't stop what happened."

She takes a shaky breath, letting the rage and pain leave with her long exhale.

"So, no. I never planned to betray them, as you say. I did, however, make sure the person in charge had the power to protect Aerash from what would be coming. I made the only choice that made sense. I took the crown."

She finishes her story, opening her eyes to watch his thumb rubbing circles into her arm. The press of his thumb and finger on her chin guide her gaze up to his. He's so close to her that he blocks out the forest behind him. She can only see him, the green eyes, the blond hair. Is it possible that she sees forgiveness in his eyes? No, but maybe...understanding. Her heart stutters in her chest and her breath catches, the sobs of her pain from recounting the uncontrollable tragedy that was her fault trying to escape.

But she doesn't want to cry, and there's one person that can comfort her. Gentle touches and soft caresses and green eyes that know how to chase the pain away and make her strong again. The feelings aren't just memories of how she used to feel with Ren, it's somehow more. Probably too much for how little she really knows about him.

She pushes that thought away and leans forward, brushing her lips against his. He inhales sharply and she looks up to his surprised eyes. She waits where she is, their breathing mingling in the space between. After a moment that feels like another three hundred years, he squeezes her arm and she takes that as a confirmation. She closes the small distance between them, firmly pressing their lips together.

Sparks zip through her body from her lips straight down to the tips of her toes. They break apart to gasp for air and plunge back into each other, tongues clashing. His hand grazes down her arm and to her waist, pulling her in closer. She moans, this is the energy that she's been looking for. Her magic whirls around and within her, like an ocean of electricity. It's exhilarating.

He pulls away, she almost leans forward to follow him but she sees the look in his eyes. He's conflicted. The ocean that was roiling through her comes to a stop, her sparks halting in their tracks.

"That was..." Vaaren starts.

"A mistake," she finishes.

He nods slowly, looking like he believes her about as much as she believes herself.

"Your eyes, your hair, everything about you is the spitting image of Ren. Even the way you make me feel reminds me so much of him, but you're not him." A pang of sadness runs through her, but she's not sure if it's because she misses Ren or that Vaaren is conflicted about her.

"I'm not trying to be him," he says sharply, his body tensing.

She cocks her head. She didn't expect Vaaren to react like that. If only she had a portrait of Ren, so she could show Vaaren how uncanny the resemblance is. They could wonder over the oddity of Vaaren being delivered to her so close to the three hundredth anniversary of Ren's death.

"Who are you trying to be, then?" she asks him. Of course he isn't trying to be Ren, he doesn't even know who Ren is. Other than what she's told him.

At this, he looks away from her. A conflicted expression takes over his features and the tension remains throughout his posture.

"I don't know right now," he says quietly.

She nods, letting the last bit of the moment between them slip away. She doesn't want him to know how much he affects her.

"Well, when you figure it out, let me know if you'd like to be on my side." She pauses, then adds with a wink, "or underneath me."

Chapter 21

"You look well," Elayce says to Vaaren who is already seated at the table when she walks in. They arrived at the castle at dusk the night before, going straight to Merda. The healer had bustled around both of them. Healing first Elayce and then Vaaren with ease, complaining about the rough wrap job Elayce had done on her own.

"It's amazing what a healer and a real bed can do for a person," he retorts.

"Should've thought about that before joining the rebellion, then." Elayce plops down in the chair next to Vaaren, sliding a book over to him.

"Even so, the amenities I have access to here are better than I had at home."

"You're welcome."

Vaaren's expression is pained.

"What?" Elayce asks.

"I can't help but feel like a traitor to the rebellion." His head hangs, while his hands clench in his lap.

"The only person that you should look out for in this world is yourself, Vaaren. Nobody else is looking out for you, and if you think they are it's because they want something from you."

"Says the queen of looking out for herself." As soon as the words are out he shrinks back in his chair.

"I've killed people for less, you know," Elayce comments. She is slightly worried that he might retreat into himself after their kiss in the woods, but he seems quite the opposite. Emboldened, in fact.

"But you need me to help with these runes," Vaaren says, a question but not quite.

"How fortunate for you." Elayce picks at a chip in the wood of the table. "You're not wrong anyway, I've learned to look out for myself. Merely passing that wisdom on to you."

"I'm still waiting for the part in your story where you try to convince me that you aren't the villain."

"I never said I wasn't the villain, I merely pointed out that I was forced to be this way." she clarifies.

Vaaren takes a minute to let that sink in.

"Will you tell me more today?" he wonders.

"Are you ready to hear more?" Elayce asks, surprised.

"You seem to enjoy talking about yourself," he says in an almost teasing way. "Besides, the less talking I do, the less of a chance I have to get myself in trouble."

"Well, you aren't wrong, I do love talking about myself." She laughs a little, her eyes going soft. "Mostly, I just enjoy having someone to talk to."

It's Vaaren's turn to be surprised, his eyebrows shooting up. "You are the queen, you must have plenty of people who you can talk to."

"Yes, well of course I do," Elayce says, clearing her throat and shifting her body from him to face the book on the table. "If you're not dead asleep after studying the rest of this book then I might tell you more." She reaches over and lifts the open book closest to her before letting it slam back down on the tabletop. The sound echoes through the room. Vaaren's eyes are still on Elayce's face.

"You're not going to be able to study the runes with your eyes on me. Get to work before I punish you for wasting time," she says gruffly.

At that, Vaaren turns towards the book.

Elayce waits quietly. He takes occasional notes in a small notebook that Elayce had brought to him. She watches him write, looking to see if any of the loops and scratches that he produces are what she needs. Occasionally, her eyes wander to the massive bookshelves that line this library. The dark wood of the shelves are regularly dusted as well as the darkly bound books that fill them.

"This would be far less taxing if I could spend my energy looking for something that I know would help you instead of studying every page," Vaaren sighs, leaning back in his chair and rubbing one of his hands on the back of his neck.

"Why should I trust you with that information?" Elayce asks.

"Why should you trust me with anything you tell me?" he counters.

"It's different." Elayce pauses to think about how to explain it. "Telling you my personal history won't give you anything that can be used against me. It's nothing I wouldn't tell someone if they cared enough to ask."

"You don't think the rebellion would use any information they can get about you?"

"You never negotiated to leave this castle, Vaaren, how do you plan on sharing any of it with your little group of scoundrels?"

His hand moves from the back of his neck to rub the beard scruff that's grown in on his face. "Do you plan to keep me here forever?"

"I plan to keep you until you're of no use to me anymore," Elayce answers, fingering the sleeve of her black velvet dress.

"And then? Will I be free to go?"

She looks into his eyes then, her breath catching as it always does when she lets herself really look at him. Her eyes bounce down to his throat, catching the movement of his Adam's apple as he swallows. Maybe he thinks about their kiss as often as she does.

"Perhaps, when I reach the end of my story, you will understand why I have done the things that I have done. And then you will be free to stay." If he decides to stay here with her...no she won't let herself think about that.

"I could never understand a monster," he says back to her, but his words lack their usual bite.

"When you have lived as long as I have, you realize that we all have a bit of monster in us. With your Rune Magic growing and being used, you'll see that your aging will slow. You'll never sprout a gray hair or feel that ache in your bones that the older folks talk about. You'll likely live for hundreds of years if you continue to foster your magic. As long as you aren't killed, of course. Magic users aren't immortal." As she says this, she realizes that he probably doesn't know that.

A mix of emotions pass across his face before he drops his gaze down to the table so she is unable to see. "I...I didn't know that would happen." He sounds breathless.

"How does it feel to know that you're more like the queen you claim to hate than the people that you blindly follow into battle?" Elayce says, laughing.

CHAPTER 21

"I..." Vaaren starts, but he pauses. His mouth hangs open before shaking his head as if to clear the thoughts from it. "I think I can finish the rest of this book today if I focus," he finishes instead.

"Please," Elayce says, gesturing to the book.

She can't help but wonder what it was he was going to say. She would push him to tell her, but she ends up saying way more to him about herself than she means to. It's been so long since she's really had someone to talk to about things other than the running of Aerash. He has a way of making her talk, beyond the false sense of security her brain gives her when she sees him. Her mind tricks her into feeling as safe as she used to feel when she was with Ren and causes her to drop her guard that's usually up when she's around anyone else.

Maybe it doesn't matter though. Now that he's learning more about his magic, he might realize that she's the one in the right. That she's just doing what needs to be done and getting a little revenge in the meantime. She might convince him to stand by her while she takes on the Darkness. Having a Runer on her side would definitely give her an edge. He agreed to help her find what she is looking for, but if he is fully on her side, they can accomplish so much more. She will have no doubts about going into battle against the Darkness if she has someone she can count on. Well-practiced Runers can draw runes in the air and use them in battle—or so she's been told, she's never actually seen it before. There isn't much time to get Vaaren trained, but perhaps under the pressure of the battle he can make it work.

Or she might lose him. No, she can't think about that. Nothing will happen to Ren. Vaaren. Nothing will happen to Vaaren. She's much stronger this time, more prepared and trained. All she needs is to find the right rune that will help her really defeat the Darkness this time instead of just weakening him until he retreats. There will be no return for the Darkness after this battle. The Goddess had told her that she would be the one to defeat it, but in reality she hadn't said when. She hadn't failed before, she had delayed. Casting the Darkness away while she learned and grew into her powers. Her light, the antithesis of the Darkness and the only power that would be able to devour it in the end.

Vaaren closes the tome with a loud thump. Outside, the sun has begun to set and an orange glow comes in through the windows.

"Done already?" she asks.

"Unless you think runes that can mend clothing, create a lock, or make your rings sparkle brighter can help you, I don't think anything in this book is what you're looking for," he says through a yawn.

"Perhaps we could put a pin in some of those for later," she says, tapping her long nail to her chin.

"Are you ready to share more of the story?" Vaaren asks.

"Whatever I must do to stop you from begging me," she sighs.

"I wasn't—"

Elayce launches into her story.

Chapter 22

"I don't want to do this. I told you what the Goddess said. She said that all of Aerash would be swallowed by a never ending night. How could I possibly stop what's coming, Ren? How could I possibly ensure that you and I make it out of this alive? I have no way to control this power she's given me. Please, Ren, don't make me do this." I had begged him. Begged him to leave with me while it was still night. I wanted to steal away into the dark and leave Aerash, get as far away as possible. What little faith I had in myself had dissipated quickly once I started training.

We had told the rebels that the Goddess had granted me my powers, my light, in order to overthrow the king. That I was meant to end the suffering of the kingdom and bring a time of peace across Aerash. That wasn't wrong, it just wasn't the whole truth. The only person I had told the whole truth to was Ren. I trusted him to have our best interests at heart. I still believe in him. I still believe that what he wanted from me and from the rebellion was because he truly believed that we could do it, together.

We trained for weeks. Not nearly as long as we should have. Neither Ren, nor I were soldiers. The rebellion didn't have any Magic Wielders that I could train with, though they did have several books they had kept safe in the instance that they recruited anybody who could use them. They weren't the same as the rune books that you have now, no. They didn't rearrange and tell me how to use or not use my powers. Clearly, Magic Wielders wanted to keep the knowledge to themselves.

The books themselves did next to nothing for me. They explained that I needed to dig deep within and feel the magic from the inside. That I would find a well of power within myself and I needed to pull the magic from it. I needed to control it and demand what I wanted from it. I would find later that this is a much more difficult way to use magic, but not until it was too late.

Staying with the rebels was rough. They didn't have a lot of supplies. Ren and I had never lived quite as much on the wild side as the rebels did. We were constantly on alert, afraid of being discovered and raided by the king's army. We trained mostly underground and in caverns. I watched Ren grow in his skills as a warrior, but I could see that that wasn't what he was. An adventurer, sure, but a scholar too. The night before we were supposed to move on the castle, I approached Ren. I begged him to leave with me.

"Ren, this isn't us. This isn't you!" Tears streamed down my face, I remember the cool tracks they left behind on my warm skin. "I've watched you in training Ren, you aren't ready. I'm not ready!"

"Laycie, this is what we have to do. Even the Goddess said that you could," he'd replied, cupping my face in his hands while his thumbs brushed across my soaked cheeks.

"Something is wrong, Ren. This isn't going to go the way that they've hoped." I could feel something in my gut. It almost felt like my powers were resisting me. I still didn't

CHAPTER 22

have great control, but I felt a regression. Like my magic was trying to tell me that now was not the right time.

"I know you're scared, Laycie. But you can do this. Everything is going to be alright." He kissed my forehead. "I'm not saying it will be easy, but we can do this. Together. You, me, and the entire rebellion will be behind us."

After that, he told me that we needed to rest for the upcoming battle. He'd never pushed back so much before. Normally, he'd really listen to what I was saying and let us make decisions together. It was the first time that he didn't trust me. I felt uneasy and had been unable to sleep much. The whirling emotions caused the time to pass quickly and before I knew it, we were marching on the castle.

Chapter 23

"Are you going to tell me what the Goddess really said to you?" Vaaren asks once Elayce finishes the next part of the story.

"When the time is right, I might," Elayce says.

"What are you waiting for?"

"For the right person, I guess."

Just then, Tydas enters the library, marching towards the queen. He looks like a one man army about to deliver the final blow.

"Your Majesty, we've just received a messenger. Theis, the King of Selna, will be arriving tomorrow." His quick breaths indicate that this isn't the first place he looked for her.

"Tomorrow? Well isn't he eager. I thought you said the invitations were accepted with arrivals beginning three days from now." The smile is long gone from Elayce's face. She's barely just gotten back.

"I imagine he seeks to spend some time here before the other kings and queens arrive from the neighboring kingdoms. Likely to continue your courtship without the distraction of other royalty," Tydas muses.

"Interrupting my regular schedule will hardly do him any good." A thought occurs to Elayce. "Vaaren, perhaps you could accompany me for the next few days."

CHAPTER 23

"The prisoner?" Tydas sputters. "That is highly inappropriate, Your Majesty!" His face grows red in the dim light.

"As a buffer, obviously. I have other means of deterring King Theis on his quest for my hand in marriage, but I hardly think a dead King of Selna is what we need right now."

"A dead king—Queen Elayce, really! We discussed the good this union could do for the kingdom—"

"Tydas." Elayce's voice goes cold and calm. Her sparks began to circle around her. He stops sputtering and bows his head. "I thought I made myself clear when I said I do not need or want this union. The best outcome for King Theis is that he walks away with a 'no' and his life."

"As you wish, Your Majesty." Tydas's head remains bowed with his eyes locked on the ground.

"Have new clothes made and brought up for Vaaren, he will need to look presentable for our guests. I imagine he could accompany me to most of the festivities," Elayce says, standing and giving Tydas a dismissing gesture. "And Tydas? Do not forget your place again."

Vaaren, who has remained in a shocked silence until now finally speaks up. "You want me to attend the celebrations with you?"

She watches to make sure Tydas has left the room before answering him. "It's good to keep Tydas on his toes."

"So you don't want me there, you just want to rile up your advisor?" Vaaren asks, more confused than before.

"All in good time, Vaaren." She gestures for him to follow her. Neither of them say anything while they stroll back to their rooms, trailed by a few guards. Vaaren looks at everything around him, silently taking in the decor and grandeur of the castle. When they reach Vaaren's door, he turns around as if to say something but instead continues into his room without saying anything at all. Once his door is shut, one of the guards trailing them stations himself outside the door, and Elayce and the rest of the entourage continue the few steps down the hall to her rooms.

~

The next day, Elayce, dressed in a light gray pouf of a gown with black swirls adorning the train that drags when she walks, paces back and forth across the dais in front of her throne. The silver crown atop her head is adorned with shining yellow gems that match the sparks trailing behind her.

"You seem agitated, Your Majesty," Tydas observes.

"Why isn't he here already?"

"Perhaps they couldn't pull together the proper clothes in time for him to be presentable on such short notice," he answers.

"If they cannot *find* the proper clothes, then *perhaps*," she says mockingly, "I can provide a dead body for them to pry some off of." She folds her arms across her chest, interrupting her pacing to glare at Tydas. He grimaces.

"King Theis will be here any minute, my queen, please sit and at least try to look welcoming. We are the ones that invited them here, after all." He stands at the foot of the dais, trying to maintain his distance.

She opens her mouth to retort when the door to the right of her throne bursts open and Vaaren comes out, being rushed along by a group of servants still tidying him up. He's wearing a nobleman's outfit in gold with gray accents, the perfect picture of an Aerash lord. His hair is trimmed and swept back from his face and his beard is cleaned up as well.

"Finally!" Tydas exclaims. "Here, here." He ushers Vaaren

to a seat down on the throne room floor.

Elayce begins to object, but her words are cut off by the opening of the throne room doors. A small entourage of guards followed by the King of Selna and his advisors sweep into the room. The crowd splits as they reach the stairs leading up to her throne, allowing King Theis to come forward to bow to her.

Straightening, he reaches out his hand to the queen. "Queen Elayce!" he exclaims in a booming voice. "Our time apart has been far too long. Allow me the pleasure of feeling the warmth of your hand once again."

She smiles coyly, the emotion not reaching her eyes, and sits on her throne, her dress pillowing out around her. "Theis," she drawls, "you're early." A statement that doesn't invite an answer, she holds her hand out to him.

Scrambling up the steps, he says, "I couldn't wait to visit the beautiful Kingdom of Aerash and to see you again. I was delighted to receive your invitation to the castle." He bows his head and kisses the back of her hand. It takes all her strength not to look over at Vaaren.

"Hmm, and how did you find the journey here?"

"The countryside is beautiful, traveling through Flora made me feel quite at home."

"I trust you didn't encounter any trouble, then?"

"No, no. Uneventful and scenic." He releases her hand and turns to gesture to his entourage. His advisors move to sit in the chairs on the side of the room with Vaaren and the guards line the walkway up to the dais. "Our advisors can chat about whatever it is the advisors do, let us catch up on more important things."

"He is not an advisor," she says to Theis, pointing to Vaaren.

"Oh?" He looks a bit confused, glancing between the table

where Vaaren is sitting with Tydas standing stuck behind his chair.

"The one standing next to him is my advisor. Vaaren needn't converse with your advisors," Elayce explains. Hardly seems necessary, but she's already said it.

"Lord Vaaren of..?" King Theis's cheery demeanor returns.

"Uh," Vaaren pauses, unsure how Elayce would want him to answer this question. His eyes flick to hers, but she only offers him a blank look. "Vaaren of Flora," he replies before he bows to King Theis.

Elayce mulls over this answer in her head, not quite a lie. "Vaaren will join us, then."

"Any friend of the queen is a friend of mine as well," King Theis says, and Elayce detects a hint of disappointment.

"I have some time today if you'd like to see my newly rebuilt greenhouse?" Elayce suggests to Theis.

"That would be wonderful, you could show me where you've planted the small pieces of Selna that you brought home with you."

"There was a fire shortly after I returned, but fortunately the gardeners hadn't replanted the Selnan specimen yet for me so they were saved."

Theis offers his arm out to Elayce as they walk towards the greenhouse and she loops her arm through his. "If you would've arrived when you were supposed to, the rest of the plants and flowers would already be planted, but since you're early..." she trails off.

"Don't you worry, Queen Elayce, you can describe your vision to me instead. We can watch it come to life over the next few days together." He pats her hand that's looped around his arm.

CHAPTER 23

They stroll all the way to the greenhouse, Vaaren a few steps behind. A crease of concentration splits his forehead.

"Have you given more thought to my marriage proposal?" King Theis asks.

"Marriage proposal?" Vaaren blurts out, his eyes bulging.

"You've only just arrived, Theis, is this the way you want to start the trip?" Elayce says, ignoring Vaaren's outburst.

"I have told you many times, my queen, that when it comes to you I don't wish to wait."

"You shall have your answer before you leave, Theis, but it wouldn't be wise to push me," Elayce replies sweetly.

Vaaren scoffs and Elayce turns to glare at him. "Something you'd like to say? *Lord* Vaaren?"

"No, nothing at all. I just wasn't aware that there was a proposal. I mean, uh, a potential union between the two kingdoms."

"I didn't think it important information to share with someone of your station," she snaps back.

"Don't let him rile you up; I'm sure he's just disappointed that his beautiful queen is no longer available," King Theis says, guiding Elayce towards the greenhouse in the distance while she stares behind her at Vaaren.

"Hardly," Vaaren murmurs, rolling his eyes.

Elayce narrows her eyes and her sparks shoot across the ground and up behind Vaaren, undetected by either of the men. Suddenly, Vaaren yelps and jumps, grabbing his ass. Elayce gives him a saccharine smile before turning back around just as they arrive at the greenhouse.

The new greenhouse is larger than the original, rows and rows of plant beds and newly added spaces for small trees to grow inside as well. Most of the beds are empty, ready to be cultivated and planted over the next few days before the guests arrive. Elayce breathes in deeply, allowing the smell of fresh dirt to flow through her. She mourns the loss of the original structure where she spent so much of her early days as queen, but she loves all the new space that this new greenhouse gives her. She can host even more plants now, and the new workshop space is larger than the old one. She can continue to harvest and mix flowers, buds, and small berries and she can also do some experimenting now. She might attempt some grafting if she ever finds the time.

A flash of her at a workbench, Ren sitting on the bench next to her plants pops into her mind. No, that's a rune tome, it's Vaaren sitting beside her. She shakes her head to clear the thought away.

She doesn't hide the way she truly feels about her gardening and her greenhouse as she walks through with King Theis. Her face lights up in ways she doesn't usually show as she gestures to the new spaces, commenting on which plants will go where and why. She feels lighter since her trip, like the future might not be so dim. She doesn't need prompting to unload all the details and King Theis barely gets a word in.

"Your extensive knowledge on plants is quite impressive, Queen Elayce," King Theis says. "I'm a little embarrassed that I couldn't answer your questions about my own gardens." He rubs his fingers along his wrist self-consciously.

"My Floran heritage has stayed with me through the years," Elayce sighs, brushing her fingers along the sides of a planter.

"For someone who loves torture and death so much, you seem to really enjoy life and growth as well," Vaaren comments from behind King Theis, causing him to startle.

"It's all about balance, dear Vaaren," she responds with a

CHAPTER 23

smile.

"Speaking of your other love, will there be...entertainment of the sort as a part of the festivities?" King Theis asks.

"Surely you'd like to be surprised, King Theis, as the rest of the attendees," she says, turning her attention back to the king.

"I wouldn't be surprised if someone in this room earned himself a seat at that table," King Theis chuckles. "He certainly has a mouth on him."

"I'm right—" Vaaren starts, taking a step forward. Elayce's sparks shoot upward from where they were circling lazily around her skirts, on high alert now, stopping Vaaren in his tracks. He knows what the sparks can do, but he doesn't know that it's not him the sparks are threatening, but Theis.

"I so love a good sparring partner, keeps things fresh. It's why I keep him around," she says, giving Vaaren a warning look. If her fierce expression doesn't tell him off, the sizzling sparks are a good back up. He takes a step back and fixes his gaze on the floor, his lips pressed together in a thin line. The last thing she needs is a fight between the men where she has to reveal the lengths she would go to protect Vaaren.

"Sometimes the feisty ones need a little reminding," King Theis comments, the dark look in his eyes not matching the joviality of his face. When Elayce doesn't laugh along with him he says, "Come now, I'm only suggesting a bit of fun that I know you love."

"You don't know me, King Theis."

"Certainly I know you well enough to know you wouldn't tolerate his comments from anyone." He looks back and forth between the queen and Vaaren. Neither says anything, and the silence stretches into something awkward. "Well," he clears his throat, "I think I should head to my rooms and make sure things are settled after the journey here. I'll see you for dinner?"

"I have things that need to be attended to before the arrival of the other kingdoms, but if I have the time I may join you," Elayce answers.

His face darkens and he glances over at Vaaren. She thinks he might say something else, but he bows his head, kissing the back of her hand. He exits the greenhouse, leaving Elayce and Vaaren alone.

"You can't just say whatever you want, whenever you want," Elayce hisses.

"You're the one who brought me along for some reason! I don't even understand what I'm doing here." He throws his hands up in the air.

"Well that makes two of us," Elayce snarls back.

"Just because you feel like you can spill your guts to me, doesn't mean I can." Regret crosses his face before he's even finished speaking.

"Trust me when I say that if I wanted you to spill your guts," she pauses, emphasizing her words with slow menacing steps towards him, "they would be all over the floor before you could stop it." She is so close to him by the time she is done speaking that it could be seen as improper. His eyes flick down momentarily to her lips and then back up to her gray eyes. The warmth she feels when she's close to him pools low in her belly. The memory of their kiss springs forward, wrapping itself around her brain.

With intense effort, she takes a step away from him and then another. Once she's out of such close proximity to him, her head clears and she whirls around to stomp out of the

CHAPTER 23

greenhouse, leaving him with just the guards.

Chapter 24

"You cannot hole yourself up in here when you have a guest, Your Majesty," Tydas pleads with Elayce. She's been in her study for the past few days, claiming that paperwork has kept her tied up.

"You know I have things to do, Tydas, you are my advisor."

Things that could have waited. She is absolutely hiding. These ridiculous requests from the council members could have gone unanswered. She suspects that they send her every request that pops into their head, just hoping that one sticks. Elayce doesn't make it easy for them to be very strategic, though she doesn't ignore anything with actual substance behind it. Usually.

"Yes, I *am* your advisor, so I do know what you have to do. I know that it can wait until after the celebration and the guests have all left."

"Tell that to Council Member Gresha, who thinks that Nicen should be compensated more for the alcohol they're providing for the celebration. Or to Silia's council member..."

"Perry."

"Council Member Perry who thinks that because the Kingdom of Don Kemt will be tromping through their forests to travel to the castle grounds in Vleck, that we should pay for the damages." Just wait until he sees the damage from the fire she started.

"You can remind them all at the next council meeting that the festivities are to celebrate the great service you have done for Aerash and they can absorb the costs on their own," Tydas suggests.

"Or I can take care of it now," she retorts.

"Rarely are you so dedicated to your work," he says.

"On the contrary, I am so devoted to Aerash that I have chosen to serve longer than the lifetimes of three ordinary men."

"I must insist that once the rest of our guests arrive tomorrow you set this aside and commit to your duty as host for the kingdoms." Tydas lightly bangs his hand on the table to hammer his point home.

"Fine," she relents, still focused on the papers in front of her.

Tydas's eyebrows rise in surprise. "Oh," he says. "Great."

"Is there anything else you'd like to test my patience with today, or could I have a few more hours of peace before the visitors arrive?"

"I will make sure that Darla has you ready on time tomorrow for their arrival," he says and leaves her study.

Phin reaches out and shuts the door behind Tydas. "No one else will be coming in, Your Majesty."

"Where was that fifteen minutes ago?" she asks. He gives her a sheepish shrug.

After that moment in the greenhouse with Vaaren she knew she needed space. She had spent time in the training room sparring with Harkn, but she had turned him down when he suggested going back to her rooms together. Now, she sits in her study no less irritated about what had happened between her and Vaaren. He isn't Ren and he isn't here to help her of his own accord. She made a deal with him and that's all it is. Why does she have to keep reminding herself of that?

Regardless of the thoughts swirling in her head, she has to keep preparing for what is coming. Not the celebration—although, that took some preparation on her part to be ready to be around so many people—but the coming battle. She has to stop being so childish and work with him to keep going through the rune tomes. Sighing to herself, she gets up and heads towards her rooms, trailed by Phin.

When they arrive, she says, "Don't let anyone in. If they try, tell them I'm bathing and then heading to bed and I'm not to be disturbed." She waits for Phin to nod then shuts the door.

In her rooms, she stands in front of an old heavy tapestry that covers a back wall. It depicts the Goddess of Light, the Goddess that everyone else believes gave her her powers. A gift from an old king long dead, she had it hung here to replace the old tapestry that had been a family tree of the previous royal family. The Goddess's eyes seem to stare down at her, screaming, "Thief!" But she isn't the real thief, that title was for the Goddess who had really given her the Goddess of Light's power. She was just the unfortunate receiver of the stolen gift.

She reaches behind the tapestry and pulls a thick cord that causes the thick fabric to fold upwards, revealing a door behind it. She pulls a key out of her pocket, one she grabbed from a drawer by her bed, and fits it into the keyhole. The lock clicks and sighs, the door swinging open to a dark tunnel hidden behind it. She lets her sparks flare around her and steps in, closing and locking the door behind her.

The sparks light the would-be pitch black tunnel, but she

CHAPTER 24

trails her fingers along the dusty wall to keep herself steady anyway. After a short walk, she reaches a fork and takes the left tunnel that leads to another door. She knocks first, though nobody will answer, and then uses the same key to open the door. Another thick tapestry hangs in front of the now open door, and though she's looking at the back of it she knows it's an identical tapestry of the Goddess of Light that she commissioned to hang in front of this door. Pushing it aside, she reveals herself to the man sitting at a table with a fork poised halfway to his wide open mouth.

"Vaaren," she says by way of greeting.

"Elayce?!" he sputters, dropping the fork and standing from his chair so suddenly that it topples over behind him, sending a stack of books careening off another small table.

"Please, address me by my first name," she mutters, closing the door behind her and letting the tapestry fall to cover it again.

"Well I wasn't expecting a human to appear from behind a tapestry in my room!" he exclaims, attempting to pick up the chair and the books that fell and instead knocking over his plate of food, muttering expletives under his breath.

"I have been downgraded from Queen to just Elayce, but now at least I am human instead of a demon," she points out.

He makes a grunting sound, finally righting the chair and setting the books on the table. He picks up the plate and fork, but the food is a loss.

"What are you doing here? How are you here?" he asks.

"I came to see if you had anything to share regarding your research. There's a tunnel behind this tapestry that leads to my rooms, locked of course," she explains.

"You couldn't wait until morning or have me brought to our

regular meeting place to ask about the research?"

"I'm hiding from my advisor." She shrugs and moves across the small space to sit at the small round table he was eating at.

"You're hiding from him? Couldn't you just get rid of him?"

"Vaaren, despite what you may think, I do understand when an inconvenient time for someone to die is. Now is not really a convenient time to be looking for a new advisor."

"I didn't mean kill him, I only meant tell him to leave you alone!"

"Oh," she says, and then bursts out laughing. She doubles over in her seat, clutching her stomach while she laughs. With all the time they've been spending together, she keeps forgetting that he's not like her.

"What is so funny?" Vaaren asks, perplexed.

"I just, I don't know why I thought that's what you meant," she says between laughs. "I have too much on my mind." She finally begins to calm down, taking a few deep breaths to curb the laughter. Vaaren's perplexed expression almost sends her into another fit of laughter, so she looks away from him, instead scanning the small but well decorated room that he's staying in.

"I still don't know what you're looking for, but I found some runes that I thought might be of interest to you," he says.

Her attention snaps back to him. "Do tell."

"There's a whole section on light and expanding or contorting light properties." He turns in his chair to grab one of the books from behind him, flipping through pages to find what he was looking for.

"Here," he says, pointing to one of the pages. "This one would help expand the area that the light covers, essentially making it bigger. Or this one," he says, flipping another page.

CHAPTER 24

"This one can trap light in a container, essentially making it usable beyond the source of the light."

She considers what he said, thinking about how these runes could help her.

"Do you think that they will also expand the magic within my sparks? Not just the light that they give?" she asks.

"I'm not sure," he answers sheepishly. "The books don't say anything about light as magic."

"We could do some testing in the training room," Elayce says, a plan forming in her head.

"I'm not sure how much time we'll have for training over the next week if you are already hiding from your advisor and you only have one guest at the castle," he points out.

She slumps in her chair.

"Damn it, I knew sending out those invitations was a mistake as soon as I said it."

"It was your idea to invite them? Doesn't seem like you," he says, pushing the book aside to lean towards her at the table.

"Sometimes I surprise even myself." She sighs. "I meant to throw off my council, but it seems to be getting to me more than them."

Vaaren laughs. "Now that is funny."

She shoots him an exasperated look. "Nobody taught me how to do this, you know. I learned everything on my own. How to use my magic, how to be a queen, how to handle people who thought they could control me. They're all the same, they all want something from me. They think they know what's best for me and for the kingdom and it's always more land, more gold, more anything. I've taken care of things the best way I know how."

He opens his mouth to respond, but she waves her hand to

stop him.

"Not now, Vaaren. I'm tired of people telling me what to do today. Tell me something about yourself. I don't want to think about my world right now."

He winces. "I...I can't."

Her face falls and she realizes that she had actually been hopeful that he would open up to her the way she had to him.

"No, Elayce, I can't. Look." He begins to roll up his sleeve.

"It's Queen Elayce, actually," she says, but there's no conviction behind it. "I expect you to behave yourself over the next few days while we visit with the other royals. Unless you'd rather stay locked up in this room for the next week, just let the guards know if that's what you decide." She's done with disappointment for the day, and she has to get out of here before he sees how much his refusal affects her. She leaves through the door behind the tapestry, leaving him with only the soft click of the lock.

Back in her room, she tosses and turns in her bed, only half asleep. Just as she's about to cross the threshold into unconsciousness, she feels a coldness settle over her. Her eyes snap open and she sees a shadow looming above her. Leaping out of the bed, her sparks come alive and whirl around her. She lands, crouched in a fighting stance, her nightgown hiked up her legs.

The shadow turns to face her, although there isn't really a face where one would expect. Wrinkles form where a mouth might be, as if a curtain were folding up on either side to create a smile.

Elayce. The hissing sound is all around her, not coming from any particular spot. *I hope you have not forgotten me, for I have only thought of you these last three hundred years.*

CHAPTER 24

She breaks out into a cold sweat, her heart begins beating rapidly. She keeps her eyes on the shadow.

"How are you here?" she asks the Darkness.

I'm not really here, my Laycie. Not yet.

"Don't call me that," she snaps.

We'll be together again soon, Laycie. Soon.

The shadow disappears and the cold along with it.

She collapses on the floor, shivering and gasping. If the Darkness can project all the way to the center of her kingdom, it is far stronger than she realized. She should have known better after her fight with the shadow creatures. This battle is coming much sooner than she thought.

Chapter 25

Despite all of Darla's efforts, she couldn't hide the bags underneath Queen Elayce's eyes. She opts for the formal gold crown and a gaudy gold dress, quite different from the queen's usual attire, to distract from the sickly look that's washing out her face.

"Should I have the gardeners restock your ingredients in here, Your Majesty? You could make yourself a tonic to help you sleep better tonight," Darla suggests.

Irritation flits across Elayce's face, but she's too distracted to threaten Darla for even suggesting she doesn't look her best.

"A tonic can't help me, Darla." Given the visit from the Darkness last night, she knows she won't be getting much sleep over the next few weeks anyway. She'll have to take Vaaren to the training room at night to practice; it's the only way to both prepare for what's coming and be present for the celebratory events this week.

"There are a lot of visiting staff with the royals, perhaps I could talk with them and see if they have any remedies to help," Darla says absently, fixing the last pieces of Elayce's hair.

"Excellent idea!" Elayce says, an idea forming. "While you're scouring for tonics and tinctures, I'll need you to keep an ear out for gossip that might be useful to us."

"You want me to spy for you?" Darla asks, uncertainty in her voice.

"How's your sister doing?" Elayce counters, spinning around on her stool to face Darla directly.

Darla winces.

"There's something coming, Darla. Something bad. A few tinctures and a room in the castle have saved her until now, but she will need more than that to protect her from what's to come."

"What is it?" Darla's voice is a whisper now, dripping in fear.

Elayce stands and pats Darla's cheek; Darla flinches with each touch.

"Don't worry your little head about it. I'll send you and your sister the protection you both will need." She isn't quite sure how to procure that yet, but for now the promise is enough. Elayce doesn't wait for an answer before leaving to greet her guests in the throne room.

Everyone is already in the throne room waiting for her. Norde's King and Queen, donning light blue regalia, are an older couple with bright white hair and deep wrinkles set into their expressions. King Guydor and his Queen, Brigit, stand stiffly in their rich, deep green clothes of Don Kemt, both wearing expressions as stuffy as their outfits look. King Theis is there as well, dressed in bright magenta with a long cape fanned out behind him. He's taken up position as close to the throne as possible without being seen as disrespectful. The last royal family, Istin's reigning family, stand together in the reds and browns of their kingdom colors. King Rand, Queen Ysen, and their two adolescent sons—Prince Rand and Prince

Grinsley. Thankfully, Tydas briefed her on everyone's names again earlier in the week.

Everyone bows as she sweeps past, her sparks shining brightly, showing off a little. Out of the corner of her eye, she spies Vaaren dressed in nobleman's clothing again. She is surprised that he's here today. She assumed that he would have chosen to stay away from all of this.

"Welcome to Castle Vleck." She gestures her arms in a wide welcome and her sparks go soaring through the room. "For many of you, this is your first time here. I am delighted to show you how we celebrate here in Aerash for the tricentennial anniversary of my ascension to the throne!"

From the shadows of the pillars, the Selnan flag thrower jumps forward. He holds several sticks in each hand with long black ribbons flowing behind him that he begins to wave and twirl. On cue, Elayce's sparks dance forward and light the cinders of several vases that are placed along the room; the fire shoots up in tall pillars and the other lighting around the room dims.

The ribbons twist and twirl in the light as he dances, throwing them in the air and juggling them effortlessly. Grinning, he makes eye contact with Queen Elayce in silent confirmation. She waves her arms dramatically, her sparks trailing the ribbons that fly through the air. Zipping and diving, they catch the ribbons on fire until it looks like the flag thrower is juggling rays of fire, as if he is producing the flames from his own hands.

The crowd gasps and claps with each new flame coming to life, their eyes flit back and forth between the flying flames and the dancing sparks circling the room. She causes them to burst, sending showers of light over the guests. She sighs to herself; the magic humming beneath her skin feels so beautiful. The release of it calms her nerves.

As the flaming ribbons get shorter and shorter and start to go out, he wiggles the last few flames in the air to signal the finale. She twists her wrist and the sparks come together to surround him in what could be a suit of armor made of near-blinding light. Turns out that he does have an affinity for fire magic, as the sparks don't burn him just like they hadn't when he had come to Elayce with the idea. The bursting lights send shimmers of more light to the ground, slowly winking out as he sinks into a bow. The crowd applauds raucously and the lights slowly come back on.

"Just a taste of the entertainment and celebration to come!" One of her high ranking staff members shouts; she thinks she recognizes them from some of the committee meetings. "Please, relax and enjoy. Let any of the staff know if you need anything." They bow and musicians at the back of the room begin playing. Conversations break out across the room between Aerash nobles and visiting ones. Elayce, still standing on the dais, is quickly approached by King Theis.

"My queen, I haven't seen much of you over the past few days. Are you well?" He scans her face and reaches for her hand. She lets him lead her down the steps.

"Fine, King Theis. I have been busy preparing to welcome everyone to Castle Vleck." They make their way over to the King and Queen of Norde, respectfully referred to as King Norde and Queen Norde per their kingdom's customs. It's meant to symbolize the sacrifice of their individual selves for their kingdom.

"Queen Elayce," King Norde says with a slight bow of his heavily-crowned head, "we were quite surprised to receive an invitation to join you here in Aerash. It's been many years since we were last here." The wrinkles along his face are set in a pleasant expression, his ice-blue eyes friendly and inviting.

"It's good to shake things up occasionally, don't you agree?" Elayce addresses Queen Norde, who just nods her head and smiles demurely up at Queen Elayce. Her long, white braids swing around her body and come to rest on her shoulder. Apparently the reports of Queen Norde taking a vow of silence are true. Elayce offers a small smile in return that ends up more like a grimace.

"We are both happy to make the trip for what is likely to be the celebration of the century. Plus, the calmer weather is much easier on our old bones," King Norde answers for his queen. Queen Norde inhales a deep breath, her shoulders reaching up to her ears before she exhales in a smile. Her petite frame leans against the king, relaxed and open.

"You're welcome down to Selna anytime you'd like to make the trip, King Norde," King Theis heartily jumps in.

"An invitation I'm sure my queen would love to take you up on," King Norde says, reaching to pat the queen's hand where it is wrapped firmly around his elbow. The subconscious gesture is filled with gentle warmth, a comfort that comes from being with someone you love and respect for so long. She could've had that with Ren, if he had lived.

"I should greet the other guests," Elayce says abruptly.

"Go, go, King Theis can tell us more about a visit to Selna." King Norde waves her off, trapping King Theis. Despite her silence, Queen Norde's expressions are quite open and the excitement and curiosity is clearly written all over her face.

Elayce turns and bumps into Vaaren.

"Vaaren," she gasps, forgetting to use his fake title. "I didn't realize you were right behind me."

"Sorry," he apologizes, releasing her elbow that he'd clutched to steady her.

"You should be more careful, I could've set you aflame for running into me like that," Elayce scolds.

"You ran into me!"

"Semantics." She waves him off, brushing down the front of her dress. "Stop arguing or I'll have to have you locked up on principle."

His eyes narrow, but he doesn't say anything else.

"Move aside, I have to greet the reigning monarchs of Don Kemt before they demand something of me and I'm forced to remind them who I am."

"On principle," he says, moving aside.

She takes a few steps forward, but realizes he's following her.

"What are you doing?" she asks.

"I thought you wanted me here."

"After last night, I didn't think you would come. Now you're following me around like a pet."

Tydas sidles up to Elayce, murmuring under his breath to them both, "Now is not the time to discuss whatever you two were up to last night."

Vaaren's cheeks flame red and Elayce rolls her eyes. "Tydas, I do not care how others think I spend my time. Surely everybody knows I don't live a chaste lifestyle."

"I simply pointed out that now is not the time," Tydas says, gesturing towards the King and Queen of Don Kemt who are staring down their noses at Queen Elayce from across the room. He wraps an arm around the space behind Elayce, ushering her forward without touching her. Elayce lets him, but she still hears the click of Vaaren's boots behind her.

"Queen Elayce," King Guydor greets, disdain evident in his nasally voice. "A pleasure to finally be seeing Aerash."

"Yes, I'm sure it is." Elayce smiles sweetly at the royals. Tydas inhales sharply on her right.

"Queen Brigit of Don Kemt," he says by way of introduction.

"A pleasure, Your Majesty," Queen Brigit says, though her tone conveys that she thinks this is anything but a pleasure. She curtsies slightly, her gloved hand pressed to her chest. Her black hair is piled high on her head, pinned with sparkling emeralds to create a crown.

"I was expecting to see more of a guard presence on the way in," King Guydor comments. "With the rumors of your growing army, I'm not sure where you're hiding them all."

"I have nothing to hide, surely a tour of the training grounds can be arranged if you'd like to see my army."

"There will be time for business, of course, but let's enjoy the welcome for now," Tydas says, a high false chuckle falling from his lips. They all turn to him, Queen Brigit sniffs, her mouth pinches into a small circle as if she smelled something unpleasant.

"I wasn't aware the Queen of Aerash needed someone to speak for her," King Guydor says, interlacing his fingers and planting his hands across his large belly.

"Oh I assure you, King Guydor, it is not me he's protecting," Elayce replies menacingly. The sparks that are swirling around her skirts on the floor begin to rise in response to her mood. Elayce vaguely picks out the sound of armor clinking in the background, likely her guards responding to the situation. She feels a light touch on her elbow again and jerks her arm away. She turns to see Vaaren's hands held up like he meant no offense.

CHAPTER 25

"Your Majesty, I think there might be space in the day tomorrow for a Vleck Academy tour," Vaaren says in a quiet voice.

"Who is this?" King Guydor demands gruffly.

"Lord Vaaren, sir." Vaaren gives a slight bow, glancing between Elayce and the king. He notices the seething look on Tydas's face and bows even lower to the King and Queen of Don Kemt. Elayce shifts her gaze to Tydas for confirmation.

"Yes, there should be some time in the schedule to fit that in tomorrow if you'd like our guests to experience the training facility," Tydas answers.

Elayce takes a deep breath, watching the top of Vaaren's head as he stands in a low bow. "Alert Captain Nolan that they will have guests at the academy tomorrow, Tydas."

"Yes, my queen," Tydas bows his head and scurries away.

"I'm sure that should be satisfactory, King Guydor. If you'll excuse me, we have other guests that need to be welcomed," Elayce says, hauling Vaaren up from his bow by his arm.

"What are you doing?" She leans in close to hiss in his ear while they walk away.

"I didn't think you should start the week by executing the King of Don Kemt. Plus I was given the schedule by your staff when I was given a crash course on what to expect this week." He brushes down the front of his clothes, attempting to remove the wrinkles from his long bow.

"Your lesson on etiquette could use some work," she whispers.

"I've had only a few days to learn royal etiquette, what's your excuse?" he shoots back.

"My excuse is that I've already spent centuries dealing with idiots like them."

He rolls his eyes, but doesn't answer because the royal family of Istin is approaching. The family is polite and quiet to Queen Elayce, and they all make conversation for a few minutes before the king and queen make an excuse to get away from Elayce. They must have prepared the princes because they didn't balk at Elayce's swirling magic, but they couldn't hide the nervous sweat dripping down their temples or the slight tremor in their voices.

Relieved to be done with the obligatory chatter for the day, she glides up to her throne and plops down with a sigh. Vaaren stands awkwardly at the bottom of the steps, unsure what to do with himself. He clasps his hands in front of himself, then switches so they're behind him instead and rocks back and forth on his feet. One of the court ladies, dressed in Norde blue, approaches him. She curtsies and introduces herself, holding out her hand waiting for Vaaren to reciprocate the proper greeting. Eventually he takes the cue and clasps her hand, bringing his lips to the back of her hand briefly.

"Ah, Lord Vaaren, madame," he mumbles out.

Elayce tries to ignore them, watching the crowd instead, but the tittering sound of the Lady's laugh grates on her nerves. What are they talking about? Why won't she go away? What if she's some sort of spy for the rebellion and they're making contact with Vaaren? She snaps up from the chair, her skirts billowing around her. She flies down the steps and grabs him by the arm, forcing him to follow her.

"What—" he tries to say.

"Be quiet," she snaps at him, dragging him out a side door and into a hallway. As soon as they're in a shadowed corner she asks, "Was that a rebel contact?"

He rears back, shock evident on his face. "What are you

talking about?"

"Are you gathering information and passing it on through a rebel network?"

"No! I don't even know how I would get a message out to them!"

"What could you possibly have to talk about with that woman?"

"You think that the only things I could have to talk about are whatever secrets you've shared with me?"

"Well?" she demands. Her agitated sparks swirl around her.

He stares at her incredulously. "You—you're jealous?"

She scoffs. "Absolutely not!" She has nothing to be jealous of. "I will not be double crossed by you."

"I'm not trying to double cross you, Queen Elayce, I swear I don't know who she is." His voice is much calmer now, and she can see a gleam in his eyes.

"Why is your face like that?" She should throw this infuriating man back into the dungeon.

"Like what?" He rolls his lips between his teeth.

"Are you laughing at me? I am not jealous!" She jabs her finger into his chest.

"Alright, alright, you're not jealous," he says, holding up his hands in mock surrender, but she can still see the upward twitch of the corner of his mouth.

"Gods," she says in exasperation, pushing past him and heading back into the throne room.

Chapter 26

Later that evening, after the guests had all retired, Elayce creeps down the cold, dark hallway that leads to Vaaren's rooms. It's going to be a long night, but it's important that they start training. She hasn't received another visit from the Darkness, but she isn't stupid enough to wait until his army is knocking on her door before she starts preparing.

She pushes Vaaren's door open, knocking at the same time. A rustling and then a thump and a grunt sounds before the door is fully open. When she walks in, he's lying on the floor wrapped in blankets next to his bed.

"That's not how you use a bed," she comments.

"That's not how you use a door," he replies, rubbing his arm where he fell.

She smiles flirtatiously. "Well, Ren, you could teach me how to use a door and I could return the favor by teaching you how to use a bed."

He immediately turns a deep shade of red and busies himself with untangling from the covers instead of looking at her. "Vaaren," he corrects her.

She didn't mean to call him that, it just slipped out. How can he get her guard to drop so easily? His presence and his actions draw her in, but his words clearly tell her that she should be putting distance between them. Her smile falls to a slight frown instead. "Should I add your fake title, too?"

"No, just...Vaaren is fine," he says, finally standing and pushing the blankets back up on the bed. The color hasn't fully left his face yet when he turns toward her again. "What are you doing here?"

The question seems to pull her back to herself, reminding her that she came here for something. "Training," she says. "We have to start training using the runes we've discussed."

"Right now?" he asks, looking down at the pajamas he's wearing.

"Yes, now. Get dressed, then we'll head to my training room."

Once there, she watches Vaaren take it all in. His eyes run over the mirrored wall, the weapon stands, and the targets that line the room. He turns slowly in a full circle until he's facing her again.

"Where do we start?" he asks.

She grins.

They're both sweating from exertion when Vaaren finally croaks, "Enough." Doubling over, he slowly rolls onto the floor, breathing deeply to catch his breath. They'd been attempting to use the light amplifying rune for several hours already.

"We can't stop now, we haven't gotten it yet," Elayce complains through her own heavy breathing, but it's clear that Vaaren doesn't have the stamina to keep going. They spent the first half of their training session just getting Vaaren to write the rune correctly before even adding her magic to it.

"Why do we have to keep going tonight? I need to rest for tomorrow." He throws his arm over his head, shielding his eyes from the light like he might go to sleep right there on the hard floor.

"We don't have time, we need to figure this out. You saw the shadow creatures out there," she says. She throws back her shoulders and lifts her hands, calling to her magic again. She can feel the strain in her body, but she pulls from the pit within her and light appears at her will.

"Elayce," he sighs, "I can't give you anything else tonight."

Frustrated, she throws the light at a target across the room.

"We can try again tomorrow, if you insist, but I need to rest. I can feel my magic within me, and there's not enough to pull from."

Her own magic is so depleted, he must be worse off than she is right now. She's had years to practice and this is probably the first time he's used any of his own magic. Surprise ripples through her as she realizes how hard he must have worked to keep up with her tonight. She sits on the floor next to him.

"What does it feel like? Your magic?" she asks him.

He takes a moment before answering. "Like I'm reading the pages of a book, and as I read, the ink disappears from the pages. Like the ink is my power and as I create runes using the ink, I have less and less ink to use in order to keep going and more and more blank pages that need to refill." She's silent after he finishes, so he asks, "What's it like for you?"

"Nothing like that," she says quietly, a touch of breathless jealousy hangs on her words. His magic sounds so peaceful.

He shrugs and stands, reaching a hand back down to help her up. She hesitates, looking from his eyes to his hand, before reaching out slowly and grasping his hand. She braces herself to feel trembling in his fingers, but his grip is strong and sure as he pulls her to her feet. The warm, strong grasp feels just as surprising as the cold that slips through her fingers again once he lets go.

"We'll try again tomorrow," he says, gesturing to her to lead the way back to their rooms.

She wipes her hand down her training shirt, attempting to forget the feel of his skin against hers. "Tomorrow," she agrees.

~

The next day she sits at a dark table across from King Guydor and Queen Brigit. Queen Brigit's face is pinched up again. Elayce had to sic King and Queen Norde on King Theis to distract him after the tour of the training facility, so that she could have time to talk with just King Guydor. Vaaren sits uncomfortably at Elayce's side. He probably shouldn't be in this meeting, but she likes having him around and it irritates Tydas to not dismiss him, so she doesn't say anything.

"Quite an impressive facility," King Guydor comments.

"As I said." Elayce keeps her tone conversational for now. She needs to get information from him today so she needs to keep him chatty.

"Queen Elayce has had many years to build up the proper training and with a multitude of new recruits coming in, we've had the opportunity to expand and test new things," Tydas says.

"Maybe too many years," Queen Brigit mutters under her breath. But Elayce knows that Queen Brigit doesn't care how long Elayce has been running her kingdom, only that Elayce's age doesn't show while Queen Brigit is starting to develop wrinkles that she can't hide without magic of her own.

"Let's cut to the chase, King Guydor," she says, "tell me what your army is fighting."

"Fighting? Don Kemt's borders are well protected and maintained. Including the ones that border your own country." His arms are resting on the table, hands clasped tightly. He doesn't blink or fidget.

"You and I both know that is a lie," she replies. If she hadn't battled the shadow creatures on her own, she might even believe his performance.

"Do we?" he challenges, his deep brown eyes bore into hers.

"I can offer you something in exchange for the information, King Guydor," she says. She worries that she is laying her cards down too early, but having spent the morning with all the visitors at Vleck has worn her patience thin.

"You still assume I have information to offer."

She lets some of her sparks slowly drift along the table, playing with a few of them and running them through her fingers, showing off. "So, there is nothing that you might need protection from?"

She sees Queen Brigit's shrewd eyes flick to Guydor before catching herself and looking back out over Elayce's head.

"If there was, would you be offering it?" Guydor still hasn't moved an inch.

"A powerful ruler as benevolent as myself? Of course." She smiles, knowing she has him on the hook now. Vaaren shifts in his seat beside her, but fortunately, keeps his thoughts to himself.

"You certainly have the men to spare," Queen Brigit says, looking down her nose at Elayce.

"We—" Tydas tries to cut in, but Elayce silences him with a wave of her hand.

"You misunderstand me, Queen Brigit. I said you, as in the king and queen."

CHAPTER 26

King Guydor cocks his head to the side, pretending to think about the offer, when Elayce knows he's already decided.

"We could stay here in the castle until you've...handled it?" King Guydor asks.

The trap is set. Elayce smiles, gesturing to the room. "Yes, of course. Right here under the protection of myself and my royal guard."

"We'll have that in writing," King Guydor says.

"I'll have the contract written up," Tydas offers, bowing his head.

"I've already taken the liberty of having something written up for us." Elayce gestures to a servant standing in the shadows of the room.

King Guydor's eyes narrow. Tydas tugs at the collar of his shirt, clearly displeased that he had been kept in the dark.

The servant places several stacks of papers in front of Elayce and she shuffles through to find the one that she is looking for. In truth, they are all the same because she knew how this would play out in the end. She slides the contract across the table to the royals, and they lean forward to look at the contract. One of their own advisors steps forward, eyes full of concern.

"Your Majesties—" he starts, but King Guydor shushes him with a single hand gesture.

"No tricks?" King Guydor asks and she hears the desperation in his voice now. It must be worse than she thought in Don Kemt.

"I am offering you two protection, here in my castle, in exchange for the information about the army of darkness that you are fighting," she says, finally acknowledging what they all know is really happening. If possible, Queen Brigit's face pinches even tighter.

The king flips through to the last page and signs for both him and the queen. Elayce's face lights up and she reaches for the contract, signing her own name as well. When she's done she slides it along the table to Tydas, so that he can stop making huffing noises and read over it himself. Elayce waves her hand and the servants and guards all leave the room. Captain Nolan steps forward to stand behind her at the table.

"The information, Guydor," she says, smiling smugly.

His lip lifts in disgust, but he begins. "As you know we've been fighting what we now know is the army of the Darkness." His voice drops when he says "the Darkness." Does he think saying it out loud will call the Darkness to them?

"They used to only come in the darkest part of the night and could be deterred by fires, lamps, and even barricades. It's gradually become worse. The front lines report that the monsters have gotten braver and tend to sacrifice themselves to the light to take a few men down with each beast.

"We've lost ground to the army. Where they rule, thick, dark shadow spreads across the land, blocking out any sun and dampening any light source. The men we send in there, they don't come back. No surviving villagers have emerged from the towns the shadows cover." Now that he's protected, the information pours out of him right along with any confidence he might have had in winning the war against the Darkness on his own.

"The beasts. What do they look like?" Elayce asks. If what he says matches what she faced in the woods, she'll know he's telling the truth.

"I haven't seen any for myself. If we manage to kill them, they dissolve into shadows that retreat back to where they came from. Reports that we have are few, but they say the beasts move like wraiths, dodging light or heat. They have claws longer than a regular man's fingers and teeth half as long in some cases. Their eyes are soulless black pits and if you come close enough to see them, you won't be making it out alive. The screams...the screams you can hear from afar. I have heard those. It was my last trip out to the front. I had to see for myself that the reports were true."

Captain Nolan's frown is set deep in his face.

"Have you successfully killed any or staved off any attacks?" he asks, his deep voice has a lethal edge to it.

"Light or fire. We have developed weapons that hold fire or a light source. If you can stab the beast with it before being ripped to shreds, the beast turns into a harmless shadow that disappears," Guydor responds, grimacing. Queen Brigit is actually trembling.

Out of the corner of her eye, she sees Vaaren sit up straighter. She can see the wheels turning in his head, like an idea is ready to burst forth. She reaches for his leg under the table and places her hand on it, hoping that he understands she wants him to stay quiet. He stills at her touch and she sees a blush creep up through his neck to his cheeks. The king and queen don't seem to notice.

"Your information should prove useful as we prepare for battle against the Darkness," Elayce says. "Captain Nolan, if you have anything else you'd like to chat with our guests about, you know where to find them." She rises, having already gotten what she needs from them. Tydas stands quickly enough that his chair almost topples behind him, but he doesn't even notice, already clinging to her side as she heads to her study.

He peppers her with frustrated questions down the hall until he realizes she's not going to answer anything. Once the study door is closed behind them, Tydas glares at her, his arms crossed over his chest. Her ass is planted on the edge of her desk, her face smug.

"What was that?" he shrieks in an almost whisper to her. He insisted that Vaaren and the guards wait outside, closing the door in their faces before anyone could protest.

"Tydas, surely you know a political move when you see one. Isn't that your job?"

"My job? Yes! It is my job, Queen Elayce. But I can't *do* my job if you don't tell me what's happening. The Darkness is back? How long have you known?"

She shrugs. "As long as the rumors about Don Kemt have been circling. And when I was attacked in the woods by the shadow creatures."

"You said it was a group of rebels!" His eyes bulge and he gasps, clutching at his throat.

"I did what I needed to to protect the kingdom. If I had confirmed what I suspected there would have been mass chaos. Instead, I have been preparing my army for a battle and gathering intelligence when I need it."

He begins pacing the room, though it's so small he can only take about four steps before he has to turn around and pace the other direction. "And you've secured us an alliance with Don Kemt, yes, yes this can work."

"I did no such thing," she objects.

"You just offered them protection in exchange for their information," he points out.

"Again, I offered the king and queen protection. In fact, I specifically said I would not be sending my men out to Don Kemt. It's a lost battle. We need to concentrate our forces here.

Captain Nolan agrees."

His hands clench and unclench. He looks as though another surprise might cause him to explode. "My queen, I am sure you have thought this through—"

"Obviously."

"But, we could have been more aggressive with our approach. We could have easily negotiated Don Kemt to be under the protection of Aerash, assimilating the country into our own borders. Then with the marriage to King Theis, we'll also have Selna's borders!" His eyes alight as he talks himself through this scenario, still pacing and nodding to himself.

She rolls her eyes. "Tydas, I will not be defending others' borders when I have my own to watch out for."

"They will be our own. Our own new borders."

"They will be nobody's borders. There will be nothing left by the time the Darkness makes it here."

He finally stops to look up at her, surprise written across his face. "Nothing left?"

"The shadows may recede once I defeat the Darkness, but what's already been taken by the shadows will be decimated. Life and light snuffed out. Nothing left to rule."

Tydas blinks, processing this information. "Then why keep the king and queen here?"

"Their lives will still be spared," she says casually. "It's not my fault they're so short-sighted as to believe that they will have a kingdom to return to once it's over."

He frowns.

"Hard to expand the borders if there's nothing to expand to, hmm?" she says. "As I've told you, I have no interest in expanding. If only you would listen to me when I speak." She fake pouts and leans forward to slide off the desk, leaving him to stew in her study.

Chapter 27

When Elayce enters Vaaren's room, he is pacing the small space. She's just barely closed the door behind her when he starts talking.

"I know how we can prepare the army to fight the Darkness. Well not, the Darkness, but his army. We can infuse your light into the weapons that they use, using my runes. King Guydor said that they use light sources, but that they go out easily in fights. He never mentioned a magical light, just regular light. We don't need an extension of your magic, we just need the light to stick." He's breathless, talking so fast she can barely keep up.

"Okay," she says, drawing it out as she takes in what he's saying. "When are we going to find time to do that in between training me for the fight with the Darkness and all the activities this week for the celebration?"

"Nothing else matters besides giving the army a real fighting chance; we have to do this," he says, determined.

She cocks her head to the side, considering. "You want me to win this fight?"

"Well, I mean, I want the people to win this fight. I want as many people as possible to survive. Don't you see? The king gave us exactly the information that we needed to have a real chance." He finally stops pacing and looks up at her. He crosses to where she is standing and reaches out to grasp her crossed arms. "Elayce, this is what we've been searching for."

She glances down at his hands on her arms, the right side of her mouth crooking up in a smile as the warmth from his touch floods through her body. His very presence calls to her, as if the warmth is meant to convince her that he belongs near her. "It won't help me against the Darkness. We have to keep working on ways to strengthen my power."

His face falls, and he removes his hands. She can't bear that look of disappointment from him.

"But," she says, reaching forward and catching his hand, "we can practice stretching your magic skills by working on infusing some of the weapons like you said."

His face immediately brightens, and he squeezes her hand. He grabs the rune tome from the table behind him and they leave his room out the front door, startling the guards.

In her training room, Elayce grabs a beat-up sword from the rack and brings it over to Vaaren. He's sitting on the floor in the middle of the room, studying the book.

He moves the sword closer to himself, looking from the page to the gray metal. She watches intently as he drags his fingers down the length of the sword, coming to a stop just below the tip. With a deep breath, he begins to draw lines with his finger on the metal. She sees the rune lines that simmer into the sword like he's branding it. They stay lit while he continues drawing. When he gets to the end of the fourth line, he holds his finger still, reaching for her with his free hand. She bends down to the floor, and places her hand in his.

She always feels warmth through her body whenever she touches him, but this time his hand is scalding.

CHAPTER 27

He flips her hand and places it on top of the burning rune and nods to her.

Deep breath in, and deep breath out.

As she releases her breath, she pushes a few sparks into the rune beneath her palm. The rune glows even brighter and both she and Vaaren rear back to cover their eyes. When they lower their hands, they see the rune is glowing the same color as her sparks.

She reaches deep into her pit of power, trying to sense if this is like the wards where it takes a piece from her in order to work. She feels full and complete, nothing was taken from her. She looks up at Vaaren, and he's smiling from ear to ear.

"It worked!" he exclaims.

"You didn't think it would?"

"I had my doubts."

"Well, that doesn't mean that it will work against the shadow creatures. But there's really only one way to find out." This could give her army a fighting change against the shadow creatures. It could help her protect those that are important to her while she focuses solely on the Darkness. She knew that runes were the answer to winning this battle once and for all. Maybe Vaaren being sent to her was less of a trick and more of a blessing.

"Let's keep going," he says, getting up and running over to the wooden rack that holds several more weapons. He gathers far too many at once in his arms and rushes over, dropping them on the ground where she sits.

Immediately, he begins drawing the rune again, much faster this time. When he gets to the end, instead of grabbing her hand, he says, "Try just shooting your sparks into it."

She does as he asks, wiggling her fingers to send a few willing sparks to the shield he is working on. They disappear into the rune, the bright light appearing again before it settles into a low glow like the sword.

She smiles and removes two rings from her hand.

"Do these," she says, holding them up.

"I don't think these will make very good armor."

She just winks at him, and he does as she asks. He begins drawing the rune in the air, once it's drawn he taps it and drags it through the open space before pushing it onto one of the thin golden bands. She takes it from him and holds up the other one. Once the rings are finished she drops them in her pocket.

"Ah-hah!" he exclaims, joy and a little bit of disbelief radiating off him. "Can you imagine how different things would be if we had figured this out during your first fight with the Darkness?"

"I wasn't ready then," she answers.

"What?"

"I wouldn't have been able to do this the first time I fought him, I didn't have control of my magic the way I do now." She shrugs.

A shadow crosses his face. "Right. Like you said in your story."

She nods, her eyes sad. "You're right though, it would've been much different."

He leans back on his knees, giving her space to think, to talk.

Chapter 28

By the time Ren and I were marching through the castle gates, the rebellion had the battle under control. The guards were on their knees, hands tied behind their backs. The siege was done, and they were marching us straight to the king who hadn't yet surrendered.

It was horrifying to see the destruction, and it was hard to tell the difference between the heroes and the villains. Maybe there weren't any heroes at all.

My mind was still whirring with what I'd seen when we burst into the throne room where the king was sitting behind a large table. A few guards were circling him and standing in front of the table. We marched right up to him, confident that the rebellion had already won, this part was just a formality.

But he didn't look scared or defeated even. He looked annoyed, like we were just bugs flying around his head instead of a force come to remove him from the throne.

"You have no idea what you're doing," he said, directly to me.

"We've come to take back the kingdom. For the people," the rebels replied. But he didn't look at them. He only had eyes for me.

"You, Light Wielder, have come to remove me from my throne when I am the only one who has been working to keep this kingdom safe." His eyes were so dark, I couldn't tell where his pupil ended and the iris began. His breath reeked so heavily that I could smell it from across the table that sat between us, like he was rotting from the inside out.

"How do you know who I am?" I asked him.

"The Darkness whispered to me, that you would come and try to take my throne. I have been waiting to meet you, young one."

"What is he talking about?" One of the rebels said, turning to me. As soon as his eyes were off the king, a shadow zipped out from beneath the king's throne and smacked the rebel right in the heart. The rebel crumpled to the ground before anybody knew what had happened.

"You're in league with the Darkness?" I asked.

"It took a while, but eventually I realized what I could do with the Darkness on my side. I will be unstoppable. Once I've taken care of you."

Shouts rang out around me as rebels were captured by guards who had been hiding in the shadows. I flung out my arm, shooting a spray of sparks directly for the king. An arm of shadow curled in front of him, protecting the king from harm but disappearing in a cacophony of shrieks. I dropped to the ground and covered my ears on instinct, not sure how I could continue fighting through the noise.

I lashed out from where I lay, sending flurries of sparks at the king. I was uncoordinated and not well-trained, but my light cut through the shadows like butter. All I needed to do was make contact. Some of the rebels had broken free and were fighting the guards. I kept rushing forward, trying to ignore the pain in my ears from the screaming shadows. I couldn't defend myself well while I was attacking him, so I was covered in my own blood by the time I came close to the king. For a minute, I thought I could do it. I might win the fight and save everyone. I was almost close enough to make the killing blow, the shadows that protected him became sluggish as I beat them back.

The smug look hadn't left his face.

I was soon inches from him. I raised my hand, ready to send my sparks straight into his heart. But the king, he just laughed and cocked his head to the side.

That was when I heard Ren scream, "Laycie!"

I spun around to find Ren standing with a coiled shadow wrapped up along his body, around his neck and covering his mouth. I reached for him, sparks shooting out of my hand, but as I did the shadows wrapped tighter and grew thorns. Blood seeped from the holes that now peppered his skin.

I was terrified, frozen in place. But Ren's eyes were defiant. He wouldn't ever back down even in an impossible situation.

"Let him go!" I shouted at the king.

"Surrender to me, first," he said.

I whimpered, looking around at the dead rebels on the ground and the ones still alive, held by guards and shadows alike. When I met Ren's green eyes again, he was pleading with me. Pleading with me to make the right decision. Save the kingdom from the king and the Darkness.

I tore my brown eyes away from him and turned back to the king.

Another scream from Ren rang out and my resolve crumbled; I rushed to his side. His body slid limply to the floor, released from the shadow that had been holding him hostage. I caught him as he fell, but he was gone. The light that used to live within him, the one that I could see in his green, green eyes. It was gone.

I brushed his cheek with the back of my hand, his body still warm to the touch. Then I reached up and I closed his eyes, gently. I choked on a sob, thinking about how I would never get lost in them again. The life we planned together would never come true—the adventures, a marriage, a family. The sadness quickly turned to rage, the light bubbling up inside of me. More than I had ever felt it before. Laying his head down gently on the floor, I stepped away from his body and towards the king.

"You made your choice," he sneered at me.

"And you made yours."

This time when I sent my magic at him, it was a solid wall of light.

The wall of light burst forth from my entire body at once, destroying everything in its path to the king. Fires popped up where furniture had once been sitting. Dead bodies turned to ash. And the shadows turned to light.

The king was dead, but the Darkness was still within him. His jaw moved like a puppet on strings, and the Darkness spoke to me.

"You may have killed this body, but you have not gotten rid of me, Light Wielder. There will be another corrupt ruler to manipulate. It will be all too easy to come back again and again and again. Greed will always be the downfall of mankind."

I knew that he was right. The only person who should have the crown is someone who didn't want it in the first place.

Then the Goddess appeared again. She appeared as the Darkness lay in scraps of shadow within the dead body of the king, sneering at him.

"You have won the battle, Elayce, but this is not where you finish this war."

Just as quickly as she appeared, she was gone again, and when I looked down, so was the Darkness.

Chapter 29

"So, you crowned yourself because you knew the Darkness would be back?" Vaaren asks.

"Among other things. I was lost with the death of Ren. Completely. I was afraid that his sacrifice would be for nothing if the kingdom ended up under another selfish ruler who succumbed to the Darkness." She looks down at her hands to find that Vaaren's hand rests in hers. With his other hand he reaches up and brushes the tears from her face; tears she didn't even know she'd been crying.

"Your eyes are gray," he says, staring into her eyes, inches from her face.

"What?"

"In your story, you said your eyes were brown. They're gray."

"Oh. Well they used to be a light caramel brown. Ren used to say they looked good enough to eat."

"What happened?"

"I guess," she says, stumbling over the words on a soft sob. "I guess the light has left my eyes as well." When her eyes first started changing color she had been concerned, but over time she was grateful that the last reminder of who she was faded away. Her home, her love, her entire self—devoured by the light within.

His hand returns to her face, stroking her wet cheek. Her breath catches when she notices his eyes snap down to her lips and back up. She feels a heat begin to coil within her. It starts in her fingers and toes, warming her and then moving to gather low in her stomach. She feels time slow again, the same way that it did when she first saw Vaaren in the throne room. Only this time, there is nobody else there.

"Elayce," he says in a low, quiet voice.

"Call me Laycie," she says.

"Laycie," her name leaves his lips on the exhalation of his next breath.

The nickname envelopes her in warm comfort. It pulls her from the present and thrusts her back to before, when Ren was still alive. When Ren stood by her side or held her in his arms. Or when he brushed his lips against her neck, her cheek, her lips.

But this isn't Ren, not really.

And she's not that innocent young girl anymore.

She lurches forward, firmly planting her mouth on his. She grabs his shirt collar to pull him closer and deepen the kiss. Her tongue finds the seam of his lips and he opens for her, letting her choose how this will go. His hands fly down to her waist, gripping her tightly to him. He sighs, like it's a relief to finally be touching her again.

After a few moments that feel like years and seconds all at once, she breaks apart from him. A step backwards has his hands falling from her waist and back to his sides. Elayce touches her lips, her breath coming in hard pants. Vaaren says nothing, waiting for her to make the next move, while he fights equally as hard to catch his breath.

For a moment, they stare at each other. Both of them waiting for Elayce to decide what to do next. She's not letting the moment pass this time. She grabs his hand and he gives her a lopsided smile.

"I can't pretend to not want this, want you, anymore," he says.

Together they run from the training room. They move quickly, pausing only to pull each other into shadowed corners to hide from guards passing by and to steal hungry kisses on the way to her rooms.

The door slams shut behind them, leaving a bewildered set of guards who hadn't even known she'd left her room. They're crashing together instantly, kissing and tugging at clothes as if they've been waiting forever for this.

Her skin isn't smooth underneath her clothes. It's rippled with pockmarks, and scars, and goosebumps. He runs his hands up and down her thighs, reveling in the feel of her body. She slowly moves her hips back and forth, grinding on his lap. He breathes a sigh of contentment into her hair while she kisses and sucks his neck.

She has no idea what caused his change of heart, but he's grasping her like she's his lifeline. There's just a few small pieces of fabric separating them from finally joining.

She moves her hands from his neck down the front of his shirt and all the way to his belt buckle. She looks up at him through her eyelashes as she undoes the buckle, pulling the belt through the loops and dropping it to the floor. She's moving surprisingly slow now, with intense control. But that's what she wants, no, needs. Control.

She pushes him back until he's leaning back on his elbows on the bed, never breaking eye contact. Her palm grazes over the bulge in his trousers before flashing to the button and ripping them open. The button flies across the room but neither of them watch it. She slowly shimmies his trousers and underwear down and leaves them in a pile on the floor. Her eyes flash down to his cock, standing straight up and waiting for her.

Reaching behind her, she slowly undoes her tight, black dress and lets it fall to the floor, revealing nothing underneath. As he lays on the bed, she stands before him in nothing but her silver, spiked crown.

Her body is perfectly toned and lethal, only there are more scars than her stories let on. She stalks towards him, and when she reaches the bed, crawls to hover over him. The heat from their bodies warm each other despite being naked. She reaches down and strokes his cock a few times and watches as his eyes close and his head pushes back into the bed. Then she slams herself down onto him. Gasping as she takes him all in one go. His eyes fly open and his hands fly up to grab her hips as she begins to rock back and forth on him.

"No," she hisses and his hands fly above his head, chased there by her magic. She begins to rock again and places her hands on his chest, throwing her head back as she finds her rhythm. She can tell he wants to touch her, his eyes are pleading, hungry. His hands twitch under the sparks that threaten him if he moves. He breathes her name, and his words curl around her like they did the first time that she laid eyes on him. She opens her eyes to look at him, her eyelids low and heavy with passion.

She leans forward and kisses him as she continues her rhythm on top of him. He thrusts his tongue in her mouth, trying to claim as much of her as he can. She moves her kisses from his mouth and runs her tongue along his jaw, leaning forward to whisper in his ear, "You are mine."

He moans against her neck and thrusts his hips to meet her building rhythm. His eyes roll closed in pleasure and she sits up again to take him deeper. Her walls start to clench around his cock and she's screaming her pleasure into the room. He follows her release with his own.

Afterwards, she climbs off of him and walks to the bathing room, her sparks following her and releasing him so he can move freely again. She hasn't felt this connected to someone in a long time. It feels like, like she's losing control again. The intensity with which her senses are overtaken when Vaaren is around is too much. She needs space, time to think. Time to get her head on straight. She can have some fun, but she isn't meant to have a partner in this. The images of Ren's lifeless body flash through her mind, squeezing the air from her lungs.

She steps back into the bedroom, holding a towel out to him. He crosses, cautiously taking the towel from her. She lifts the tapestry that leads to his room and pushes the door open, gesturing for him to enter. His eyes grow wide.

"You want me to leave? Now?" he says incredulously, glancing back at the bed where the sheets lay rumpled and his pile of clothes sits accusingly on the floor. His disbelief feels like a punch to her gut.

"You don't want to stay," she says. The words to brush him off feel wrong to her, causing her stomach to churn with an empty cold. They got swept away in the moment, but now they both need to come back to reality.

"But I do want to stay, even if that goes against everything I stand for. I can't explain it, but I can feel my magic pulling me towards you," he says, trying to explain. He runs his hands through his hair in frustration.

"Like calls to like. Your magic is just reaching out to another powerful source of magic. Hopefully, we've gotten whatever it is out of our systems, and we can get back to focusing on how to defeat the Darkness."

"So you feel the pull too?" he asks quietly, his eyes full of hope. It's almost worse. She is trying to shut him down and kick him out, not reveal that her innermost soul is yearning for him. As usual, she can't control herself, including her mouth, around him. She needs to get away, clear her head. She leaves him to walk to his room on his own, escaping to her dressing room and closing the door behind her.

~

"This is for you and your sister," Elayce says, handing Darla the two rings that she and Vaaren worked on last night. This is the best protection she can offer them right now to follow through on the promise she made to Darla. They are preparing Elayce for the party tonight and now is the perfect opportunity to ask Darla if she has any gossip to report on.

"This is too much, Your Majesty," Darla says breathlessly, inspecting the gold trinkets.

"You should each wear one. They can offer some protection." She attempts to make eye contact with Darla in the mirror, but Darla is fitting one ring on her finger and tucking the other into her pocket.

"I've been talking to some of the servants from other kingdoms," she starts. Elayce makes an encouraging sound for Darla to continue. "The servants from Selna say only good things about King Theis; it's clear they love working for him. They think that they will be preparing for a royal wedding soon."

"It's easy to love a king when he doesn't have to make any tough decisions," Elayce mumbles, rolling her eyes. Love can be taken away at any time, it can be faked or used against you. Love is conditional. Fear lasts longer—is more stable.

"Your hair is done, my queen, let's get you dressed." Darla walks over to the dressing room, Elayce close behind.

After dinner, most of the royals and nobles in attendance are well into their third or fourth drink and the music is low and sultry. Dinner was a lavish spread of Aerash delicacies with the finest alcohol supplied from Nicen. Council Member Gresha is still boasting about it, talking loudly into the open space in front of her, guests near her doing their best to ignore her.

Elayce is draped across her throne, lazing in the energy of the room without having had a drop to drink. She doesn't want to be caught unaware if she gets another visit from the Darkness tonight. She isn't sure what to expect, as this is new since the last time she fought him. Vaaren is once again standing at the foot of the dais as if that's his post and he is determined to guard it. He has maintained a polite, quiet attitude this time, dissuading any of the lively, drunken women from engaging with him.

"A dance, my queen?" King Theis asks from above her, his hand outstretched to Elayce. She glances down to Vaaren, but he doesn't look up.

"Why not?" she answers, accepting his hand and letting him drag her down to the floor.

The crowd parts for them as they enter the dance floor, never missing a step. He twirls her outward and spins her back in, pulling her body flush against his and immediately falling into movement with the crowd around them. She lets him lead her through the steps, noting that he holds her much closer than necessary.

"You've been avoiding me," he murmurs into her ear as they dance.

"I've been distracted with other things," she says playfully.

"Other things like the plaything standing at the foot of your throne?" he says, subtly nodding his head in the direction of Vaaren who is staring intently at the dancing couple.

"Plaything?" Her mood sours instantly. She doesn't keep her extracurricular activities a secret anymore, but something about Theis accusing her of using Vaaren for sex rubs her the wrong way. Now isn't the time to dissect that feeling.

"He hasn't left your side since I've arrived, Elayce, I wasn't born yesterday."

"What I do on my own time, doesn't concern you. I haven't accepted—"

"Don't worry, my queen. I'm not jealous. I'm well aware of what I have to offer while he has nothing. My advisors couldn't even find records of a Lord Vaaren anywhere in Aerash or the surrounding kingdoms."

"You were looking into Vaaren?" With her focus on the Darkness and the deal with the King and Queen of Don Kemt, she forgot to keep an eye on Theis. Truthfully, she didn't think she had to.

"I had to make sure there wouldn't be any competition." He winks at her, either unaware of her shift in mood or ignoring it.

"An alliance with me is not a game, Theis. In fact, I'm done playing." She tries to push from his grip, but he holds her tighter, crushing her hands in his.

"I will not be giving up on protecting my people so easily, Queen Elayce," he whispers to her forcefully. Abruptly, he lets her go, stepping back from her.

"Big mistake," she growls. She reaches for her magic and feels it surge under her skin and then...sizzle out.

"What?" she gasps. She looks down at her hands, flipping them over in front of her as if her skin will tell her what's wrong. By now, the crowd has realized that something is wrong and have backed up to form a circle around the queen.

She looks back up to Theis's smug face, but he's looking at Vaaren like they're both in on a secret. When she looks over at Vaaren, his face is a mask.

"Shall we go somewhere private, my queen?" Theis asks, his emphasis on what was once an endearment now sounds possessive.

"This way," she hisses, leading him off the floor and to a small private chamber off the dais. If Elayce wasn't so distracted trying to figure out why her magic wouldn't come forth, she would have likely made a smarter move. Now it is just her, Vaaren, Theis and two of his guards in the overcrowded space. Why did Vaaren follow? Where are her own guards? What had Theis done, where is her magic?

She spins to face Theis once the door shuts behind them all, wringing her hands. She could fight if she needed to without her magic. It's why she did all that physical training with Harkn and other soldiers, but she isn't about to tell him that. Let him think that he had the upper hand here; she could still salvage this.

"What is going on?" she demands as the music resumes in the room behind them.

"As I said, I will not be giving up the only option I have to protect my people. I could tell from the moment I arrived and this *trollop* was following you around that you had no intention of accepting my proposal. So I switched over to Plan B." He smiles and gestures to Vaaren, who seems just as confused as Elayce does.

"Your dearest Lord Vaaren here is a Runer," Theis says, pausing for dramatic effect but when Elayce fails to react, he frowns. "I see you already know that."

"Of course I know that," she snarls. "Why do you think I've been keeping him close?"

"I see you've had to improvise," he says, addressing Vaaren.

"Improvise?" he asks.

"What *are* you going on about, Theis? Get to the point," she snarls, crouching like she's about to pounce. The guards behind Theis move to protect him, but he holds out his hand to stall them.

"I've seen her fight, she relies on her magic and she doesn't have any right now." He smiles smugly again, proud of himself.

Going along with it, she straightens and crosses her arms across her chest, feigning a momentary surrender. She lifts her eyebrow, waiting for him to go on.

"You see, your little rebellion approached me some time ago. They had hoped that I could help them in their fight to overthrow their ruler, but I knew I couldn't win against you. I also was more concerned with the rumors of the Darkness spreading in Don Kemt, and I knew that you might be the only hope of ridding the world of it again.

"They told me that they had a Runer. That they could imbue a piece of jewelry with a rune that could contain your magic without killing you. All I had to do was get you to put the ring on." He looks down at her hands.

She holds her hands in front of her again and sees that she

has an extra ring—on her left ring finger. She wears so much jewelry she didn't even notice it. He must've slipped it on her finger before she pushed him away while they were dancing.

"He's the Runer that made this for you?" she asks.

"Yes," Theis says simply before continuing. "Obviously, my original plan had been to marry you and slip this little thing on your finger at the altar. That way I had legitimate claim to your throne, before we stripped you of your magic.

"I was told that they would send Vaaren here in case anything went wrong with the rune. I thought at first he was here as one of your advisors. I was surprised to see him following you around like a little puppy dog." He spits the last few words at Vaaren, shooting him a look of disdain and giving Vaaren the space to explain himself.

Vaaren's mouth opens and closes, no sound escaping, his head swiveling back and forth between Elayce and Theis.

Elayce is desperately tugging at the ring, but it doesn't budge. This is why she doesn't get close to people. She should have ignored whatever was drawing her to him because obviously her feelings were wrong about him. She should have had better control of herself.

"Do you know all the things that Runers can do? Infinite things, really. Anything you can imagine. Runers can figure out a way to do it. Dim the light, hold it, block it out. And things as easy as make sure your jewelry can't be stolen. Such useful things," he says, reaching forward to stroke Elayce's cheek. He rears back when she snaps at him with her teeth, laughing it off once he's out of her reach.

"Get this off me," she says low, menacingly.

"Only the hand that placed the ring can remove it. So don't go getting any ideas," he says, shaking his finger at her as if she was a child.

Oh she had many, many ideas about how she was going to kill him. First, she had to figure out how to get this ring off her hand.

"Now that you have accepted my proposal, and my engagement ring is on your finger, I think we can tell everyone to start planning the wedding. I hope you don't mind that we have it here at your castle? It's just that all the guests are here already. We could end this week with our wedding," he prattles on without waiting for her to respond. "I think your Head of Staff should be well-prepared for this."

Her eyes flash, Loras is in on this scheme. Figure out how to deal with Theis now, everyone else later.

"We'll have much to discuss, but I think for now we should perhaps, retire to our rooms?" Theis asks, once again not looking for an answer from anyone. He nods to his guards and they step forward, reaching to grab Elayce.

"You will not drag me through my own castle," she grits out.

Theis's eyebrows raise. "Can you behave?"

"Lay hands on me and find out," Elayce challenges.

Theis chuckles, and steps away from the door. He gestures to it, allowing Elayce to walk out on her own. When she goes, the guards follow but don't touch her. She breezes past Vaaren, making sure not to look at him on the way out.

Chapter 30

She's pacing back and forth across the shattered glass and dried leaves that cover the floor of her room. Out of the corner of her eye she sees the Goddess of Light tapestry rustle. She runs to her bedside table and quickly pulls a dagger out of the drawer and crouches behind the bed, ready to surprise an attacker.

Vaaren shuffles out from behind the tapestry. Damn it, she forgot to lock it.

She throws the dagger anyway.

He throws himself to the ground, screaming. The dagger lodges itself in the tapestry right where his head had been moments before.

She grabs a second dagger from her drawer.

"What are you doing in here?" she hisses at him.

"I came to explain!" His shout is muffled by the rug.

"Explain?" she sputters. "The only reason you're still alive right now is because I need you to get this ring off of my finger."

She looks at the dagger in her hand, then to the ring on her finger. Her magic is worth more than just one finger. She positions the dagger against her finger just below the ring...

"No!"

Blood beads around the dagger, but she pauses and swings her attention to him.

Still pressed flat to the floor, he says, "I need to explain, Elayce. I...I don't remember doing what he said I did. But I don't think that will work."

"How could you not possibly remember?" she spits at him.

"Look," he says, sitting up. He starts to roll up his sleeve and another dagger whizzes past his head and sticks in the wall next to him, small drops of her blood trickling from it. He looks up at her with a shocked expression.

"There's more where that came from, so don't try me."

He grimaces and rolls his sleeve up the rest of the way. On his arm are faint pink lines etched into his skin.

"What is that?" she asks.

"A rune," he answers. Another dagger sails through the air, hitting the wall above his head this time. "It's a memory loss rune. I don't remember anything from before this mission with the rebellion. I remember waking up in a room, a man with a green cape told me that I had volunteered to have my memories wiped. That I was being sent to the castle under the guise of a rescue mission and that I was meant to get close to you."

Green cape—that must be Loras. "Why?"

"I don't know why, or maybe it really was what Theis said and that I was meant to be here to help him in case he needed anything. I just know that my goal was to get close to you and—" he stops suddenly, grimacing again.

"What? Get close to me and what, Vaaren?" she says. Hurt and disgust lace her words.

"And, uh, let you discover that I was a Runer. So that I could get access to the books you have here."

"Damn," she says forcefully, her stomach clenches and she thinks she might throw up. She kicks the side of her bed. "Damn it! I knew that you were sent here for a reason. What about what you told me of your childhood?"

He has the gall to look ashamed. "They gave me information to feed to you. I don't know what's true or isn't. What I do know is that cutting off your finger is more likely to quell your magic permanently than free it."

She's too incensed to say anything else. She throws the rest of the daggers in her hands, Vaaren flinches but they don't hit anywhere near him. She screeches and runs into her workshop grabbing anything she can get her hands on and throwing it to the floor around her. Shards of glass cover the spaces on the floor where the previous shattered pieces hadn't yet. She screams until they turn into rage filled sobs, the emotion too much to contain. Maybe it's a good thing her magic is restrained right now, or she might've burned everything to the ground.

She let her feelings cloud her own judgment. She never should have opened herself up to him. Elayce rounds the corner back into her room, where Vaaren sits on the floor looking miserable and scared.

"Get out." Her voice is low, but filled with so much malice that he flinches.

"Elayce, please. Let me help get the ring off," he says.

"You sat on your high horse and pretended like I was the monster who had betrayed everyone. Well look who's joined me in the mud now, soldier!" Her voice raises as she goes on. "At least I never pretend to be someone that I'm not. I am the villain. This is who I am. But you? You're the real monster. The one that acts like the hero, when his true nature is hiding in the shadows."

"I don't remember what I did I—"

"I said get out!" She's shouting again, pointing at the tapestry where he came from, "You're alive because I need you to get this ring off, but I don't want to be near you."

He looks at her, searching her eyes for something other than the burning hatred he sees there, but there is nothing. He holds up his hands, moving slowly, and disappears behind the tapestry and back down the tunnel to his room.

Chapter 31

The next morning Elayce is standing in her dressing room, being measured for a wedding gown. The anger has passed through her and she's moved on to one-track determination. This is an unexpected setback, but she's faced worse.

When Darla tries to place more rings on her fingers, Elayce waves her away. She wants the singular cursed ring on her finger to guide her focus. The unadorned gold band around her left ring finger feels cold against her skin. Every time she tries to call to her magic she feels the sparks dissolve, as if her own magic is trying to escape from it.

She ignores the hurt she feels in her heart from Vaaren's betrayal. She locks it away with the other feelings she had about him—trust, contentment. Their relationship never should have developed past that of a prisoner and executioner, but she let her lonely heart reach out to him. She let his blond hair and green eyes pierce through her armor and into her soul. It has been three hundred years since she was able to share herself so openly with someone, and the anniversary of Ren's death made her vulnerable and stupid.

She won't let that happen again.

Donning a plain, dusty gold ballgown, she heads to the throne room where she and Theis are expected to make their engagement and wedding announcement to their guests. Tydas didn't waste any time.

When she enters, she sees her throne is moved off to the side and a second throne now shares the space. Without missing a beat she takes a seat on the right side. Theis strolls in shortly afterwards, wearing an ensemble that marries the gold of her kingdom and the magenta of his own. Elayce takes note of the well-coordinated outfit and thinks that maybe she will wear those colors one day after all. Once Theis is out of the way.

"Good morning, my queen," he says to her as he plants himself in the throne next to her.

"Theis," she says in greeting.

"I see you've abandoned your stray puppy."

"On the contrary, I've locked him up back in his cage." She did, in fact, have his rooms locked and gave strict instructions to her staff and guards that he was not to exit the room.

"It's for the best, I'm sure. Once we've made our announcement, I wouldn't want another man to be associated with my future wife."

"I didn't know you were so insecure, King Theis."

"Hardly. But I'd hate to have to sentence our Runer to death due to any nasty rumors circling. Or perhaps a public execution would be the perfect way to celebrate our union?"

"I would love to perform an execution; remove this ring from my finger and I will happily oblige." She smiles coyly, reaching her hand out to him.

He chuckles. "We'll have to find another way to celebrate then, Queen Elayce." He takes hold of her outstretched hand and brings his lips to the ring on her finger. She doesn't let her smile falter when she rips her hand from his grasp. Too bad there isn't a gemstone embedded in the ring, she would've ripped right through his lip.

At last, the final guests arrive and Tydas sweeps to the center of the room. Horns sound, signaling the beginning of the announcement. Elayce doesn't pay attention to anything Tydas says, she'd been prepared with her portion of the announcement earlier.

Tydas finishes his part and gestures to the queen, bowing low as she stands and signaling to everyone else that they should bow as well. Elayce takes a deep breath and launches into her speech.

"I have chosen to unite Selna and Aerash through a marriage contract. King Theis will stand beside me as the king consort." She smirks as Tydas visibly stiffens and King Theis shifts next to her. King consort was definitely not part of the prepared speech. "I'm sure our kingdoms will thrive with our new king consort and his knowledge and expertise on the music and entertainment that Selna can bring to our kingdoms. In exchange, Aerash will begin to send many of our newly trained troops to bolster Selna's defenses."

Finally, she looks over at King Theis. Good luck following that.

"Selna is quite looking forward to this partnership. And I am looking forward to celebrating our wedding with you all before you leave at the end of this week!" He throws his hands up in a wide, celebratory gesture, grabbing Elayce's hand on the way up so they seem united in their celebration.

Cheers and clapping break out across the ballroom, although when Elayce scans the crowd she can see that King Guydor is less than pleased. She will have to follow up with him and ensure that he understands their agreement still stands.

Music breaks out and servants begin to bring out trays of

CHAPTER 31

breakfast foods and morning drinks. The crowd breaks up to find their seats and dig into the delicacies. King Theis and Queen Elayce step down off the dais together and find their seats at the head table.

"It seems you went a bit off script, my queen," Theis murmurs in her ear as he helps her sit in her chair.

"Is king consort not what you offered to me back in Selna when you first proposed this union?" Elayce asks innocently, quietly enough so just the two of them can hear.

"Not in so many words. It was my understanding that things were different now." He says 'different' with emphasis at the same time that his fingers brush over the ring on her finger.

"Then I am glad I made the announcement, so that you didn't get it wrong in front of everyone." She pops a forkful of food into her mouth. "King Guydor," Elayce says, "isn't the breakfast spread this morning delightful?"

It feels like hours before Elayce is able to escape the guests. Rounds and rounds of people come to congratulate her and King Theis on their engagement and she endures all of it while standing next to him. She forces herself to be okay with it in front of everyone, so nobody can tell it wasn't her idea to begin with. There are many who express their relief to know she was building her army to send protection and enforcement to Selna rather than to start a war. She's not going to tell them that they are wrong. Let them believe what they want, and maybe they'll get off her back about the growing army and the draft. She could find some positives to this situation after all.

Once in her room, she walks straight to the door behind the tapestry, unlocks it, and marches through to Vaaren's room. When she enters, he's sitting at the table staring at the door as if he was waiting for her.

"Elayce—" he starts.

"*Queen* Elayce," she cuts him off.

"No, I have to talk to you." His shirt sleeve is already rolled up, the memory loss rune etched into his skin on full display. "I told you last night that I volunteered for this. That my job was to get close to you and that I don't remember much of anything."

"Yes, please remind me of the circumstances of your betrayal." She rolls her eyes and crosses her arms in front of her.

"Will you let me speak?"

"I'm not sure you deserve it, but if I must." She gestures for him to keep going.

"I've been here for a few weeks now, and I've watched you and I've listened to your story. It took me a while, but I think I understand what you're trying to do. You're trying to protect your people from the Darkness. Nobody was there to teach you, and nobody was there to help you. Not even the Goddess who gave you those powers. You've been alone and you've been doing things the only way you know how, afraid to enjoy it too much so that one day you weren't tempted to align yourself with the Darkness. You've lived a life longer than most and watched everyone around you care about trivial things and then die. They've asked more and more from you, when you are giving all you have to make sure that you are ready to defeat the Darkness when it comes back, and all along nobody has even known or cared." He pauses, and takes a step forward to lay his hands on her crossed arms. He gently tugs her arms until he can take her hands in his.

"But I do. You've let me see you. I wanted to tell you last night that I don't believe the things they told me. Something about what they said doesn't ring true for me. I feel... something...inside me that calls to you. I've tried to cling to what they told me, but it doesn't feel right. When I'm near you, I know that my purpose is to help you. We'll figure out how to get the ring off and we'll figure out how to take care of the Darkness. And then you'll be free."

Elayce tries to absorb everything, thoroughly turned around by his words. They crack the pitiful lock she put on her feelings and they start to leak out again. Consuming her heart and warming her body. All she ever wanted was to be seen—for herself, for what she was doing—and for that to not be a weakness.

She pulls her hands from his and pushes him squarely on the chest, away from her. His face has a look of disappointment until the back of his legs hit the bed behind him and she smiles, stalking towards him. He breathes a sigh of relief when her body presses up against his and her hands come up to the buttons on his shirt. She begins slowly undoing them and pulls his shirt out of his trousers, leaving his chest fully exposed. She crouches in front of him, kissing his abdomen and then dragging her tongue up his middle all the way back to his neck, before coming back up to kiss his mouth. Their mouths and tongues stay connected while her hands work their way up and over his shoulders, pushing his shirt fully off.

He flips her around, her ass pressed into his groin. He groans as she grinds into him, losing focus on undoing the buttons of her dress. His hands slip around her, helping her grind into him harder. He tugs up her dress enough to slip his fingers between her thighs, finding her already wet.

Elayce moans, "Dress. Off. Now." She needs everything between them to be laid bare, to feel their joining and to know that he is really with her.

His fingers find their way back up to the multitude of buttons that line her back with renewed focus. Finally, he has the last button undone and the dress slips down to pool at her feet. She gasps at the cool air that wraps around her body, a contrast to his warm lips that press kisses down her bare shoulder. She spins in his embrace and reaches between them to unbutton his trousers and push them off of his hips, leaving him just as naked as she is.

She pushes him slightly and he falls back onto the bed behind him. Eagerly, he reaches up and tugs on her hip until she joins him on the bed, laying against him, naked flesh to naked flesh. Their bodies press so closely together, each curve finding a place against the other's. It feels as though he was made for her.

Carefully, he traces his fingertips down from her hip to behind her knee. Never breaking eye contact, he hitches her knee up to his hip and flips her so he's on top.

Her eyes flash in surprise and a dangerous smile spreads across her lips. "What are you going to do to me?"

"I'm going to take it from here, Laycie," he breathes into the crook of her neck. He starts kissing her collarbone and slowly works his way down her body, picking up speed as he goes. Kissing the inside of her thighs and getting closer and closer to that sweet bundle of nerves. He suddenly takes her in his mouth, and her back arches in pleasure. She grabs the sheets and squeezes them in her fists as he sucks and licks. She fists his hair and cries out his name.

She's almost there when suddenly he's not between her legs anymore and she opens her eyes to find him hovering over her instead. She pulls his lips to hers so she can taste herself on them. Their movements feel fast, but the moment feels like it's happening in slow motion. Almost like time is speeding up and slowing down at the same time. She feels his cock at her entrance and she bites down hard on his lip.

"If you aren't inside me in the next moment, I will gladly finish without you," she growls.

"Anything you wish, my queen."

And he thrusts into her. Their breaths come heavy and she tightens around him. He leans back into a sitting position, holding onto her ass and pulling her with him. He sinks deeper into her and she lets out a guttural moan in response. With both his hands on her hips, he helps move her up and down along his shaft. Their movements are quicker now as their release comes closer. She looks down into his eyes, keeping contact as she bounces on his cock. Her hands pull tight into his hair and she rips his head back to kiss his neck.

She whispers into his ear, "Mine." And then they both scream out as they find their release together. Her magic sings within, telling her that she'll find herself again in the moments she's lost to him. In a tangle of sheets and flesh on the bed, they fall asleep.

Chapter 32

Elayce lay in the bed next to a still sleeping Vaaren. It's been a while since she's woken up next to anyone. In fact, the last person she woke up next to looked exactly the same, only it was three hundred years ago and these two men are similar, yet not. In the end, Ren had stopped listening to her too. He believed he knew what would be best for them. She wishes she had the chance to ask him about it, to really talk it through. Maybe she would have been able to let him go before now if she had had some closure.

She is capable of many things, but she can't change the past. Now Vaaren is here. He sees her. He sees past the violence and the tyranny and he sees that really she is just trying to protect them. The thought makes her almost giddy. If only she could stay in bed all day with him instead of attending to the myriad of other things on her schedule. Thankfully, the week is coming to a close. Now, to just figure out how to get this wretched ring off her finger and rid herself of King Theis.

She gently moves the covers, so she can sneak out without waking Vaaren. Her toes hit the ice cold floor and she shivers in her night dress. She slides to the edge of the bed and makes to stand before she sees the shadow. Him.

The Darkness hovers in the corner of the room. Eyes look

out from the mass of shadows, phasing between solid black and familiar green eyes.

She freezes in place, somehow managing to hold her scream in. She can't access her magic right now, but she can't let on. Maybe he won't be able to tell.

Laycie, she hears. The familiar voice is a whisper, but it feels deafening. *You have betrayed me. I fought my way back to you for the last three hundred years, and when I find you it's in bed with another.*

"You will not trick me, Darkness. Ren is gone. You are not him." She tries to keep any trembling from her voice.

My sweet, Laycie. Ren is here with me. He is me. I am him. We have been looking forward to being with you again.

Elayce feels something skate across her skin and she flinches and twists back to brush it off, finding Vaaren reaching for her across the bed. His eyes are large and full of confusion.

She glances back to where the Darkness waits, but when Vaaren follows her gaze, he keeps searching. As if he cannot see anything.

"Who are you talking to, Elayce?" he asks.

She turns back to the Darkness, less afraid than she was before. If Vaaren cannot see the Darkness, then perhaps the Darkness is not yet strong enough to hurt them.

I am here only for you, Laycie. But soon enough, I will be here for everyone else. Then. You will join me, and it will be our turn to rule.

"The only thing you will meet when you return is your end. Leave!" she shouts, throwing her hand out and calling her sparks. Nothing answers her call. Her feint seems to do the trick though, and the Darkness disappears in a puff of black shadows.

"Elayce?" Vaaren asks again.

She stares at the spot where the Darkness had stood a moment before, maybe to convince herself that he has left.

"The Darkness. He came to visit again."

"Again?"

"Yes, he must be growing stronger. I expect he will be moving towards the kingdom within the month. Maybe sooner than that, I'm not sure. Last time, we approached the Darkness already within the king. This time, he approaches me." She looks down at the ring she is twisting on her finger.

"We need to get this off of you," he says, grasping her hand to stop her fidgeting.

"Any ideas?"

He stands from the bed, still naked, and starts flipping through the pages of a rune book on the table across the room. She crosses the room and reaches out to drag her nails down his bare back. He stiffens under her touch.

"You should at least put some clothes on. If anyone comes in, I can explain that I'm here to talk strategy against the rebels, but they might not believe me if you're naked," she jokes, wrapping her arms around his torso.

"I do not have time," he says, still flipping through the book.

"Surely, you have time to put some trousers on."

"No! Don't you see that I don't? The Darkness was just here. In this room! You were defenseless and it's my fault." He grabs the ring on her finger that's wrapped around the front of his body. "I did this to you."

His outburst surprises Elayce and she pulls her arms from him, taking a step back.

"You did not put this ring on me, King Theis did."

"You know what I mean." He sighs, flipping the next page.

"Look at me." He flips another page. "Vaaren, look at me."

He sighs deeply, his head hangs between his hunched shoulders. She steps towards him again, and gently grabs his chin between her fingers, twisting him to face her.

"I need you here, with me. Now."

His eyes move back and forth between hers, before he nods.

"You're right, my queen. I am with you," he answers with a small smile, leaning forward to give her a peck on the lips.

"Unfortunately, I will have to leave you. I don't want King Theis to know that we are working together. I'll be back to see what you've come up with later." She turns to head back to her rooms.

"Where are you heading?" he asks.

"I'm off to see the King of Don Kemt," she calls out as she walks through the door, dragging her golden dress behind her.

~

"Queen Elayce, I've been expecting you," King Guydor says when she enters the room. She had Tydas gather the king and queen for her meeting with them and they seem to have been eager to meet. To her surprise, King Theis is also present. Tydas must've expanded the guest list.

"Our deal still stands, there is nothing to worry about King Guydor," she says breezily, taking a seat in a chair across the table from the king and queen. They share a look of discontent.

"Is there anyone here that you are not forming an alliance with?" King Guydor says, momentarily shifting his gaze to King Theis.

"I haven't formed an alliance with Don Kemt, I have offered you and the queen protection while the Darkness spreads across your abandoned country." Her long, black nails twirl through her hair that drapes over her shoulders.

Guydor's face turns red, "Queen Elayce, that is not—"

"King Guydor, it is only us here, and apparently the future king consort. You don't have to pretend that you care more about your country than yourself. I am only interested to know if you have received any updates on the battle against the Darkness in Don Kemt."

Elayce hasn't confirmed any information about the Darkness with Theis, but he doesn't show any surprise. She'll have to double check that Tydas's loyalties still lie with her instead of Theis. The king continues to bluster and mumble about the audacity, while the queen fans herself and her pinched face with a handkerchief. Elayce rolls her eyes. Ridiculous. Who are they pretending for? Tydas wipes the sweat off his forehead with a handkerchief.

"Enough, Guydor. My patience wears thin. Do you have any updates on the state of the country that you abandoned to protect your own skin?"

"Oh, just tell her!" Queen Brigit shouts, then clears her throat and continues fanning herself as if she didn't say anything at all. She doesn't turn to see her husband's glare.

"We received word that the Darkness has gained ground. Most of Don Kemt is under shadow right now. It seems to be spreading this way," King Guydor finally says. The last part a bit accusingly.

"Hm," she says, noncommittally.

"Will you do nothing to help Don Kemt?" Queen Brigit asks.

"You'd have to speak to my betrothed, as currently all of our extra troops are headed to Selna." She turns pointedly to King Theis.

"Selna and Aerash are our top priorities right now, King Guydor. Unfortunately, we will be unable to send troops to

Don Kemt. Though, Don Kemt will be our first area of recovery once we have things handled," Theis answers smoothly.

Elayce raises an eyebrow at him, but he doesn't look in her direction.

"And when will you have things handled?" King Guydor asks, shifting uncomfortably in his seat.

Elayce shrugs. "When I have them handled."

Theis chuckles next to her, a sound that gets under her skin, causing her to roll her neck and flex her fingers.

"We're done here, I believe. If you receive any other news, have Tydas contact me. The more we know, the faster we can get this handled. Tydas can escort you out," she says, gesturing to the door and dismissing the King and Queen of Don Kemt.

As soon as the door closes behind them, she whirls on King Theis. "What do you know about the Darkness?"

"Mostly just the rumors that I knew about before you came to visit Selna," he replies.

"You were not surprised to hear about the extent of it in Don Kemt this morning?"

"Surprised? Absolutely, my queen. However, some of us were raised to be king and understand how to play the game," he says, rather smugly.

She narrows her eyes and purses her lips, thinking over what he said. Whether or not he is telling the truth doesn't seem as important right now.

"How do you expect me to fight the Darkness with this ring on my finger, then?" she challenges.

He shrugs. "That will be something for us to discuss after the wedding, I suppose."

"It seems rather counter intuitive for you to trap me into a marriage to protect your country by not allowing me the magic I need to protect your country."

"A player does not reveal all of his tricks at once, my queen. Don't you worry, but my Runer and I have things well in hand." He smiles and gets up to leave her, sending Tydas back into the room.

"Tydas, I expect my invitations to be extended to only those I specify in the future."

"You did not want your king at this business meeting, Your Majesty?" Tydas asks.

"He is not *my* king. He is the future king consort, and since I didn't say that I wanted him here, then no. I did not." She leans back in her chair, giving Tydas a stern look.

"Yes, my queen. Of course." He bows slightly.

"You have done well as my advisor in the past, Tydas. But I have no need for someone who makes my life more difficult. With access to all of my new subjects in Selna, it may be that I could find someone more...agreeable to my needs." She cocks her head to the side, letting her comments wash over him.

"I...I understand, Your Majesty." He bows lower and backs out of the room without standing.

As soon as he's gone, she stands and heads swiftly back to her rooms and through the tunnel to Vaaren.

"How is he expecting to utilize my magic without freeing me?" she says, sweeping in without a hello. He's at the desk, hunched over a stack of books, writing notes.

"What do you mean?" he asks, distractedly, still copying down his own notes.

"He said that 'his Runer', presumably you, had a way of allowing me to use my magic without harming him." She comes to a stop behind him, looking over his shoulder at the notes he's taken. Although, they mostly mean nothing to her.

"I imagine whatever he's referring to is something I did before they locked my memories away. I have no idea what he's talking about." He sits fully up and moves his chair back, and Elayce takes advantage of the space he's created and sits on his lap.

"How do I plan for something when I don't know what it is?"

"The same way I imagine you've been trying to plan for the Darkness's return before you had me," he says simply, wrapping his arms around her waist.

"By killing anyone who gets in my way?"

"I would have said by staying one step ahead." She searches for the judgment in his eyes, but doesn't find any.

She contemplates the ring on her finger. "Look at the runes. What are they exactly?"

He picks up her hand to examine the ring. His hands are much softer than when he arrived, the callouses from training with the rebellion starting to soften. She rests her cheek on his head, inhaling the clean scent of soap and the floral undertones that linger in all the palace toiletries.

"This here," he says, riffling through the pages. "This rune is the one he was talking about that keeps the ring on your finger. It's like a locking mechanism almost, and only the person who locked it can unlock it."

"Can you…erase the rune? Remove it?" Elayce asks.

"Not while it's active. It's meant to prevent theft of precious items. This rune next to it is a light dampener, it won't let light past the item it's drawn on. But there's a third rune, it looks like a light holding rune? It would've been used to trap light into a container to use past sundown."

"An extra precaution?" she asks.

"Yes," he answers, dragging out the word. "It's actually the same rune that we used to infuse your light into the weapons, just drawn in a different order. Look, you can tell by how deep certain lines are." He holds the ring closer to her face, but when she looks she can't tell the difference.

She shrugs. "Must be a Runer thing."

There's a crease between his eyebrows and his green eyes flick back and forth between the page and the ring. "I think," he pauses, scrutinizing the ring again, "I think they might be funneling your magic somewhere else."

Chapter 33

"What?" she asks, standing from his lap.

"What does it feel like when you try to use your magic? With the ring on?"

"It feels like, when I call to it, it answers but instead of growing bigger and exploding outward, it dissolves." She flicks her fingers through the air, testing to see how she feels when she tries to use her magic.

"What if it's not receding back into you, wherever it comes from. What if it's leaving you and being pulled to another source somewhere in the castle?"

"Can that happen?"

"I suppose it could. If they had a matching rune somewhere that connected with this one."

"So if we destroyed that store, we could convince him to take the ring off to fight against the Darkness," she says, her words coming faster with excitement. Finally, a plan. Something they can work towards.

"And then you'll be free from Theis," he adds.

"Free to make him pay," she says, grinning. She studies Vaaren to see how he responds. Theis is trying to control her; surely Vaaren would agree that he needs to pay.

"I'm sure he'll get what he deserves," he nods, smiling

briefly at her.

He reaches for her hand and squeezes gently before dropping it again. Not exactly the support she was hoping for, but not nothing. She sits next to him and they begin flipping through the rune book together.

~

Later that afternoon, Elayce finds herself in the training room with Harkn. She has so much energy built up from planning with Vaaren that she had to come burn it off before the festivities tonight. Tonight would be a competition between participating soldiers in her army. Hand-to-hand combat, archery, and swordplay, all while the royals and nobles watched, placing bets.

Harkn steps forward, catching Elayce off guard and punches her in the side. "My queen, you are distracted."

"There's a lot on my mind," she says, rushing him to catch his arm and twist it behind his back. Her body is pressed up against his back as she holds him while he struggles to get out of her grasp.

"I could think of a better way to distract you," he says to her, twisting his head so he talks to her over his shoulder.

She releases him and thrusts him forward, putting her arms back up to indicate she's not done fighting yet. "This is the only distraction I need from you, Harkn."

His eyes momentarily stray to Vaaren, who is in the corner of the room, pouring over his notes.

"Ah, yes, you will have a king by the end of the week," he says, circling her on the mat, searching for an opening.

She narrows her eyes. "King consort."

"Of course," he answers, nodding his head slightly but never removing his eyes from her.

CHAPTER 33

She maneuvers along the mat so that she's standing in between Harkn and Vaaren and then she launches at Harkn. They go several more rounds before she starts to feel calmer. Harkn bows out of the training room with a smile on his face and sweat running down his temples.

As soon as it's just Vaaren and Elayce, the temperature in the room drops. Elayce runs over to Vaaren, searching for the Darkness. But there's nothing. The Darkness doesn't show himself. Instead, a deep malicious laugh echoes through the training room, and then the temperature rises again.

"Are you okay?" Vaaren asks, staring up at Elayce from the floor.

"The Darkness is teasing me. It's unnerving," she answers, grimacing. She extends her hand to Vaaren to help him up. He pops up from the floor, clutching his notes in his other hand, his face only inches from hers.

"We'll figure it out," he says quietly.

She hums in response, caressing his cheek. They head back towards their rooms, hands close enough to touch but not quite. Elayce continues towards her own room, allowing Vaaren to enter his suite through his own door. Being engaged to Theis now, she is careful not to give anyone reason to declare a betrayal and demand Vaaren's head. She's got enough on her plate.

When she enters her own room, Darla is there waiting. Red faced and breathing heavily, she jumps as soon as she sees Elayce. "Oh, my queen," she says, curtsying quickly before continuing. "I've discovered something I think you'll want to hear right away."

"Go on," Elayce says, taking a seat at her vanity.

Darla rushes over, frenzied and nervous. "I've been searching for information like you asked me to. Trying to befriend the other attendants from the visiting countries, so they would trust me. It's been difficult, as though they've been told *not* to trust anyone from Aerash. It drives Cook mad actually, they're always testing the food more than once before it goes anywhere."

"The point, Darla?"

"Right. Sorry, my queen." Darla shakes her head. "Well I think I finally broke through to one of the men that serves King Theis, I think he fancies me." She clears her throat. "He says that King Theis and his advisors knew the proposal would be accepted. They started making security adjustments to the throne room before the proposal was even announced, just in case there was any dissent. Said that's why they showed up before the rest of the guests. Apparently, they've been making many changes to the security—"

"The throne room, you said?" Elayce interrupts her again.

"Yes, that's what he said. For King Theis's safety," Darla confirms, nodding her head vigorously.

What would he be doing in the throne room, and why? She hasn't been consulted about any changes. Now that she thinks about it, it was maybe too easy to sequester herself when Theis showed up. Perhaps she had played right into their hands. She'd been so stupid. Three whole days, she let Theis and his entourage move about her castle without anyone watching them. Some of her staff were likely even helping them.

She sighs, there are way too many things on her mind and things keep slipping away from her. She's so distracted by the Darkness that she let King Theis roam about to do as he pleased. Yet, now she's trapped by King Theis and unable to do anything about the Darkness. Then there's Vaaren, a welcome

CHAPTER 33

distraction, but maybe not timely. Which was likely the point all along and she played right into the rebels' trap.

The rebels. She hasn't even thought about them, and King Theis had flat out told her that they had approached him in an insurrection attempt. Hopefully, her problems would collide and the Darkness would take out the rebellion for her.

"Queen Elayce?" Darla asks, a look of confusion taking over.

Elayce waves her hand for Darla to get to work on her tangled hair. Darla's face falls a bit before her fingers continue their work.

"What could he possibly have done in the throne room?" Elayce murmurs.

"He did mention that there was a tunnel below the throne room that leads directly to King Theis's rooms. Maybe they were fixing it up as an escape route in case of an attack?" Darla offers.

Elayce sits up straight. A secret tunnel below the throne room would be the perfect place to hide something. The throne room is where she often displays her magic or conducts executions. It would make perfect sense to keep it nearby.

"Go get my clothes ready," she says to Darla, trying to get rid of her.

"But, your hair isn't done," Darla says, pausing with a pin partially shoved into Elayce's long hair.

"Go. Now."

Darla drops into a curtsy, letting Elayce's hair fall and backing away from her.

"Darla," Elayce calls out. "You've done well."

Darla's face beams and she turns towards the dressing room, disappearing around the corner. As soon as she's out of sight, Elayce rushes to Vaaren's room. She runs down the hallway and bursts in and finds him half dressed for the event tonight.

"Vaaren!" she exclaims, though this time he doesn't startle.

He raises an eyebrow at her. "We only just parted, what could have happened?"

"The throne room. He's storing my magic under the throne room," she blurts, a little breathlessly—from rushing over and maybe a little from finding him half naked too.

"How do you know that?" he asks.

"My maid, Darla, she said that one of Theis's men told her that they had made 'adjustments' to the throne room. That there is a tunnel that leads directly to his quarters for a quick exit."

He nods his head, throwing his shirt back on over his head. "I'll go check it out."

"But what about the competition tonight?" Elayce says, disappointment runs through her.

"It'll be the best time to go searching for what we need. Everyone will be at the competition and you will be able to keep an eye on Theis and make sure he doesn't leave before we find it." He comes to Elayce and puts a hand on her cheek. His eyes are searching hers for agreement. "Do you trust me?"

She leans into his touch. Vaaren's touch, not Ren's. This man who somehow went from hating her and cursing her to listening to her and then to standing by her. He was sent here to get close to her and trap her, and while he may have done both of those things she's stronger with him by her side, trapped only by his warmth.

"I do," she says, twisting her head to kiss his palm.

He nods. "Then let me handle this. Do what you need to do to keep Theis away."

Chapter 34

"What a beautiful night to be out watching this competition," Theis comments. Elayce is wearing a gold and magenta pant suit with a lengthy skirt overlay attached to her waist. Clearly, it's some sort of fashion from Selna, but she doesn't mind. While she loves her dresses, the leggings will make it easier in case she has to fight something on a moment's notice. She already had Darla request more be made.

They are sitting on a dais at the top of the stands that frame the training yard. The other visitors are all spread throughout the seats around and below them. The sun is slowly setting, sending golden rays across the yard and glinting off of the soldiers' armor as they move around the field.

"Quite," Elayce replies, briskly.

"It will be nice to see the sunset every night once I have my things moved over to our castle here in Aerash," King Theis says.

"You could always just stay in our summer house in Selna," Elayce suggests.

"I couldn't possibly spend so much time away from you, Queen Elayce," Theis replies, patting her arm.

"Pity." She focuses on the fight happening in the center ring.

"Besides, how will we produce an heir if we are so far apart?"

She snarls at him in response and rage pits in her stomach, but King Theis just chuckles. When she has finally removed this ring from her finger, she will start by showing him exactly what she thinks about having his heirs.

After that, King Theis doesn't try to talk with her, instead interacting with the royals that sit around them. Talking about his plans for moving their army once the marriage is done and how they plan to open more trade routes between Selna and Aerash. Elayce rolls her eyes, but lets him continue. As if he has any idea what's coming for him.

She glances at the space next to her where she wishes Vaaren was. By this time, he is probably in the throne room. Hopefully, he can figure out how to destroy whatever is stealing and holding on to her magic. She's been trying not to call upon her magic since they discovered what is going on, but old habits die hard. She doesn't want to give Theis the chance to take anything else from her.

The fight down in the field comes to an end and Captain Nolan names the winner and then calls up the next two soldiers. Polite clapping comes from the stands and several hands go up, calling for servants to take bets. The wooden scoreboard is updated with the most recent fight's results, pushing a new contender into first place. She doesn't recognize any of the names; nobody in her personal rotation is partaking in the festivities.

She shifts in her chair, her thoughts drifting to Ren and the training that they did when they first joined the rebellion. This was their preferred form of training, active combat. You learned quickly how to defend yourself, or you spent a lot of time with the camp mender. She and Ren had never been fighters, but Ren adapted quickly. Because of her magic she was able to argue her way out of being involved, claiming that she needed to focus on that instead of combat. Maybe if she had focused on both, things would have turned out differently.

Captain Nolan shouts again, calling the end of the fight. Murmurs and bid papers exchanging hands rustle through the crowd and the wooden board shifts once again. The fights are the last portion of the night, just in time too, because the sky is quickly becoming too dark to see.

"It is unfortunate that I can't light the braziers for our guests," Elayce says to Theis, drawing his attention back to her.

"If only you were feeling better, darling." He pats her hand. He raises his hand in a signal to the castle servants and the lights around the courtyard are lit all at once with fire torches. She grimaces at the unfamiliar red-orange of the flames. "Lucky for us, there are other ways of lighting the courtyard."

A scream comes from the fighting ring, cutting off Elayce's retort. She turns quickly to the ring, and then she feels the chill creep over her.

The Darkness stands holding a shadow dagger with blood dripping from it and onto the limp body that lays below it. Captain Nolan is floating a foot above the ground, his feet jerking and his hands scrabbling against the shadow wrapped around his neck. The shadow shies from the rune etched into his chest plate, expertly avoiding the light flowing from it. The other soldier cowers on the ground, his hands covering his head.

Elayce is already on her feet, her fingers twitching at her sides. If she tries to use her magic, everyone will know that she doesn't have anything right now.

The voice of the Darkness booms across the field, sending the people in the stands to their feet, cowering and covering their ears. Shadows creep their way up the stands, forcing everyone to remain where they are, lest they fall and break something. "Queen Elayce, the time for our reunion is almost here. How wonderful of you to throw a party to welcome me home." A smile forms in the shadow. The shadow shifts and twists, and then a body begins to form. First feet, legs, a chest and arms, the body slowly reveals itself from the shadows. It joins the smile that was floating alone just a moment ago and then eyes that she's loved for over three hundred years. Suddenly, Ren is standing in the ring, holding a bloody knife and a shadow rope wrapped around her captain's neck.

But Ren is dead, and...

"Lord Vaaren?" someone whispers, causing more whispers to build and spread. Hands come away from eyes to see that Queen Elayce's trusted Lord now stands in the ring, having killed a guard, threatening another. People shriek and shout, one lady even swoons.

King Theis stands. "Seize him!"

A few guards rush forward to obey. The smile on the Darkness's face grows wider, impossibly wider than that of a human's face. Shadows dart out from around him, striking the guards to the ground. Screams erupt from the crowd. A few nobles take their chances and try to run, but shadows find them too.

She whirls to Theis, speaking in a low voice only they can hear. "Remove this ring. Now."

He doesn't move to obey her and his mouth opens and closes like that of a dying fish. More guards rush forward, and instead of striking them down, the Darkness creates a shadow wall that they crash into, unable to penetrate or move forward.

"Soon, my love," the Darkness says, before disappearing into a swirl of shadow. Captain Nolan goes crashing to the ground, gulping air and touching his neck. Good. She can't lose anymore allies.

With the Darkness gone, the crowd jumps into motion, screaming and running to get to the castle. To a place where they might feel safe. It's chaos, everyone pushing to get out of there quicker than the person next to them. Elayce isn't even sure the woman who fainted was retrieved from the floor before the stampede began. Tydas appears near the king and queen and directs them to exit off the backside of the dais, quickly leading them to the castle and into a small room with no windows. She glances at her personal guards and sees that Phin is with her.

Before she steps into the room and as Phin is stepping into place to guard the door she grabs his hand and hauls him off to the side.

"Phin, I need you to do something for me," she starts. His eyes widen, but he nods.

"That wasn't who everyone thinks it is. It wasn't Lord Vaaren. I need you to go to the throne room and bring him into my rooms. Nobody can know where he's gone or where he was. He needs to be kept safe, Phin. Do you understand?"

He doesn't hesitate. "Yes, my queen." He bows and heads off in the direction of the throne room. She hopes that she can trust him, but she doesn't have another option right now. After that show by the Darkness, everyone will demand Vaaren's death.

She enters the room where Tydas, King Theis, and King

Theis's advisor are already talking and plotting as if it didn't matter that Elayce wasn't there.

"We will be ready next time, he just caught us off guard," King Theis says.

"Queen Elayce," Tydas says, clutching at his chest. "Why didn't you use your magic?"

Elayce's eyes slide over to King Theis. "The timing wasn't right. He would have been able to see an attack coming and to block it."

"As I said, we will be ready next time. Now that we know his strength is building and progressing so quickly." Theis paces across the room, tapping his finger to his chin. "The wedding should be moved up."

"The wedding? That's where your priorities are right now?" Elayce asks.

"Yes, that makes sense. We need to show everyone else that we're not alarmed and that we have things under control. Put a warrant out for Lord Vaaren's arrest. Anyone who sees any trace of him will report it and we might get a better picture of where he's hiding out," King Theis's advisor says.

"If only he was still locked up in the dungeons, this wouldn't have happened," Tydas says.

"Though the Darkness appeared as Lord Vaaren, he is not Lord Vaaren," Elayce answers through clenched teeth.

"Queen Elayce, obviously he used your promiscuous nature to seduce and deceive you." Tydas scoffs.

Her expression hardens, but she lets her body go languid. "Oh, is it obvious?" She saunters over to where Tydas is standing.

"Perhaps King Theis should be in charge. You...you let the Darkness into our midst and you couldn't even defend us when he finally showed his true nature." His face remains indignant, but he shakily backs away until he's pressed up against the wall and she looms over him.

"It is a good thing you're not the one to make decisions around here then," she whispers. She drags her sharp fingernail down his chin and to his throat, and suddenly it's no longer her fingernail, but the tip of a dagger. "Seduction can be such a useful tool. For instance, you didn't even notice my dagger appear. My slow walk over here made you believe that you didn't need to run. I've trapped you here, like a little rat. Now, you will die in this corner like the pest that you are."

She shoves the dagger into his throat and rips it swiftly across his neck. Blood spatters across the wall behind Tydas and his body starts to sink. With her other hand she grabs hold of his shirt, to stop his descent.

"You know how much I love to watch the light leave the eyes of my victims," she says in a low murmur. Her eyes glint, but she makes sure to hold back her magic. When his last breath ekes out, she lets go of his shirt and his body crumples to the floor, blood pooling around him.

She straightens and turns around, finding both King Theis and his advisor rooted to their places in shock.

"Find someone to take care of this," she says to the advisor. He gulps loudly and leaves the room to find one of her staff.

"Was that necessary?" King Theis asks.

"Likely it came later than it should have," Elayce replies. "Now, I would like to know how you plan 'to be ready next time' without removing this ring from my finger."

"Once we're married, I'll tell you how I plan for us to defend our kingdom."

She rolls her eyes, and wipes the dagger off on Tydas's

body before returning it back to its sheath in her clothing. "A marriage will mean nothing if we're all dead."

"We will not be dead. I have a plan, and that plan includes me being king of both Aerash and Selna."

"Fine. Have it moved up to tomorrow." Over her dead body will he rule her kingdom. "I refuse to remain defenseless against the Darkness."

"What happened last time? Why is it back?" King Theis asks.

His questions surprise her. Maybe the attack has rattled him more than he is letting on.

"I wasn't ready last time."

"You knew he wasn't gone?"

"Of course I knew," she snaps. "I just didn't know how long until he would return."

"Are you ready this time?"

She hears a hint of vulnerability in his question, maybe he truly does just want to save his people. Too bad caging her and trying to use her like his own personal weapon was the wrong way to go about it.

"I don't know."

Chapter 35

A sigh of relief escapes her lips when she sees Vaaren sitting on her bed among his books. He looks up at her and smiles.

"Your guard found me, told me to wait in here for you."

"The Darkness showed up at the competition; he took a form this time. Ren's form...or your form," she explains.

"Ah," he says, his green eyes clouding over.

"The wedding is moved to tomorrow, we're out of time. Were you able to find what you were looking for?"

"It took me a while. Theis's new throne covers the entrance. When I entered the tunnel from the throne room, there was a huge canister underneath. It was glowing."

"Glowing?"

He nods. "I think that's where they're storing your magic. I was able to find the runes that they had drawn on it and I drew a counter rune. It should cancel out the connection."

"That's amazing!" Elayce leans forward, planting a kiss on his lush lips. A warm hum runs through her, once again her magic is just hers.

"I still don't know how to get the ring off your finger, though." He stares at her hand with a look of frustration.

"Can't you use the same counter rune?" She holds her hand up, so they can both look at the ring.

"It doesn't work like that, the only way to deactivate the rune on your finger is the action of the correct person removing it." He shrugs.

They solved one problem at least.

"Let's hope that Theis can be convinced to remove the ring now that I'm his only option for fighting the Darkness." The plan is flimsy at best, but right now she isn't sure they have anything better. They sit in silence for a moment. So much less time than they needed to prepare properly. She still doesn't know how she will actually defeat the Darkness. Her light hadn't been enough to completely destroy him last time, he just retreated and regained power. She has to figure out a way to wipe him out completely or lock him away. An idea starts to form in her head, a dark one.

Before she can figure out the right words to voice her idea, he speaks. "I wish we had more time to infuse light into weapons and armor, so that more people at least had a chance to fight." He flops back on her bed, pulling her with him. She lay partially on top of him, tracing the curls of hair on his chest peeking out of his slightly open top. The books make for an uncomfortable bed, but she doesn't want to draw away from him to move them.

"What if you drew the runes now, and I infused them when we get this ring off of me?"

His hands tighten around her waist, pulling her into a kiss. "Elayce! You're a genius. I could draw them now, while everyone is sleeping. We won't be able to protect everything, but it would be better than nothing." His eyes light up and his body vibrates underneath her with excitement. She's a little disappointed that her own idea means that they have to leave the bed, but it's probably for the best. He kisses her temple before shifting her all the way onto him and sitting up. She's now straddling his lap, cursing the pant suit that she thought she liked only a few hours ago.

He clutches her ass, still holding her to him as he stands from the bed. "Where should we start?"

Her eyes slide to the bed, and he chuckles. "Come on, Laycie, we need to spend as much time as we can preparing."

She slides from his grip, her feet coming to land gently on the floor. "Queenly duties are never done," she sighs. She should really leave all the responsibilities to the heroes.

He squeezes her hand, glancing at the bed longingly. "Maybe there's a little time for that later."

~

Phin follows close behind them and she's glad it's Phin on duty. He's proven himself trustworthy.

They make their way to the armory, making sure to avoid anyone else. Vaaren spends several hours drawing runes on shields, swords, and chest plates. He even draws one directly onto Phin's chest plate and sword. Phin doesn't ask any questions, but his eyes grow big watching Vaaren work. Once a rune is placed, Elayce thinks it looks empty. Just waiting for her to fill it with her light. Frustration courses through her, knowing that she still can't reach her magic.

They make it through a good chunk of what's stored, but it doesn't seem like enough. There are tons of weapons and armor that soldiers are holding by their beds, camps that are stationed around the kingdom that they will never reach, and civilians who will never even see a rune come near them. She can tell that Vaaren is growing tired, but he's done even more than she could have imagined. Sheer determination is keeping him going at this point.

"Let's head to the throne room, you can show me what you found."

He nods his head, sleepily. Not only has he expended a ton of his energy through magic, but it's also far into the early morning hours and neither of them has slept. Once in the throne room, they lock the room behind them and he drops to the floor by her throne. She starts to tell him that it's the wrong one, but he begins drawing runes all over her chair.

"For extra protection," he explains.

He leans against the other throne, trying to push it forward. When it doesn't budge, Phin immediately jumps to assist him. The chair tilts forward on hinges and a staircase appears in the space below.

"How did I not know about this?" she asks out loud.

To her surprise, Phin answers, "It's an old tunnel system that was covered up and out of use."

"You knew this was here?"

"The royal guard knows about several passages within the castle in case we need to move any royal family quickly. But as I said, this one was deemed unsafe and with you on the throne, it wasn't considered necessary to rebuild it."

"Who gave the order to fix it recently?"

"I wasn't aware that any order was given, my queen," Phin answers. His eye contact is direct and unwavering, making her believe what he says. She isn't sure what changed in him and why he doesn't seem to be as afraid of her anymore.

Someone had to have given the order. If the royal guard knows about this, she wonders who else does. And who told Theis about it, but not her personal guard. Unfortunately, Tydas is no longer capable of answering her questions.

She begins walking down the stairs and Vaaren tries to follow.

CHAPTER 35

"Stay here, Vaaren. Rest." Then, addressing Phin, "Stay here with him. Get him to safety if anyone comes in."

She continues into the dark, once again, cursing that she can't use her magic to light the way. This is one of the simplest things she should be able to do for herself. As she feels her way along, finding the bottom of the stairs a faint glow comes from the other side of the room. She crosses to it and finds herself walking around a large metal barrel. The glow is coming from the largest one, and she can see smaller barrels scattered around the room. Some of the smaller ones glow as well, although some remain void of any light.

The largest barrel, the one that takes up the majority of the room, has a pipe that leads from it and down the dark hallway. Elayce shoves one of the glowing barrels and grunts as she rolls it down the hallway with her like a giant lantern. The barrel isn't as light as she expected it to be, but once she gets it moving, it's easy to keep it going. She stares at the ceiling of the tunnel, tracking the pipe that suddenly turns and goes into the wall to her left.

She rolls the barrel to the side and feels along the wall. There's no door handle that she can see or feel, but this pipe has to lead somewhere. Her hands graze over the cold brick of the tunnel wall. In a huff, she backs up to try to get a wider view of the area. The space is narrow and she only takes a few steps back before she's pressed up against the wall on the other side. Her elbow presses into the wall further than the rest of her body, and she realizes that she's actually pushing the brick backwards. She twists to get better leverage and continues pushing the brick, watching in triumph as a panel in the wall across from her slides down into the floor below.

She hears a grind of stone on stone and the brick stops

moving, the panel seeming to be completely flush with the floor now. She grabs the barrel and shuffles it slowly inside. She can see the pipe ends here in a wide funnel. There is a singular metal chair in the center of the room. It looks similar to one of the thrones above them in the throne room, but there aren't any cushions on it. The hard surface has thick straps attached at the feet, arms, chest, and head. She traces a strap with one of her fingers, feeling lines that must be runes drawn along them. She hisses, dropping the strap, unsure what it could do to her.

Were they planning on bringing her down here? Or maybe the Darkness? She scoffs at the idea that this could hold him. They could all see that the Darkness could come and go in the shadows. Unless...Unless he was trapped inside a physical form. She'll have to ask Vaaren if that might be a possibility. She backs out of the room and into the hallway again, staring down towards where the barrels of light are sitting. Her eyes track down the pipe, follow it back into the room with the chair and the straps.

If the Darkness were tied to the chair, and they moved the light into this room, would it kill him? Would the concentration of light be enough to rip him to shreds and finally be rid of him? It's a risky plan, they only have one shot. If it didn't work, they'd have to go to Elayce for more magic. Theis is delusional if he thinks she'd help, considering he made an enemy out of her too.

She has to get back to Vaaren and Phin. Elayce attempts to pull at the brick that she originally pushed to get the door open, but she can't grab hold of anything. She starts pushing on all the bricks surrounding it until she finally finds one that slides inward as the first one slides back out. When she looks over her shoulder, she can see the brick panel sliding upwards to close the room. She rolls the barrel back down the hallway, heaving it into a position by the other barrels.

At the top of the stairs she finds Phin standing next to her throne, Vaaren slouched in it.

"He tried sleeping on the floor," Phin explains.

She rounds the throne and reaches out to gently caress Vaaren's cheek.

"I'm awake," he mumbles, not opening his eyes.

"We have to go before someone finds us," she says gently, tugging on his hand.

With a deep sigh, he rolls up and out of the chair. His eyelids droop and he sways on his feet, but he stays standing. Where are all the guards? Phin seems to get more and more on edge the closer they get to her room without running into anyone.

"Something doesn't feel right, my queen. We should have passed a few guard rotations by now," Phin says, quietly.

Elayce is helping Vaaren into her room when she hears the pounding of footsteps coming down the hallway.

"Queen Elayce! Queen Elayce!"

She quickly stuffs Vaaren into her bedroom and shuts the door closed behind him.

A young woman with long red hair runs up to them. Immediately, Phin takes a defensive position in front of the queen, unsheathing his sword to threaten the woman running towards them.

The woman drops to her knees, breathing hard. "Queen Elayce, forgive my interruption, but there's been an attack. Staff have been searching for Tydas to send to you, but he hasn't been found, so they sent me."

"An attack? Where?" Elayce says, perhaps she should tell

her staff that Tydas is dead.

"On the borders of Aerash. The Darkness must have broken through your wards, Silia is being overrun."

Chapter 36

She would have felt it if her ward fell, but this is the same ward that wasn't where it should have been when she went looking for it. The shadow creatures had already been in the forest, but now a whole army was making its way towards the castle. Elayce sits at the head of the emergency council meeting. All the council members and King Theis had been roused from their beds and called to meet with the queen. With the absence of an advisor, she'd told the red headed woman to stay with her as a messenger.

"What are we going to do about this? It will spread to Donnen!"

"We should be worried about what's currently happening in Silia. Drive it back to Don Kemt."

"It's going to reach us here in Vleck! Where is Lord Vaaren and why hasn't he been apprehended?"

The council members talk over each other, speculating about where the Darkness would spread and how long it would take. Elayce locks eyes with Captain Nolan, standing just to her left.

"Report," she says, and the council members, thankfully, grow quiet.

"We're unsure when the army crossed the border, but the guard tower was completely overrun. The sole survivor made it because he took off immediately to warn us," Captain Nolan answers.

"Is he here?" a council member asks.

Captain Nolan nods.

"Bring him in."

Captain Nolan signals to a guard standing just inside the door of the tight meeting room. The guard opens the door and a disheveled soldier walks through. He doesn't have any armor on, and his clothes are ripped and covered in dark stains. He clutches a dagger in his hand, twisting and twirling it like a toy.

"He won't drop the dagger, captain," says the guard.

"It's fine," Elayce says. "Just tell us what you saw."

He gulps, and his body is visibly shaking. He locks eyes with the captain as he speaks. "It was…" he starts. His voice is raspy and weak. "We didn't stand a chance. A shadow rolled in, thick. So it couldn't be fog, but you could feel it around you. It was so hard to see, wiped out the lanterns." His eyes begin to drift to a point over their heads, like he's seeing it all over again. "We were scrambling, trying to relight the lanterns and armor up. Then…then the monsters came. Dozens of them. Maybe more. They were like, like deformed animals. Darker than the shadows, so you could barely make them out. What you could see though…" He squeezes his eyes shut and shudders. "You could see the shining, white teeth and then the blood. Pools of it."

A sob escapes him and the guard walks up to put a hand on his shoulder, but the soldier flinches and jumps away. He holds the dagger up to cover his face in a defensive pose before seeing that it's not an enemy.

"I left them. That was my duty. To come here and inform the

queen." He slaps his chest with the hand holding the dagger, coming dangerously close to cutting himself with it. "I did my duty. The shadows, they followed. I rode as fast as I could to get here and the shadows followed as far as Village Durst, when the sun started to come over the horizon. The barest sliver caused the shadows to stop. But I heard the screams. I still hear them." The last bit comes out in a rush, picking up speed and volume right at the end. "I can still hear them!" he shouts. Before anyone can make a move towards him, he raises the dagger and slits his own throat. His body slumps to the ground and the stench of blood permeates the air.

Elayce watches a thin black shadow seep from the body and dissipate into the air around them. A soft, low laugh bounces along the walls and this time everyone seems to hear it. It's a warning. Just like what happened last night at the competition.

"Gods help us," Council Member Gresha whispers.

The guard is momentarily frozen until Captain Nolan grunts. He goes to call for assistance with the mess.

"Queen Elayce, surely you can protect us. This is why you are our queen," Council Member Arvij says, panic and hope present in his voice. This is the reason she's been here the whole time, but only now are they going to acknowledge it.

"King Theis? What are your thoughts?" she asks, bile rises in her throat. She shouldn't have to answer to anyone.

"We need to lure the Darkness back here. His army will fall when he does. We shall continue with the wedding today as planned, at sunset. We can expect that he and his army will mobilize when the sun goes down. Until then, send word out to light as many fires and light sources as possible. King Guydor informed us that his men were more successful when using light against the Darkness. That's where we should start,"

King Theis finishes.

The council members nod and head out to give the orders and make arrangements. Anger floods through Elayce that they listen to him without question. Is she the only sane one around here? Why is everyone okay with continuing with this charade of a wedding?

"Your obsession with this wedding is obscene," she hisses to Theis once they are alone.

"Clearly, the Darkness is seeking you. What better way to lure him right here than to throw a lavish party in the wake of his destruction."

"What are you going to do once he's here?"

"Once we're married, I'll tell you," he answers, not meeting her eyes.

"I am not your weapon to control." Her voice is deadly and low, all the anger she's attempted to suppress coming out. He's whittled her use down to that of a weapon. A magic weapon. She is not a placeholder for a true ruler.

"Elayce, now is not the time." He begins walking out of the meeting room. "Only once I am declared the rightful king of both of the kingdoms will I let you in on my plans to save us." The door slams shut behind him before she can even respond.

She could chase after him, but chooses instead to heed his words. There's too many unknowns right now and it feels paralyzing to not have control. She hears the soft swish of a dress and realizes that they are actually not alone, that the red-headed girl has been present for the whole conversation. Elayce arches an eyebrow at her.

"I've heard nothing, ma'am," she says, curtsying low.

"What's your name?" Elayce asks.

"Asha," she answers, still not looking up from the floor.

CHAPTER 36

"How long have you been here at the castle?"

"Long enough to know what will happen to me if I... disappoint you," she answers.

Elayce hums in approval. "Lucky for you, I am in need of someone."

Asha's eyes bounce up to Elayce, wide and surprised. "I can't be an advisor, ma'am."

"I think I'm done with royal advisors for now, I simply need a messenger I can trust," Elayce says.

"That I can do, Your Majesty," Asha says, standing up straight.

"Great. Now, run along and let Loras know about the changes."

Asha nods and rushes from the room, determination replacing the surprised look on her face. Elayce has no idea if she can trust Asha or not, but she doesn't have time to find a replacement advisor. By tonight, everyone in this castle will either be reminded that she is the Queen of Aerash or dead.

~

Elayce is woken by Darla several hours later. After the morning meeting, she had come back to her rooms to find Vaaren fast asleep. Harkn is posted outside her rooms, perhaps he's the reason nobody has been able to enter her room to search for Vaaren. She had laid down beside him to feel his warmth and comfort and she must have dozed off as well. If Theis is right, tonight will be a long night and she needs the rest.

Vaaren doesn't stir even when she swings out of bed and heads to the bath to ready for the wedding. Her wedding, at a time like this, is ridiculous. She knows that her people don't like her, but surely they will be rioting in the streets now.

Ignoring the curfew that's in place for their own safety. She's hosting a wedding, while so many others are likely planning funerals. If there's anyone left to plan them.

Regardless, she needs to get this over with so that Theis will tell her what he's planning. Then she can figure out how to convince Theis to take the ring off her finger, and she can fight the Darkness with her full power. Without any time to prepare.

No pressure.

A splash of water lands on her cheek, and she turns to find Vaaren entering the bath next to her. His naked body sinks below the water line before she has a chance to appreciate it. She reaches for him under the water, connecting with his arm and drags him towards her. He slides across the bath, not stopping until his body is pressed along the side of hers and he wraps his arm around her shoulders.

"There would surely be a scandal if anyone came to find you in here with me, the morning of my wedding no less," Elayce teases.

"I'm sure you'd take care of any whispers. Anyway, surely their focus is elsewhere with the Darkness's approach," he says, nuzzling her ear.

"Nobody can keep their priorities straight around here, so I can't even begin to guess what they might find important at a time like this." She leans backwards into him, sighing with contentment.

They sit in silence in the bubbles, soaking in the feel of each other. It feels like the calm before the storm.

"Any chance you've discovered a rune that could help me with the Darkness tonight?" she asks, gently.

"Actually, after last night, I had the thought that we could place more light capturing runes around the throne room. You could lure the Darkness to the throne room, and then infuse the runes laid out in the room once he's there. Perhaps hitting him with light from all sides will trap him there, without a chance to escape the light that withers him."

"So, similar to what Theis had planned for him?"

He blushes a bit. "I may have followed that line of thinking."

"What if it isn't enough? What if we get to that point and he survives in the barest of shadows. We'd only have one chance."

Vaaren's head falls backwards.

Elayce clears her throat and spins so that she's facing him. "What if," she starts, "we use another idea that King Theis had."

"What do you mean?"

"What if we siphon the Darkness's power like he did mine?"

"Even if storing the Darkness's power somewhere was a good idea—which it isn't—where would we store it?"

"Within me," she says tentatively.

His eyes widen and he sits up straight, causing Elayce to slip away from him in the process. "No. That doesn't even make sense, Elayce. We need to keep the Darkness away from you, not offer him a way in."

"I am the embodiment of light, Vaaren. If we cage the Darkness's shadows within my power source, there is no way for it to escape. We can lock him in and there will be no way he survives," she explains.

"What if you're just allowing the Darkness in and it takes control? No. We would lose you and there would be nobody powerful enough to defeat the Darkness once combined with your power." He gets out of the bath, water trailing behind him as he walks. "I would lose you, Laycie, and I'm not doing that. I just found you."

"But Vaar—"

"No. I'm not discussing this."

"This is what I was given these powers for, Vaaren. My whole purpose is to defeat the Darkness," she pleads.

"Don't ask me to draw those runes for you. I can't do it."

"I'm asking you to trust me," she responds.

He doesn't say anything on his way out of the bathing room. Her stomach clenches with the feeling of wrongness. She only hopes that he learns to trust her before time runs out. For once, if someone could just choose her. There are so many people working against her, betraying her and worming their way into situations that only benefit them. They deliberately choose to not look at the whole picture simply because they don't like that she's a queen without a king by her side.

This whole time, Theis has been trying to be the hero and instead he's ruining their only chance for survival. How fitting that a jealous man would be the reason that the Darkness, born from jealousy and rage of some long ago fight between the Gods and Goddesses, would succeed. But Aerash is not his to take, and this is not his legacy to leave. He may be keeping her in the dark, but she is the light. All she needs to do is burn brighter.

Chapter 37

The doors open to the ballroom and all of the guests rise from their seats and bow as Queen Elayce walks down the aisle. Her dress is a silky white sheath with a tulle black over skirt that drags far behind her as she walks. There is heavy, dark beading along the top of the dress with sheer, loose sleeves that come all the way down her arms. She wears a heavy black veil that drapes down her back and covers her face as well, making it hard to see.

She walks down the extravagantly decorated aisle alone to a song that sounds more like a funeral march to her than anything marking a supposedly happy celebration. When she reaches the stage where Theis is standing in full Selnan regalia, he holds out a hand to help her up. Instead of taking his hand, she holds out her left hand to her side and a guard rushes forward from the wings to help her walk up the stairs gracefully. Only she can see the darkening of Theis's eyes.

"Interesting attire," he murmurs to her.

"I've never been one to follow the customs," she answers.

The ceremony itself is short and uneventful. They don't exchange any further jewelry and the kiss to seal the deal is barely a grazing of skin. Nobody interjects, despite a brief fantasy that Vaaren would come running down the aisle for her.

He is hidden away, guarded by Phin, for his own safety. They are still searching for him, but most think that he has fled the castle only to return when the army of Darkness shows itself. They are announced the Queen and King Consort of Aerash and Selna, turning to face the cheering crowd. Theis holds the tips of her fingers up in the air to join in the celebration.

"No quick-wit for me today?" Elayce whispers out of the corner of her mouth, while they allow the guests to rain their praise upon them.

"I've gotten what I wanted, Elayce, the ceremony is enough of a gloat," he responds.

He grasps her hand more firmly, to lead her to the next part of the wedding. Together they walk through the halls, followed by a parade of guests and a retinue of guards. They make their way to the throne room, and take their places side by side on the thrones. They will be here for several hours where anyone is allowed to come forward to swear their allegiance. With both kingdoms coming together, it will likely be longer than normal. Because of this, they have arranged for food and drinks to be offered by servants walking around with platters. Quiet music also sounds through the room.

"Is it safe to have so many people here still? Should we be cutting this part and moving everyone to the other ballroom for the official reception and dinner?" she asks.

He glances over to the window, where the last sliver of light from the sun is about to disappear. He nods. As he stands, a hush falls over the room.

"Gathered guests," his voice booms, "please join us in the ballroom for the more celebratory part of the evening." He smiles and the crowd chuckles, shuffling out of the throne room. As soon as everyone has cleared out, Theis turns and walks to the back of his throne. He gestures to a nearby guard, who steps forward and heaves against the chair. It grinds against the stone floor, revealing the steps down to the secret tunnel that Elayce and Vaaren had already discovered.

She cocks her hip and crosses her arms, loudly tapping her foot. His expression turns to a slight frown.

"Well come on then, dearest, we haven't got all night," he says, leading the way down the steps.

She follows behind without hesitation, understanding that they have very limited time before the Darkness shows itself here tonight. When they reach the bottom of the steps, Theis goes to the large container of light, his frown deepening.

"I thought it would be fuller by now," he mutters to himself.

"I'm sure it would be. If we hadn't already found it and cut the connection between the container and my ring," Elayce says, excitement rushing through her. It is finally time to get the ring off her finger and get her magic back. "I am the queen of this kingdom and now Selna, and you are nothing but a walking dead man. You can die by the hands of the Darkness or you can take this ring off and die by my hands. But trust me when I say you are not getting out of this alive." Perhaps threatening him with his imminent demise is not the best way to get the ring off her finger, but she's beyond that now.

"How do you think the Darkness gained access to Aerash?" The gleam in his eye makes her worry. He should be more disappointed that he has no other choice but to take the ring off. He should be quivering at the knowledge that his death is coming. Her mind stutters and scrambles to keep up, trying to understand.

"You're working with him?"

He scoffs. "No, of course not. But I did direct him away from

Selna. By allowing the Darkness through Silia, he halted his spread down the walls of the wards and towards Selna. The force that was slowly crawling its way into Selna retreated and rushed towards the opening they had been given. I told you," he continues calmly, "it's you he's after."

"How did you take down my wards?"

"Did you really think the ring was the only thing that the Runer of yours helped with? The rebellion knows where all of your wards are. Turns out Runers are well equipped to find runes, similar to a hunting dog." He smirks. "When the time was right, the rebellion took down your ward on the east side of Aerash to direct the Darkness in the right direction. Here, towards you."

"Like bait," she finishes for him. That's why she couldn't feel the ward stone when they were in Silia's forest. It had already been moved.

"When did Vaaren move the ward stone?" she asks. It was at least before she left on her trip with Vaaren and he had already been in the castle by the time she left for Selna.

"Thankfully, before they put that ridiculous memory rune on him. The rebels did it to protect their own operations, planting stories in his head about who he was before they sent him out. I'm sure they had no idea that he would turn on them, reverting back to his delusional belief in you."

"Belief in me?" she asks, her heart hammering in her ears.

His lip curls in disgust. "It was like he was on a one-man crusade to defend you. They had to torture him every step of the way to get what they needed before they were finally able to get the memory loss rune on him. But you can't keep evil locked away for long."

Her mind whirls with this information. Vaaren had been on

CHAPTER 37

her side before they tortured him and turned him against her. It makes sense now when he said that what they said to him didn't ring true—he had always believed in her.

"The ward is currently reset on the border between Silia and Donnen so the Darkness doesn't go any further south," he adds, smiling at his own cleverness.

"You've murdered all those people," she throws at him. Just like the rebels when she first joined them. You can't save people without sacrificing others. They scream their outrage about the way that she rules, when all rulers are the same. She just doesn't hide her choices in the shadows.

"As if you care about your people being murdered. Mine, on the other hand, I do care about." He pushes back from the table, ready to leave her to mull over everything he has revealed. How is he always so many steps ahead of her?

"What are you going to do about it once he gets here?" she asks, her fury pooling in her stomach.

"This will be enough I'm sure, although it would be better if it was full like I had planned." He pats the container, giving her a look as if he was chastising a child.

He moves over to a small chest partially hidden behind in the shadows. He pulls a key from his robes and bends over to unlock the chest with a soft click that echoes against the stone of the chamber. She stretches to her tiptoes so that she can see what he's collecting. She should have paid closer attention when she was down here the first time. She kicks herself for not thinking ahead. Her hands twitch toward one of the many knives hidden beneath the fabric layers of her dress.

When he spins around to face her, he's clutching a wand with both of his hands, presenting it for her to see.

"Take a look," he says, a crazed smile overtaking his face.

She reaches out to grab the wand, but he quickly pulls it out of her reach.

"Ah, ah, ah, Elayce, I said a look. Not a touch." He slowly extends his arms again, so that she can see it clearly in the light from the container. His tone has the joking, smugness that she was waiting for all night. The sound grates on her ears.

She focuses on the wand. It is smooth and looks to be plated in gold. It's longer than any of the daggers she has attached to her body, but it doesn't look sharp. She can see that there are runes inscribed along the body of it, but without Vaaren here she has no idea what they mean.

"It is obvious that you discovered the runes on the container and that they were connected to the ring you wear. But the ring is also connected to this wand here. I can wield your light through the connection." He waves the wand gently towards an unlit sconce on the wall and a soft gleam of light shoots out and sticks to the sconce, casting a bigger glow over the whole room. A soft twitch of pain echoes through Elayce's hand at the same time and she hisses, clutching her hand to her chest.

He smiles before continuing. "Yes, well, taking magic is going to be painful. As would forcefully taking or removing any other part of your body or soul."

She lunges for the wand, but Theis is quick and steps back, holding the wand high above his head. Guards' hands close roughly around her arms, pulling her back away from Theis. She could easily throw them off of her if she wasn't wearing this infernal dress.

"Will you ever learn to play nice?" Theis asks her with a tinge of exasperation. "The wand only works for me. It really is a pity Runers aren't more common. Thank you for keeping mine safe, though we will have to do something about his allegiances." He strokes the wand in his hand, examining it with pride.

"You will not touch Vaaren," she snarls, struggling in the arms of the guard.

He just smiles, pausing a beat before moving past her comment. "You have another option here, Elayce."

"I could just kill you and let the Darkness take over the world?"

"Gods, no. I once offered you the chance to work together as partners. You refused, and pushed me to this. But we could still work together. If you push your magic through the connection and to the wand, it won't be painful. Just as it was when you were filling the container with your light, you didn't even know it was happening."

"What makes you think that I would ever help you after everything you've done?" she asks.

"You've been preparing for this fight since your last encounter with the Darkness, I doubt you'd give up now."

She scowls at him, annoyed that he's right. He nods to the guards and they release her, and she stays in place. Scowling, but listening.

"I need you to channel your magic through the wand, so that I can get the Darkness into the chamber down the hall. Once he's strapped into the chair, the runes will hold him in place. We can bombard him with the light we've collected in the container. He'll have nowhere to run, he'll be defeated. Finally. And we will be the heroes who defeated him and saved our kingdoms."

Her breathing accelerates and the walls begin to feel like they're closing in around her. The temperature is dropping and she knows the Darkness is growing nearer and nearer. She can't even pace because the size of this ridiculous dress takes up the extra space in the room. Three hundred years to plan for this moment and this fool steps in and ruins everything. Not that she really had much of a plan until Vaaren came along. Even now, Vaaren didn't agree to help her with the plan she came up with.

She sways on her feet. Would Theis's plan really work? He seems quite sure that this could really be the end of the Darkness. This can't be what the Goddess meant for her to do. This was her task. Right? Was the Goddess wrong? Maybe she was never meant to do it alone. Maybe she's been waiting for Vaaren for three hundred years to come along and give her the runes that she needs. But he was discovered by the wrong side and now this is what she has to work with.

"Might I remind you of the time constraint?" Theis asks, breaking into her panic. She grunts and faces the wall, just for some semblance of privacy. She is being ridiculous and Theis is right. There is no time left and this plan—it could maybe work.

"Show me the chamber," she says, spinning around to face him again.

He smiles, slightly bowing and gesturing for her to head down the hallway first. She begins walking, the tulle layers dragging and snagging on the stone walls and floor. She makes a frustrated sound, whipping out a knife and slicing through the belt that keeps the tulle attached around her waist. It flops to the floor behind her. She's not quite done though, leaning to the ground to grab the bottom of the sheath. She sticks the knife in and drags it up along the fabric, cutting a slit up to her mid-thigh, making it easier to walk.

CHAPTER 37

"Take care of that," she says to a guard, pointing to the abandoned tulle before strutting down the hall.

Chapter 38

In the chamber, Theis picks up the straps on the chair and points to the runes. "We need to infuse these with your light to make sure that they can hold the Darkness."

Vaaren might not have access to his previous memories, but clearly some things must have broken through. It's the same idea he had for the weapons and armor for her army. Maybe he was able to draw a weakened memory rune so that he could find his way to her somehow.

Theis stretches the strap out across the chair and points the wand at the runes. "Okay, Elayce."

She hesitates, wracking her brain for one last option that isn't working with Theis. This man who has caged her and is already using her like his own personal assistant.

"I do this with you, and you don't hurt Vaaren," she says. She'll do it anyway, she wants to defeat the Darkness and she doesn't have a better plan. But, she'll take anything that she can get.

Theis exhales through his nose. "If it gets you to do this faster, then fine. I will not hurt Vaaren."

She scowls at his sarcasm, flushing. Of course he's not going to harm Vaaren, not as long as he can use him too. She takes a deep breath and calls to her magic. The warmth wells inside of her, a feeling that she hasn't felt in several days. The longest she's gone without feeling her magic since it was bestowed upon her.

This time, instead of feeling it fizzle out when she tries to call it forth, she tries to direct it toward the ring on her finger and push it through. It feels wrong, like it's being squeezed instead of released, but it works as she watches her light burst out of the tip of the wand instead of around her. Theis was right, she doesn't feel any pain. It's strange, to feel her magic in use, but watching it come from somewhere that isn't her own body. She feels a detachment, like she's actually watching herself from above.

She tries to call to it. Now that it's outside of her body and beyond the lock maybe she can control it. It doesn't feel natural, like the sparks themselves are lifeless. The magic doesn't respond to her, but it does respond to the wand and Theis's movements.

Hope begins to build within her, maybe this could work. Darkness today, Theis tomorrow? One enemy at a time. She watches Theis slowly direct the beam of light from rune to rune, each one accepting a small piece of her and beginning to glow. Theis's face gleams with the light from the wand, but also with a look of triumph.

"I've done it!" he cries out; he tilts the wand and the beam of light tapers off. Every rune on the straps is now glowing as well as various ones that line the chair. She isn't sure what they all mean, but she is sure that Theis has actually done none of the work.

"Now what?" she asks, crossing her arms.

"Now we lure the Darkness down here and trap him in this chair. The runes will lock him down. Then we release the light from the container, snuffing him out." Theis is smug. Not a shred of doubt within him.

"And how do you plan to lure the Darkness down here with us?"

"Keep up, my dear, as I've already told you, he is looking for you. He will come directly to us." He slips the wand into a sheath attached to his belt. The wand disappears into the folds of his cloak. He marches past her and back down the hallway, gesturing for her to follow.

"Don't you think he will grow bored of me quite quickly once he realizes I don't have my magic?" she says, shuffling down the hall and up the stairs behind him.

Instead of answering, he slows as he gets to the top of the stairs. There is a black fog creeping over the edge of the staircase and falling down into the depths where they are hiding. Unfortunately, the stairs aren't wide enough and she can't see past Theis.

Maybe she doesn't need to see though. Because she feels him, instead. The temperature dropped before during his visits, but that was nothing compared to the icy cold that greets her now. She flashes back to all those years ago when she stood in this same room and faced him. She won that battle, but did she really? She lost Ren. Her mom. She lost her right to choose her path. Everything she's done in the last three hundred years is because she's been preparing for this moment. She's not quite sure it'll be enough.

A trail of blood leads from their feet to the doors that are now shut tight, coated in shadows. The guard that was here with them isn't any longer, and she assumes that it's his blood that coats the floor.

A loud, deep laugh echoes around them, nearly masking the

screams coming from beyond the throne room doors.

"Laycie," the Darkness says. The sound is low with layers so deep that it feels as though you could fall into it.

Theis steps aside, letting her get her first full view of the Darkness in three centuries. He stands wreathed in shadows, casual in his stance. The face he's wearing is that of Ren's, except the eyes. The eyes are a deep, endless blackness. When he sees her, his smile stretches into a too wide grin that contorts Ren's image in ways that she's never seen on a person before.

A sob crawls its way up her throat and she attempts to cover it. Her knees wobble slightly, but she remains standing. She remembers the feel of his warm skin as it turned cold in her arms, clutching him after he died. The soft, papery skin of his eyelids as she closed them never to see that gorgeous green color again.

Until Vaaren.

The thought of Vaaren fills her with strength, her fear and sadness warming into a white hot fury.

"You," she whispers. "You will not live to see another night."

He chuckles, shaking his head. "All this time, and you still have not learned the truth?" He begins taking slow, languid steps towards her. His steps don't make any noise.

"We could be better together, you know. We would be unstoppable. This world would be ours. And perhaps other worlds as well." His path begins to circle around her, toying with her.

"Other worlds?" she asks.

"The worlds where the Gods reside. The Goddess of Night created me to take over this world and the next and the next.

As a punishment to her lover, whom she found in bed with her sister, the Goddess of Light—"

"Thankfully, the Goddess of Light blessed our Queen with her gifts to defeat you," Theis shouts with a flick of the wand in the Darkness's direction. Much quicker than the beam of light, the Darkness disappears with another malicious laugh. Theis and Elayce swivel back and forth, searching.

She feels five cold fingers squeeze around her neck, his cold presence pressed up to her back. Her body stiffens as his rotten breath snakes into her ear from behind.

"You haven't told them where your power comes from, then. Naughty, naughty."

Clutching her chest as soon as she's released from his grip, she gasps and leans forward. She looks over at Theis whose eyes flash with confusion and then fear when the Darkness appears beside him instead with one arm around Theis's shoulder like they're good friends.

"Why don't you ask your little wife here who she is really blessed by?" A finger drags down Theis's face before giving him a quick slap to the cheek that leaves a red mark.

Theis's eyes drift from the Darkness back to Elayce. He presses his lips into a thin line, as if defying the Darkness. The Darkness just watches Elayce with a hungry look.

"It wasn't the Goddess of Light who visited me." Elayce drops her hand from her chest and stands up straight. If she's going to say this out loud for the first time, she's going to do it with a little respect.

"It was the Goddess of Night. She gave me a small drop of a gift she had stolen from her sister to clean up the mess that she made." She spits out the last part at the Darkness.

His wide smile falters and turns down into a sneer. "I am

the greatest creation the Goddess has ever made."

He takes a step towards Elayce and she takes a step backwards. Out of the corner of her eye she sees Theis side step so that he's directly behind the Darkness. All she has to do is keep his focus, so Theis can use the wand to trap him and push him into the chamber. The bait. She can be the bait.

"If you were the greatest creation, she wouldn't have realized that she needed to rid the world of you," she says, taking another few steps backwards. The Darkness follows, his shadows twitching and flickering.

"If she really wanted to be rid of me, she would have come herself. Or sent someone more powerful than a mortal with a drop of stolen magic." He lunges towards her, only able to grab onto her long hair that flies forward with the sudden motion of her dodge backward.

She cries out in pain as she runs down the stairs, yanking her hair out of his grasp. She flies down the stairs, knowing that he's following her. Hoping that Theis is right behind, but unable to hear anything over her own panting.

She's moving so fast that when she makes it to the chamber, she runs into the stone frame trying to make a sharp turn. She clutches her arm and comes to a stop in the far corner. She needs to get him in far enough for Theis to trap him.

The Darkness whooshes in, his shadows filling up every corner making the already dark room even darker.

"You can't hide in the shadows, Laycie. I am the shadows, the darkness that fills the corners and shades your secrets." He moves slowly, again, with purpose. He stalks her, like she's his prey.

"I'm not hiding from you," she says, "I'm leading you to the light." She pushes all of her magic towards the ring, which explodes in a burst behind the Darkness. She sees Theis straining to hold onto the wand, directing it at the Darkness. The light hits its mark and branches out to wrap around him. Screams erupt from all around them as the shadows battle with the light.

Theis grunts and shifts his whole body to direct the light and the Darkness towards the chair. The Darkness is screeching and writhing while pillows of smoke eke off him where the light is wrapped around his figure. He loses his hold on Ren's face and Elayce watches in horror as Ren's face decays rapidly. The skin stretches and peels away to reveal muscles pumping and pulsing with black blood before the muscles dry up and shrivel, leaving clumps of sinew clinging to bone. All three hundred years pass by in thirty seconds, bone finally flaking off to reveal the Darkness's true form.

He looks like a solid shadow, whorls of gray and black moving about within him. His black eyes glare out from his sunken face, locked on Elayce as he attempts to rip from the chains of light. He continues to scream in what must be another language, because she doesn't understand the words coming from his mouth. She can understand the sentiment, though. He is enraged. If they don't get him strapped down in this chair and take care of him soon, she's not sure Theis will be able to hold him.

Frustration courses through her, knowing that she can't direct her own magic to force him into the chair. The two most powerful beings in the world, and they are both caged by the same man.

"We have to get him into the chair!" she shouts to Theis. The shadows swirl and blow around them all, creating a wind tunnel that echoes the Darkness's screams.

CHAPTER 38

"Help me!" Theis shouts to her. The veins in his hands pop with the effort of trying to hold onto the wand and the magic. The thought of leaving him to watch his own failure briefly floats through her mind, but they've come too far now.

She crouches and tries to shuffle over to him, against the wind and the shadows and the ear piercing sounds coming from around her. For every foot she's able to move forward, she slides a few inches back along the hard stone. Slowly, slowly she is able to creep closer to Theis. As soon as she's within arms' reach, she reaches out and grabs him, using him to haul them both closer to each other.

He grunts and strains with the effort of holding on to the wand. She covers his hands with her own, forcing down the repulsion she feels from the skin to skin contact with him. The magic moves a bit easier, although she doesn't know if that's because she's the one directing the wand or if because the ring and the wand are so close now. Together, they are able to slowly direct the Darkness towards the chair.

Just as he's in front of it, Elayce feels Theis rotate the wand. The straps on the chair fly up in response, waiting to clutch their victim. He thrusts the wand forward, one final push to propel the Darkness into the waiting final prison. He lets out a loud "oomph," interrupting his screeching only momentarily. The straps fly over his chest, his head, his arms, and his shadowy legs.

The shadows swirl even faster and the chair shakes with the force of the fight the Darkness is putting up. Theis grabs Elayce's arm, dragging her back with him. She trips over the back of her dress, not taking her eyes off of her long-time nemesis.

Suddenly, the stone door closes just in front of her face and she realizes that Theis dragged her back far enough to remove her from the room. He's panting, but he's still in motion, running down the hallway towards the canisters.

She places her hands on the stone wall. The cold is seeping through, but the wind that surrounded her a few moments ago is gone. It feels as if the whole world has stopped moving, a stark contrast to before. The screams and shrieks from the Darkness are muted to a point where she knows that nobody above them can hear anything. She presses her ear to the wall; she wants to listen for his demise.

She hears a loud thump and then the shrieking reaches a peak before slowly, slowly fading away. She slumps to the floor, still pressed up to the door.

Theis comes running down the hallway. "Is it done? Is he gone?"

The goosebumps that lined her skin begin to fade as the temperature begins to rise. Silence permeates from the locked room.

"We'll have to open the door to find out," she says quietly from the floor.

Theis nods to himself and moves to the hidden mechanism. He hesitates.

"Maybe we should give it a few moments," he says, leaning against the wall.

They wait in silence, getting their breathing back under control. The last few minutes wash over her and she feels as though she might be sick. She can't believe that she finally faced the Darkness again. She knew the key to defeating him would be to combine runes with her magic. If only she had discovered Vaaren earlier, the terror that controlled her could have been washed away long ago.

CHAPTER 38

"Back up," he commands.

She pushes to her feet and backs up. The stone door brushes harshly against the floor as it opens. Inside the chair is empty. The shadows that were circling are gone. The icy temperature has warmed. The only sign that the Darkness was ever here are the burn marks at the edges of the chair.

She takes a step inside, followed by Theis.

"Do you...sense him at all?" Theis asks hesitantly.

She cocks her head to the side, focusing on her body. She checks in with herself from the tips of her toes all the way up through the tips of her ears. She notices the absence of the light, but she also notices the absence of the dread and cold that usually come with being near the Darkness. There is no prickle at her neck, no finger twitch looking for her magic. There is just...nothing.

"No," she breathes.

Chapter 39

Theis exhales a whoop of celebration. "I saved us!"

Elayce turns to him and crosses her arms. She should be happy too, celebrating that the Goddess's order has finally been carried out. But instead she just feels...empty? Lost? No, that's not quite right. She's relieved that the Darkness is gone, but she knows her battle isn't over. How will she rid herself of Theis, the idiot. He'll never release her on his own. They both know that she would happily melt him from the inside out once she has control of her magic again. Only, the rage that usually fills her is gone too.

"Follow me," he says confidently, and because she doesn't know what else to do, she does. She's been waiting so long to be rid of him, but this isn't how she thought it would go. Maybe she should be grateful? Nobody was hurt and they won.

Theis strides ahead with purpose, Elayce jogs lightly to keep up. A cold breeze sweeps from behind her just as they crest the stairs together to find Vaaren standing there.

"Vaaren!" she says.

"Elayce," he breathes and runs towards her. They crash into each other's arms. His eyes are wet and rimmed in red. His hands roam over her body, checking for injuries.

"I'm okay, it's okay," she tells him, planting kisses across his face. Finally, she feels something, as the warmth of being near Vaaren rushes through her to replace the empty cold the Darkness had left behind. "The Darkness is gone."

He sags into her, squeezing her as tight as he can. "You did it," he says.

"How did you know he was here?" she asks.

"He downed a few guards, leaving a trail of bodies from the front of the castle to the throne room. Once everyone realized you two were still in here, they did everything they could to get inside, but there were shadows blocking the doors. A few minutes ago they just disappeared, along with the shadow creatures roaming the castle. I'd hoped that meant that you had taken him down," Vaaren explains.

A group of guards and staff creep cautiously into the room now that the doors are open. Most everyone is covered in wounds, blood dirtying their clothes and armor. They step over several bodies strewn across the threshold, as if they were piled up against the doors before the shadows released their hold on them.

Theis clears his throat, but Elayce glares at him from over Vaaren's shoulder, clutching him even tighter. She bares her teeth for good measure.

"We both know that you have no power here, wife," Theis says, waving the wand back and forth.

A rush of frustration courses through her and she reaches for one of her hidden daggers underneath her skirt. The dagger is sailing through the air towards him, before Theis even knows what's happening. Her arm remains outstretched in his direction, so there's no mistake about her intent. Theis squeaks and ducks, clutching his ear. When he pulls away, blood coats his fingers. Outrage covers Theis's face and he opens his mouth to speak, but he's cut off by a booming laugh.

"There's that spark, Laycie," the Darkness's voice rings out. Shadows spring up everywhere, bringing the cold back with them.

"Did you really think you got rid of me? We didn't even get to have any fun," the Darkness's voice rumbles. He appears, twirling the knife she just threw at Theis between his fingers. The doors swing shut again with the sickening crunch of bodies being pushed out. She catches a glimpse of Council Member Arvij's terrified face just before it shuts—the cowards.

Elayce shoves Vaaren behind her, but it doesn't matter because the Darkness is focused on Theis. A tendril of shadow shoots out and wraps around Theis's waist, hauling him up and backwards through the air. If he dies, so does the hope of removing the ring. Her magic could be trapped within her forever.

She sprints down the length of the throne room, funneling magic into the ring. Theis is shouting and waving the wand about him. Bursts of light race through the air, sometimes colliding with shadows but mostly colliding with the room. Giant chunks of stone fall from the walls and the ceiling. She dodges to the side as a chandelier falls, but not quick enough. She screams as she's sent sprawling. Her dress is torn open and a large bloody gash runs down the side of her leg.

"Theis, you idiot!" she screams at him, pushing herself from the ground and continuing her mad dash to get to him. She longs for her magic to answer to her instead of this arrogant asshole.

Her leg stings, but she pushes the feeling down deep. Now is not the time to succumb to weakness. She lunges for the Darkness, but he reappears by Theis before she even closes her

CHAPTER 39

arms around the space where he used to be.

"You let them cage you, my Laycie," he says. He's wearing Ren's face again, but in its partially decayed state. Like he can't quite hold on to the healthy mirage of what Ren used to look like. The grotesque image makes her stomach churn. "All this time, I've waited to gain power so that I could come here knowing that I wouldn't lose. What a waste."

Suddenly, he's in front of her, fingers wrapped around her neck once again. She scrambles to clutch his fingers and feels the skin peel away from his bones. She'd gag if she could breathe properly. Her vision dims at the edges. She kicks and writhes as he lifts her higher from the ground, watching gleefully through Ren's eyes as she struggles. But Ren would never have enjoyed this.

A loud "No!" sounds from the other side of the room. For the first time, the Darkness notices Vaaren.

No, no, no, why didn't he stay hidden? Vaaren is holding what looks like a makeshift shield with a rune drawn on it. Light flares from it, but it's not quite the same as her own light. It's dim and more orange than her yellow-gold. This rune must produce its own light. But even she knows that it isn't nearly enough. Vaaren must know that as well.

The Darkness drops both Theis and Elayce to the ground. Both of them sputter and inhale deep, gasping breaths. She reaches out to grab the Darkness's shadow cloak, but he just kicks her hand, causing her to release a breathless shout.

"You didn't tell me that the Goddess sent you a gift," he muses.

"I don't know what you're talking about," Elayce gasps, trying to catch her breath.

"He's a Runer—I can feel it. I wiped all the Runers out while I was in hiding. This one reeks of the gods. The Goddess of Night must have sent him to you, even made him recognizable to you." The Darkness looks over his shoulder at Elayce. The green eye, set in lines of bare, pulsing muscle—a twin to Vaaren's own eyes.

Of course, Vaaren is a gift from the Goddess of Night! The key to finally being able to use her first gift—her magic—to really defeat the Darkness. This is why she felt such a strong pull to him all this time. It was a sign that she was meant to trust him.

"Why would the Goddess of Night send me to Elayce?" Vaaren bravely asks.

Please, please don't turn away from her now.

Elayce winces when the Darkness laughs again. "My, my, you really have kept your secrets."

Vaaren's jaw sets, putting the pieces together.

"I'm sorry," Elayce gasps, attempting to stand. "Nobody would trust me if they knew the real Goddess that blessed me. I barely have a leg to stand on as it is." Vaaren has to understand where she's coming from. "But, Vaaren. You have to remember that you were always on my side. You always believed in me before the rebels took that and hid it away from you. You were sent by her to help me finish this."

He doesn't say anything, just looks from her to the Darkness.

"Your one and only love doesn't even trust you now that he knows who you really are. But I do. I know who you are and I know who we could be together. Join forces with me, Laycie. We'll make them all pay." He reaches out towards her, palm up.

He's saying all the right things. Yet, there isn't a single part of her that wants to take his deal. She doesn't hesitate.

CHAPTER 39

She lunges for him again, a blast of light from Theis's wand accompanying her. The light pierces him this time and she's able to grasp him, bringing him to the floor with her. There's a dagger in her hand before she even has to think about it and she stabs it directly into his eye. He screeches, and quickly disappears from beneath her, reappearing a moment later next to Theis again.

"Time to get rid of you, little nobody," he says. He picks Theis up from the floor and throws him. Theis smashes into the wall and slumps to the floor, chunks of stone falling around him. Blood drips from the corner of his mouth and cuts mar any exposed skin. He doesn't move, the wand tumbles from his limp hand at his side.

She moves faster than she's ever moved, rushing to make sure the Darkness doesn't get a hold of the wand. Shadows are darting around the room, blocking out light and smashing through decorations and walls and pillars, but she doesn't see the Darkness.

She makes it there before him.

She grabs the wand tightly. She could use this to expend her own magic, but she knows that it doesn't have the same level of finesse that she does when she's controlling it with her body and soul. Nothing can compare to the way she connects to her light, deep down. She touches Theis's neck, looking for a pulse. Before she even finds one, his eyes flutter open and he lets out a weak cough.

"Take the ring off me, Theis," she says, leaning in close so he can hear. She puts her hand on his own. He doesn't move, but his glassy eyes flick up to hers and then down to the wand.

She takes a chance and lifts the wand up between their faces. With a quick flex, the wand snaps in half.

"There is no way for you or I to use my magic through this ring anymore, Theis. Take. The. Ring. Off."

"My kingdom..." he wheezes and chokes.

"I can't save anyone if you don't take it off," she says.

His head shifts in what she thinks is meant to be a nod, but he coughs before he can finish the movement, blood dribbling down his chin. His fingers twitch around hers in an attempt to close, but she doesn't think he'll be able to grasp the ring on his own. She reaches over and gently helps him close his fingers around the ring, shifting her body to shield them both from view.

His fingers are barely closed around the ring, but she pulls her hand away from him and the ring stays in his fingers. The metal feels smooth and cold against her skin and she is momentarily bewildered by the ease of which it slides off her finger. A shadow whips around them, knocking Theis's head back against the wall with a loud crack. She throws up a shield of light to block any more attacks. Her entire body warms and sizzles and it feels like it's saying hello. She revels in the feeling of having this piece of herself back.

He coughs again, slumping slightly to the side. She places her hand on his shoulder, propping him up so that his head rolls and he's looking her in the eyes.

"I will see you burn before I listen to you claim my victory again," she whispers.

His eyes widen and he begins to moan and tremble. The smell of burning fills her nostrils and she smiles. His skin begins to bubble and blood bursts forth from the boils before new boils reform to take their place. His moans turn to screams that crescendo and peter out quickly. It doesn't take long before she fulfills her promise of burning him from the inside out and she finally gets to see the light leave his eyes. Rejuvenated by the return of her magic, she's ready to face the Darkness.

She whirls around and her sparks light up the space around her. She throws her arms out in front of her and her magic answers, flying ahead of her, spearing shadow after shadow. She draws her arms back into her chest and the sparks return back to her, flipping and spinning and whirling through the darkness, clearing the space around her.

For the first time in days, she feels balanced. She darts through the room fighting off the shadows that thrash around her. They disappear with each one of her touches, but there seems to always be another shadow to replace it. She keeps her momentum going, the thrill at seeing her magic shine pushing her forward. She hits some of the runes Vaaren drew over the previous few nights, making it harder for the shadows while they dip and dive to avoid her.

"Darkness, come out to play," she calls. She is ready for this fight to finally come to an end.

He's suddenly right in front of her, so close that she almost smashes right into him. The too-wide smile is plastered across his face. His eyes reflect the sparks of her light back to her.

"I've been waiting for this moment," he croons.

He lashes out with a dagger-shaped shadow. She barely has a chance to throw herself out of the way, a small cut appearing across her collarbone, the strap of her dress hanging limply off her shoulder. She grasps the air in front of her and pulls apart, forming a spear of light in between them. She spins, letting the spear fly from her grasp. The Darkness throws a hand up, creating a shadow-shield moments before it hits him in the chest. The tip of the spear drives through the shield, and then both fall to the floor. She can see that a small drop of thick, black liquid is leaking down his front.

She smirks.

He appears suddenly in front of her again, exuding dark shadows that jolt towards her. She dodges and swipes with her light, but she isn't fast enough to escape every shadow. They're stuck, matched in a flurry of light and shadows.

He thrusts his arms out to the side and then brings them together in a loud clap, shadows and darkness converging around her faster than she can slap away. He breaks through the shadows and clenches her throat, but almost as suddenly, he lets her go. He's clutching his hand, and they both watch the steam that comes off the burn. She reaches up to her tender neck and feels the imprint of him on her. They burned each other.

She drops to her feet, swinging her leg out and kicking his feet from underneath him. Instead of falling to the floor like she intends, he disappears in a puff of shadow and glides away. Shadows from all around accost her. She swings and kicks and dodges her way out of the shadows, but she can already feel herself slowing. She's trained hard, but with the distraction of this week and the loss of her magic for several days, she knows that she isn't at her best. The worry and the fear begin to creep in; then she hears metal sliding across the floor and a dagger comes to a stop at her feet.

She looks down at the dagger and sees a light holding rune drawn in it. While continuing to fight off the shadows, she tosses an extra beam of light towards the dagger and scoops it up. Wielding the dagger along with her sparks, she fights her way out of the tornado of shadow swirling around her. Panting, she looks around to the dais to find that the Darkness has an arm and several shadow binds wrapped around Vaaren.

CHAPTER 39

"Here we are again," the Darkness says to Elayce.

Chapter 40

"It's not going to happen the same way this time," she says. Elayce throws the knife, sending sparks along with it. The Darkness must not have expected her to act so brashly because the sparks and the dagger find its mark within his chest. He stumbles backwards, clutching the light-infused dagger and disappears into a cloud of shadow once again. The shadows swirling around the room tell her that this isn't over yet.

She rushes up the dais to Vaaren, who's now kneeling on the ground. There are thick, red welts on his skin where the shadows had been wrapped around him.

"Vaaren, I need you to trust me," she says to him. Her breathing is heavy and her words are rushed. She almost thinks he'll flinch away from her touch after what he's learned about her magic, but he surprises her with a firm touch.

"I'm not helping you draw the Darkness into you, Elayce. I've been drawing more runes around the room while you've been fighting, use it to light him up from all sides," he says, pointing to the runes.

"It isn't going to be enough. He's going to find a small sliver of shadow to hide in just like he did in the chamber. Please just trust me. We need to siphon his magic into me, so that his power is dissolved within my own well of light." She pauses, clutching one of his hands between hers. "Please. Remember who you were before the memory lock rune." If the Goddess sent him to her, then he must know, deep down, that this is what she's supposed to do.

His face is covered in scratches and bruises are already forming, but he still looks perfect to her. The shadows, once distracted by their wounded master, seem to recollect and swirl around Elayce and Vaaren. Their hair blows around them in the wind created by the shadows' violent dancing. Elayce throws her hand up creating a thin dome of light that surrounds them. Loud thunks sound all around them as the shadows fight to break through.

She begs him with her eyes, silently watching him work through a whirlwind of emotions. The seconds where he says nothing seem to stretch on forever.

He doesn't get a chance to answer before the Darkness comes hurtling back. Vaaren and Elayce are thrown apart from each other. He slams against one of the thrones and collapses across the arms as she tumbles down the stairs and slides across the floor. She reaches out towards him, but the Darkness blocks her view.

"You didn't think a tiny dagger was the end of me, did you?" he says, grinning wildly.

His foot shoots out from the cloud of shadows that surround him and connects with the side of her head. She sees sparks, but she doesn't think they're her own. Gasping, she rolls over on the ground, trying to claw herself away. He takes three large steps and leans out to crush her hand beneath his foot. She screams, sending her magic through her hand, melting the shadows. She snatches her hand from underneath him.

He screeches, yanking himself from the melted shadows

and keeps marching towards her. She throws light beams and sparks at him, but his advance is constant. She's shuffling backwards as quickly as she can to get away from him, but her back slams into a hard surface. She glances up behind her to see half of a column still standing. She pushes against the column to get to her feet. The Darkness is still closing in on her, but in her attempt to get off the floor she gave away the upper hand.

He begins hurling shadows at her. Shadow whips come up from the floor and wrap around her ankles, holding her in place. She sends sparks down to combat the ties, but they keep swelling instead of breaking down.

She digs deep within her pit of power, heaving it all up. With a loud scream, she pushes all of her magic towards the Darkness. Instead of dodging, he counters with his own stream of darkness. Their magic meets in the middle, crackling and hissing. He grunts with the effort. She's grateful that the pillar still stands behind her otherwise she might be flung backwards from the force. They stay locked like that, their magic battling and tangling between them.

"Vaaren!" Elayce shouts. "Vaaren, please!" There's movement in her peripheral vision, and she sees Vaaren inching towards her against the waves of magic that are pulsing between Elayce and the Darkness.

"Draw the rune!" she shouts. A grunt comes from the Darkness and her magic pushes back towards her. She refocuses and pushes outward, sending their magic back towards the middle.

"We'll lose you to him if you do this, Elayce. You won't be able to hold on to any piece of your sanity anymore. You've seen him," Vaaren shouts back to her. He's positioned himself to the side of the pillar, shielding himself mostly from the onslaught of magic. "Nothing will be able to stop him if you let him in."

"I can stop him. I can hold his power within my pit of—" She stops and leans forward, thrusting all of her strength into holding the Darkness back. She's close to the end of what she has to give.

"I can hold him," she finishes, breathless.

She tries to push a bit more, send her light down the connecting lines of power towards the Darkness. She gains a little bit, before the Darkness pushes it right back, sending her slamming against the pillar again.

"Okay," he whispers next to her. "I trust you." She glances towards him, a bit shocked. It wasn't until right now that she realized she believed he would leave her in the end too. But he didn't. He's choosing her. He believes in *her*.

He reaches out to the bare skin just below her collar bone, but a whip of darkness comes from the clash of magic and slams into him, sending him sprawling.

"NO!" Elayce screams.

The Darkness yells from the other side of the room and she knows she has to break the connection. She tosses up a spray of light, hoping to momentarily blind him, and ducks as the beam of darkness drills into the column and shatters it. Chunks of stone smash to the ground and across Vaaren and Elayce. She covers her head, praying that Vaaren is okay.

She rolls to her feet, scanning the room for Vaaren. He's wreathed in shadows, and she stumbles briefly as she's looking at the same scene as when she last saw Ren alive. Her stumble leaves her vulnerable and she feels a shadow hit her squarely in the back, knocking the breath right out of her and tossing her forward. She's now closer to Vaaren and she begins to crawl towards him. She needs that rune drawn or they will all be lost.

Another shadow smashes into her from behind sending her careening. Her face smacks into the ground and her vision blurs, but she somehow clings to consciousness. A shadow wraps around her waist and pulls her to her feet, turning her towards where the Darkness slowly stalks forward.

"I think we've had enough fun. Time to snuff out the light," he says, his eyes glinting.

This is it. She's failed. She convinced Vaaren to finally help and trust her, but it was too late. The Darkness will kill her, Vaaren, and then the rest of the planet. Her only consolation is she gets to die first this time. She doesn't have to watch while everything she's worked for is taken from her. The kingdom she's tried to protect for three hundred years. The man that the Goddess gave her a second chance to have a life with, finally trusting her fully for who she is. All for it to come to an end.

She feels a small tug on her shoulder. Not a tug. A poke? Something warm drags along her skin, like someone is drawing on her.

Vaaren is drawing the rune on her! She sends out beams of light to distract the Darkness and tries to look over her shoulder. Vaaren is drawing the rune in the air in front of him, but she feels it being etched into her skin. She didn't know that he had mastered the rune enough to do that yet. A brief flash of pride runs through her. She feels the last drag of the marking imprint on her skin and a spark of heat before it cools. It's small, but it's there.

She braces her body, centering her energy for the Darkness's next blow. This time, she'll have to let it hit her and hope that the rune is working. She keeps fighting and struggling, so that she doesn't give anything away and he keeps his attention on her.

A strangled gasp comes from behind her and she does her best to look at Vaaren. He's struggling with the shadows wrapped around him. She can tell that the Darkness is squeezing him.

"Listen to him gasp for you," the Darkness sneers, "unable to help him. Just like last time."

"No!" she shouts, struggling against the shadows. She sends what's left of her magic to help Vaaren, but the sparks bury deeply into the shadows and disappear. She's not strong enough. Her struggle becomes desperate and uncoordinated as she watches his lips and face turn blue. His movements become sluggish and soon his head drops forward.

She told him she would keep him safe. She has nothing left if Vaaren is gone. She just has to get to him, he'll be okay. She's screaming and shouting and the Darkness is laughing maniacally. He drops Vaaren to the ground.

He doesn't move.

Time stops. Her screaming and his laughter fade into the background. It feels like the first time she laid eyes on Vaaren, those few weeks ago. Nothing exists in this moment except her and him. Except this time...Vaaren isn't here with her. It's just her. Again. Everyone she loves, dead. Ren, her mother, Vaaren—all taken from her by the Darkness. He leaves her alone again and again. His darkness filled the corners of her mind even when he was hiding away all these years. He consumed her every thought, her life, her love.

She erupts.

Light explodes outwards from every pore in her body, causing the shadows wrapping her to fade away and tossing the

Darkness back. The light ripples off of her in waves, equivalent to the despair that she feels raging within her. She's only ever experienced this once before. When she found her mother dead, and she burned the village to the ground. This time though, she's going to use it.

She screams and hauls her arms inward to her body, refocusing all of the magic around her. It crystallizes into one concentrated beam that she shoots straight at the Darkness. It moves faster than her light has ever moved. It slams into his chest.

She sees a flicker of fear cross his face. He clutches the hole in his body, black liquid gushing out between his fingers. Her breathing is heavy, the effort of controlling this wild magic is taking its toll. Elayce glides towards where the Darkness stoops clutching his wound.

"You are done taking from me," she hisses. His eyebrows raise and he opens his mouth to retort, but she's already throwing her next beam of light.

She grunts, bracing her legs and feet against the floor to hold herself steady. The light feels angry and hopeless, like it's ripping the emotion out of her and using it to fuel its own fire. It plows directly into the Darkness and forms chains around and around him starting from his feet and moving up to around his neck.

She grabs the chain of light and yanks on it, pulling the Darkness to his knees at her feet.

A crown made of pure light appears on her head, atop her battle-messed hair. Her dress is torn to shreds and she's bleeding from so many places on her body, but she feels powerful. Her eyes glow with golden light.

"I am the Queen of this castle, and I will not be caged." She squeezes her hands on the chain, causing the magic to squeeze inward on the Darkness.

He screams a thousand screams at once, pure rage. His body begins to dissolve, starting with his feet. He's writhing and twitching on the floor, but she holds the chain tight. The dark shadow form of his body turns lighter and lighter, disintegrating under the weight of the cage she's built around him. His eyes are the last to disappear, the dark blots hanging in midair before finally succumbing to her power.

The shadows go with him. The light chains disappear as well and she collapses on the floor. The fury that filled her seemed to have burned up along with the Darkness. The silence fills her ears. The silence that comes only when you're alone in a big room.

She crawls and shuffles her way back over to Vaaren's body. Elayce grabs his arm and heaves him up onto her lap. A choked sob bubbles up from her throat and echoes around the room.

"Vaaren?" she whispers to him, hoping for an answer, a twitch of a finger, a flick of an eyelid. Anything. Tears stream down her face, and sobs heave out of her. What was the point of all this if she's lost him again? The Darkness may be gone, but she wishes he had taken her with him.

She leans her head down to his chest, checking for the heartbeat that she loves so much. There's nothing. She quickly shuffles him back onto the floor and angles herself above him. Elayce places the tip of her finger on his chest above where his heart should be. Taking a deep breath, she releases the smallest spark of light directly into his chest.

His body jumps a little, and when she listens again for a heartbeat, there's still nothing.

"Please!" she shouts. She places her whole hand on his chest this time, taking a deep breath and releasing a wave of magic directly into his body. It's all she has left, but it's enough. His body heaves off the ground and his eyelids fly open.

"Elayce?" he croaks, laying back on the floor. He shifts like he's struggling to get up, but she throws her body on top of his forcing him back to the ground.

"You're alive, you're alive," she sobs into his chest.

"It seems that way." He clutches her to him and rubs her back.

"I almost lost you," she says through the tears, finally sitting up and helping him prop himself up into a better sitting position on the floor.

"I remember now," he says. "I remember that I was sent to help you. I almost—"

"The Darkness isn't a problem anymore," she answers firmly, covering his lips with the tip of her finger. She believes it too. She can feel the absence of him from the world.

The door bursts open behind them and a retinue of guards and council members rush in, trampling over the bodies of the dead that lay on the floor in the hallway. Elayce and Vaaren clutch each other, helping each other to their feet.

"Queen Elayce," Council Member Arvij says, bowing briefly. "Where's the Darkness?"

"The Darkness is no longer a threat," she says, the ethereal crown still glittering atop her head.

Gasps erupt from the group and a few guards in Selna colors rush over to King Theis's body.

"The Darkness killed Theis, I was unable to save him," she lies. He would've died anyway, she just hastened the process. Vaaren reaches over and gives her hand a small squeeze.

"The Kingdoms of Selna and Aerash are surely grateful for

CHAPTER 40

your protection, Your Majesty. Long live Queen Elayce," one of the council members says before dropping to their knee in a bow. There is a slight hesitation from a few people in the group, confused by what to do now that their king is dead. She stares them down, daring them to contradict her, holding her crowned head high until the rest of the battered group drops one by one.

Despite not having wanted to expand her rule, she takes some satisfaction knowing that the man who tried to cage and control her lost everything to her in the end.

"Rise," she commands. "There is much to do, but that will come later." She wants to move on, but a period of mourning will be required for the death of the king consort. However brief his time was.

The council members begin to call for servants and staff to take charge of cleaning the mess of the throne room. It will have to be rebuilt.

She turns back to Vaaren and wraps her arms around his neck, leaning into him. She takes a deep breath in, letting his scent consume her.

A prickling tickles the back of her neck and she opens her eyes to see the Goddess of Night standing in the shadow of a broken pillar. Nobody else seems to have noticed the Goddess in their presence.

The Goddess of Night nods her head slightly, a hand coming up to her chest to complete the silent thank you. Elayce nods back, causing Vaaren to shift to see what Elayce is looking at, but the Goddess is already gone.

Epilogue

6 months later...

Elayce's shimmering crown sends fractals across the crowd gathered for her official announcement at the foot of the dais, bowing. Her black gown is streaked through with gold and magenta, swirling together in a uniting pattern. Today, she is giving the order to remove the border guard towers between Selna and Aerash and sending her own troops to begin the assimilation of border watch on the far southern reaches of Selna. The country is officially her own, now the southernmost region of Aerash.

She glances to the right where the visiting royals from Istin and Norde are standing in their traveling finery. Several mornings after the Darkness was defeated, the King and Queen of Don Kemt were found missing and they still haven't been located. It's suspected that they fled once the reports of a beyond repair Don Kemt arrived at Castle Vleck. The first reports on Don Kemt are bleak, no word of any survivors. The land, though without shadows, is left blackened and dead. Disgraced by Elayce's declaration that they had bartered for their own safety and not the safety of their kingdom, they've seemingly vanished into thin air.

"With no royalty present to claim the throne of Don Kemt," Elayce's new advisor, Vaaren, begins, "Queen Elayce will be sending troops to search for survivors and look for ways to revive what has been lost." He turns to look at her, a smile turns his lips upward and light glints in his eyes.

She smiles down at the people before her. "It is with great humility that I take on this responsibility. Under my leadership, I hope to restore the resource-rich Don Kemt that was selfishly abandoned by Guydor and Brigit."

The crowd cheers, "Long Live Queen Elayce!"

Her sparks explode above her and spiral through the room, the crowd jumps and gasps in awe at the beautiful display. Bottles of sparkling wine pop open around the room and lively music begins to play. The guests begin to mingle and dance as banners of gold, magenta, and deep green unfurl around the room. More applause and cheers echo over the music.

How quickly they forget how much they hated her. She leans back in her throne, holding out her hand to stroke Vaaren's arm who stands proudly at her side. The kingdom is safe for now, whispers that the rebellion disbanded or vacated make their way to Elayce and the council and its two new members that have been selected to represent the new regions.

She'll enjoy the adoration while she has it. The knowledge that she'll always have Vaaren, even once the adoration of her people dwindles, fills her with a warmth and energy that forces her to her feet. She clutches Vaaren's hand, dragging him down to the dance floor and sweeping him into the middle of the dance.

He laughs, squeezing her tightly to him then letting go so they can swirl around the other partners on the floor before coming back together. Even with the packed room it feels like it's just the two of them when he looks into her eyes. She can see the depths of his devotion reflected in them, in the way he holds her and the way that he almost never loses sight of her.

After waving off King and Queen Norde and the royal family of Istin, Elayce and Vaaren celebrate with the crowd in the ballroom long into the early hours of the morning before finally returning to their rooms.

She sits in front of her mirror, brushing out the tangles before laying down. For the first time in three hundred years, she's not preparing for war.

Even if she were, she has Vaaren to stand by her side through it all.

"What's next?" Vaaren asks from her bed behind her.

She looks at him through the reflection in the mirror, her eyes locking with his gorgeous green ones. He smiles at her, beckoning her to join him and wagging his eyebrows. She laughs, setting the brush down on her vanity. She stands to join him, her reflection blocking his from the mirror.

Before she turns away, she looks into her own eyes. They're golden now, a change that came from the rush of power that flowed through her when she defeated the Darkness. She waits a moment, studying the new color. As she watches, a dark shadow spreads across her iris, starting from the pupil. She blinks, and it's gone.

"Anything we want," she croons, turning from the mirror and joining him in their bed.

Acknowledgments

Thank you to the Madison Writers' Studio and my class of 2024 that helped me to write this book. Susanna, Katie, Ti, Eric, Fae, MJ, and Max this book wouldn't be what it is without you and your feedback. You read it as the story was unfolding and stuck with it when I explained that Elayce was exactly who she was supposed to be. You helped new characters come to life and helped me realize what the full story could truly be. You all make me a better writer and for that (and all the laughs) I will be forever grateful.

Thank you to my cover designer, Bring Design, for taking the vague idea I had and creating a beautiful cover for my book. A cover I'm proud and excited to show off.

Thank you to my book club and beta readers, for constantly asking about my writing progress and supporting my dreams of becoming an author. For loving my book so much, that you've tried to recommend it before it even existed as more than a manuscript on our kindles. You gave me the confidence to take this path of publishing and I'm so grateful to be able to hold a physical copy of my work and watch it go out into the world. Without you, this wouldn't have happened. Special thanks to Shannon who made my book a playlist that showed me that my characters were able to stand on their own.

Finally, I'm grateful for the hundreds of authors that have written the books that inspired me to write my own story.

Reading all of your stories has allowed me to be transported to different worlds, learn deeply about all the different ways women can be strong, and gave me the confidence to put my own words to paper. Reading will always be a huge part of my life because it makes me a better writer and a better dreamer.

About the Author

Ashley Hintermeyer is a higher education professional and fantasy writer. She has a master's degree from Nova Southeastern University and completed two year-long writing workshops in 2024 and 2025 through the Madison Writers' Studio. She lives in Wisconsin with her husband, son, cat, and two dogs.

When she's not writing, you can find her reading in the same genre, drinking coffee, or vacationing in Disney.

You can connect with me on:
🌐 https://www.ashleyhintermeyer.com

www.ingramcontent.com/pod-product-compliance
Lightning Source LLC
LaVergne TN
LVHW091712070526
838199LV00050B/2371